HER SISTER'S LIE

Debbie Howells worked as cabin crew, a flying instructor and a wedding florist before self-publishing three books. She then wrote *The Bones of You*, which became a *Sunday Times* bestseller. Since, she has written two more psychological thrillers and *Her Sister's Lie* is her fourth. She now writes full-time from her home in West Sussex.

www.debbiehowells.co.uk

Also by Debbie Howells

The Bones of You
The Beauty of the End
The Death of Her

Her Sister's Lie

DEBBIE HOWELLS

PAN BOOKS

First published 2019 by Pan Books
an imprint of Pan Macmillan
20 New Wharf Road, London N1 9RR
Associated companies throughout the world
www.panmacmillan.com

ISBN 978-1-5098-3472-3

1 3 5 7 9 8 6 4 2

A CIP catalogue record for this book is available from the British Library.

Typeset by Palimpsest Book Production Limited, Falkirk, Stirlingshire
Printed and bound by CPI Group (UK) Ltd, Croydon, CR0 4YY

For Martin

'First one tells a lie;
then one believes it;
then one becomes it'
MARTY RUBIN

I remember running through the woods. Tall trees planted in rows. The deer that used to graze in the garden.

Party days . . . Coloured lanterns and loud music and randomers floating on the wind. I remember your free-spirited children, your smile, contagious, so that I caught it too, holding your hands, dancing barefoot on grass that wasn't quite dry, while the fairies watched us.

I painted memories of your hair shining, captured the caricature of your smile as you danced in slow motion. The cottage, flowers, music and people, twisting before my eyes to form a truth I block out of that terrible night; a scene of destruction with noiseless screaming, of darkness; Jude going from room to room, smashing things.

The accident.

A body on the floor, not moving.

Who was to know what was to come.

1

Hannah

The rain that had started as drizzle as I left home grew heavier, the closer I got to London, while the voice in my head was growing louder.

Why are you doing this, Hannah?

It wasn't because I wanted to. I hadn't felt I had a choice. An hour ago I was drawing a line under another long day, about to pour myself a glass of wine, trying not to think about Matt. But he was in my mind, constantly, his beautiful face, the sadness in his voice. *I'm sorry, Hannah. I can't do this any more. It isn't working . . .* Words I hadn't expected, the audible sound of my life changing, foreshadowing the shock that was about to hit me. Shock that was followed by agony. *You can't mean this, Matt – our relationship means everything to me.* His response, which still haunted me: *If we were that close, you should have been honest with me . . .* My apology, desperate; my attempts to explain; the sinking realization that it was too late. Time wasn't making it any easier. I couldn't think about Matt without pain sweeping through me, but nor was I ready to block him out.

Evenings were the worst time. It was March, still dark too

3

early, leaving me alone in the empty house with only my memories and the ragged emotions that tore through me. I'd been torturing myself, remembering the day six months ago that Matt had moved in, when my mobile buzzed. The call was from a Detective Inspector someone. A woman. I hadn't registered her name, just sheer disbelief as she told me that my sister had had an accident.

As she spoke, I felt the ten years Nina and I hadn't seen each other shrink to nothing, as for a few seconds my mind ran haywire. 'What do you mean? What's happened? Is she all right?' My imagination was picturing Nina involved in a car crash or a hit-and-run. 'Which hospital is she in?'

But I knew, from the hesitation in the policewoman's voice before she spoke. A silence that didn't need words.

'I'm sorry, but by the time we got to her, it was too late.'

Words that hid the reality of what had happened to Nina, but not the truth: that my sister was dead. I was numb all of a sudden, as an image of her came to me: slender, vibrant, tormented. Nina belonged in the land of the living, not a morgue. Her son Abe was at the house alone, the detective inspector went on, breaking into my thoughts. Abe's school had me listed as next of kin.

'How soon can you get here?'

I was next of kin? For a moment I was stunned. 'I can leave in a minute.' Suddenly I remembered. 'I need her address.'

Shock compounded on shock, as I wrote it down. When we'd been absent from each other's lives for so long, it made no sense that Nina had named me next of kin.

But then we were sisters. Blood was thicker than water.

The DI's voice broke into my thoughts. 'How long will it take you to get here?'

'I'm not sure. I live in the New Forest. An hour and a half maybe? It depends on the traffic.'

As I switched off my phone, a fleeting picture of Abe came to me, of the last time I saw him – a small, lost figure, standing in front of a sash window. There were no curtains, just the peeling paint framing the expanse of darkness outside. Abe had been wearing his pyjamas, his feet bare, Nina standing beside him, as though they were watching something together. I remembered seeing him reach for her hand; noticing Nina's lack of response; after a few seconds, Abe's hand falling away.

Unless Jude, his older brother, was around, which somehow I doubted, Abe had no one, as far as I knew. So I was driving. Then out of nowhere I was thinking of the Cry Babies, the band of which I'd been the lead singer – in my late teens, early twenties, when life had been simple. *Why am I thinking about the Cry Babies, with everything else that is going on?* But I knew what had reminded me. It was the many times we'd driven up this same stretch of the M3 towards London for some gig or other, music blaring, Danny's van filled with smoke from the Gauloises he chain-smoked, the scent of youth and hedonism.

The car in front slowed down suddenly, jolting me back to the present. Slamming my foot on the brakes, I felt my car skid slightly on the wet road. My heart lurched. I needed to focus.

Dropping back into the slow lane, I peered ahead through the windscreen at the car lights multiplied in the rain, thinking about Nina. Desperate to leave home, at seventeen I'd moved into her cottage in a remote part of Hampshire. Nina was nine years older than I was and, like me, had left as soon as she could get away. It was the early days of the Cry Babies – gigs had been thin on the ground and money tight. Nina had taken me under her wing. She always had, back then. My big sister, who had seemed to have her life so sorted, was used to rescuing people. At the start, they'd been happy, carefree days. But so much time had passed. So much had changed.

For a while I came and went from Nina's place, as the band worked hard and played hard, pushing ourselves ever more in pursuit of the dream. Then, after three years together, it paid off. The Cry Babies had looked set for the stars, with a nationwide tour supporting another band and a record deal being talked about. The band had taken over my life by then and I was often away, travelling around the country, spending less and less time at Nina's. Now, it felt like another lifetime.

I wasn't the same person I'd been then, but things happened, life changed people. That brought me back to Matt again, to our first meeting, two years ago, at a New Year's Eve party. It had been a meeting of eyes across a crowded room, which sparked an instant attraction. We met again, by chance, a few days later when, over cups of coffee on a park bench bathed in winter sunshine, he told me he wanted to see me again, my elation punctured by shock, as in his next breath he told me he was married.

I remembered him sitting there, as I got up and walked away, staring into his coffee cup. I'd reached the edge of the park before I heard his voice behind me, saying he wasn't sure what was happening to him, but please . . . He had no right to ask, but couldn't I give him time to work things out?

Difficult months followed, months during which Matt wrestled with himself, while I was almost forced to give up on him. But six months ago he'd moved in with me. It was a new beginning, the start of the rest of our lives together. But it hadn't been easy. Matt's ex-wife had refused to let go, trying to persuade him to come back to her, never seeming to understand that you can't force love. That it's a gift.

I'd believed in Matt, trusted him implicitly. *With the rest of my life . . .* The mistake of my life. I'd been so wrong.

Now, confronted with the latest twist that fate had thrown at me, I was finding my way towards the address the police had given me, thinking about the last time I saw Nina, hardly able to believe it was as long as ten years ago, when our interwoven lives had been irrevocably wrenched apart. It had been a brief visit, ending, as it usually did by then, in an argument, but our relationship had been fraying for some time. After the band broke up, Nina had wanted me to salvage what was left of my career, to keep trying and not give up. But, devastated, I'd done the opposite, isolating myself from ridicule, from the world; from everyone. After one hit record, fate had intervened, marking a fork in the road for the band, veering us sharply away from success towards oblivion. But life did that, I'd discovered. Presented the unexpected; tantalized with a glimpse of amazing possibility, holding it just out of reach, before taking it away forever.

The roads were still slick with the oily wash of the earlier rain. As I turned into Nina's street, I followed my satnav to a break in the terraced houses, where two police cars were parked in a lay-by. One of them had a flashing light on top. Pulling in beside it, I paused for a moment, taking a breath, steeling myself.

As I sat there, I shivered, thinking again of my sofa and glass of wine at the home that I thought of as my sanctuary. A random thought flashed through my head, lodging long enough that I considered quietly driving away, unseen, my arrival unnoticed. Concocting a story about how my car broke down; how sorry I was. Abe would be OK, wouldn't he? There had to be someone else?

I got as far as reaching for my seat belt, then stopped myself, pulled by the invisible thread that runs through all of us, which, however much we might want to, none of us can ever truly disown. *Family.*

As I walked past the front doors towards Nina's house, I looked around, struck by how dismal the street looked, the sense of despondency that hung in the air alongside the smell of fried food. Outside her house I paused, then knocked.

The door opened straight away. 'Ms Roscoe? I'm Detective Inspector Collins. Please come in.' The DI closed the door behind me.

'Thank you.' I stood inside the small hallway, wondering if she'd been watching from the window, and taking in her brown hair and creased navy jacket, feeling cold all of a sudden, not sure if it was the house making me shiver or the knowledge that Nina had died.

'Shall we go through to the kitchen?' She turned and walked along the narrow passageway and through a door into Nina's kitchen.

I followed her, shocked by what I saw. The house was dingy, unloved, reeking of neglect, with dirty carpets and chipped paintwork. In the kitchen itself, the worktops were dirty and the floor filthy. It was a world apart from the cottage I'd shared with her all those years ago, which had been colourfully, if shabbily furnished, but had felt like a home. When I lived with her, Nina had never had either the money or the inclination to spend on material possessions, but she'd always kept her surroundings clean and bright. Nothing like this.

'What happened to her?'

DI Collins turned to face me. 'It looks as though she fell and hit her head – in her bedroom. She may have been drinking.'

'Oh my God . . . ' Leaning against the door frame, I felt the blood drain from my face.

'Before I go and get Abe, I need to take some details.' DI Collins picked up the clipboard from one of the worktops. 'We have your name as Hannah Roscoe, and obviously I have your phone number . . . Could you give me your address?'

I gave it to her, waiting for her to finish writing.

'You're married?'

I shook my head. 'No. I live alone.' I realized, as I said the words, that it was a first, like other firsts: the first night after Matt left, when I'd tossed and turned, unable to sleep; the first morning that I woke up alone.

She frowned. 'You and your sister don't share the same name. Was she married?'

'No. I was, briefly, quite a few years ago.' It was just before the band split up. Nathan and I hadn't really known each other when we got married. After a small register-office wedding, we'd thrown a big, extravagant party. Nathan had been in another band, which had gone on to become a household name. The music world had been the glue that held us together. Without the Cry Babies, we'd rapidly drifted apart.

'So no one else lives with you?'

Thinking of Matt again, I shook my head, swallowing the lump in my throat.

DI Collins paused for a moment. 'When did you last see Ms Tyrell?'

'A long time ago. About ten years.' As I said it, I felt guilty for not making more of an effort. 'We fell out.' The truth was too complicated – too open to being misinterpreted – to explain to a total stranger what had really happened. 'I'd always intended to track her down. You always think there's time, don't you?' I shrugged helplessly. But it was true. Everyone thinks they have so much time, but they don't know. Not really.

You were on my mind, Nina. Always. You were my sister.

But weeks had passed, becoming months. Before I knew it, they'd become years. It happens all the time; people become estranged for all kinds of reasons. Even sisters.

'And that was before she moved here?'

I nodded.

DI Collins frowned. 'You haven't been in touch since?'

My reply was deliberately evasive. 'I suppose you could say our lives took us in different directions.'

It wasn't a lie, more a limited version of the truth. The last conversation between us had been after a few drinks. I remembered Nina shouting at me. *For Christ's sake, Hannah. You can't let what's happened destroy your future. You have to move on. You still have a chance to do something with your life . . .* After I left, we hadn't spoken for a couple of weeks. I'd called her several times, but on each occasion it had gone to voicemail. I'd assumed she hadn't paid her bill and then, when I eventually went to see her, I found the cottage empty. She'd moved away.

DI Collins didn't look convinced. 'Don't you think it's odd that, when you hadn't seen each other for so long, Nina would give your name to the school as next of kin? I'm guessing you wouldn't have known she'd done that?'

I shrugged. 'No . . . I was surprised, but then I'm her sister. People used to come and go in Nina's life. Maybe there was no one else. She had a history of sabotaged relationships.' It had begun with our parents. As far as I knew, she – like me – had never made her peace with them.

If I'd wanted to, I would have found you, but you know I couldn't.

'I asked Abe about his father, but he said he doesn't have one. Do you know who his father is?'

Oh, Nina . . . So many men came and went, never staying for more than a few months. 'There was no one permanent in her life when he was born.' It wasn't a lie.

'What about your parents?' DI Collins asked.

It was the question I'd been dreading, the one that I'd hoped she wouldn't ask. There were no happy childhood memories; no place in either my life or Nina's for the father who'd abused us; for the mother who'd known, but had done nothing to protect her own children. I tried to keep my voice steady. 'She didn't speak to them. There was a falling-out. It was a long time ago.'

She frowned. 'Do you think it's possible that things had changed between them? I did ask Abe earlier about his grandparents, but all he said was he doesn't really know them, which fits with what you just said. But it's been a considerable time since you spoke to her. Maybe Ms Tyrell had been in touch. They may well want to be part of Abe's life. We need to talk to them and, of course, they need to be told, though it might be better if it came from you.'

I wanted to shout at her. *No . . . things wouldn't have changed. Nina would never have contacted them, any more than I would. Sometimes, for your own sanity, you leave the past behind and don't look back.* But if I said that to DI Collins there would be more questions, dredging up painful memories; questions to which there were no answers. It was easier not to go there. I nodded, numbly. 'I'll let them know.'

She nodded briefly, then glanced at the notes in front of her. 'I understand Abe has a brother.'

'Half-brother,' I corrected. 'Jude.' A difficult child came to mind, one who was always getting into fights and who swore like a trooper, except that he wasn't a child now. He must be nearly twenty.

'You're not in contact with him, either?'

I shook my head. 'No.'

'Is there anyone else you remember from the time you lived together?'

I stared at her. Ten years had passed – it was hardly relevant. I'd been twenty-two when I last saw Nina. After all this time, the people I remembered were nameless faces, passing through, as I had, in the end. 'There wasn't really anyone who stayed around.'

Then, for a moment, I think about Summer. Beautiful, strong, free-spirited. But, like everyone else, she too had been transient.

The DI looked up. 'One last thing. I'm sorry to have to ask you this, but it would really help us if you could identify your sister's body.'

It hadn't entered my head that I'd have to do that. I stared at her, shocked.

2

An air of surrealism had come over me. It wasn't just the thought of coming face-to-face with my sister's body, inches in front of me. What affected me more was the reality that it was someone whose blood I shared; whom I remembered being so full of life.

'Her body has been taken to a Chapel of Rest.' DI Collins paused as she wrote something on a piece of paper, then handed it to me. 'This is the address. If you call them in the morning, they'll arrange a time with you.'

I took it reluctantly, my eyes scanning the address without taking it in. 'Could I see her room?'

Back downstairs, I felt shaky. Nina didn't belong in that dingy bedroom, where the drab furnishings and unmade bed seemed so uncharacteristic of my sister. I hadn't been prepared for the dark stain, where her blood had soaked into the carpet. The empty vodka bottle and tipped-over glass had sent another ripple of shock through me.

Now we were back downstairs, DI Collins had more questions. 'Were you aware that your sister had a drink problem?'

I shook my head. It was drugs that Nina had relied on to blot out what haunted her, but I didn't want to tell the DI that. Not unless she asked. 'No. Not as such . . . I mean, when we were together, she drank, obviously. We both did – a normal amount.'

Remember the script, Hannah. Sisters look out for each other. Keep each other's secrets.

'Normal being . . .?'

Under the DI's scrutiny, I felt uncomfortable all of a sudden. 'Wine. A bottle or two between us.' Sometimes a bit more, but there was often a party going on, and it had never been a problem in the sense that the DI was implying. Thinking of the empty vodka bottle again, I leaned against the door frame, battling light-headedness; not sure why I felt the need to protect Nina.

'I'd better go and get Abe.' DI Collins put down her pen. 'Do you have children, Ms Roscoe?'

'No.' I frowned. I'd already told her I lived alone. 'Where is he?'

'Outside.' She glanced towards the window. 'He hasn't said much. Poor kid. Imagine coming home from school and finding his mother like that.'

'God!' I was shocked. It was the first time I'd thought of it that way. 'How long is he supposed to be staying with me? I mean, I live so far away. What about contacting Jude? If he's nearer, wouldn't it make sense for Abe to live with him?'

DI Collins turned to look at me, a frown on her face. 'We're trying to trace him. I thought you understood, Ms Roscoe. Unless some other family member comes forward, he has nowhere else to go.'

I felt myself turn ice-cold as the realization slowly sank in. I knew I owed Nina. And I'd already thought about the next few days, or possibly weeks, if it came to it. I'd do it willingly. But I couldn't take Abe on. She would have known that. Not forever.

DI Collins went outside to get Abe. Alone in the small kitchen, I felt a fleeting moment of panic, as the enormity of what lay ahead caught up with me. Surely there was someone else in Abe's life. The responsibility of caring for him couldn't be down to me.

Then I was thinking about Nina again. She'd liked a drink as much as anyone, but it hadn't made her an alcoholic. Still, there were clues I couldn't ignore: the state of the house, the fact that her body was upstairs with an empty vodka bottle lying on the floor next to it.

Still reeling from the sight, I watched from the window as DI Collins made her way along the dimly lit path to the communal patch of grass behind Nina's house, where I could just about make out the silhouetted figure of a boy, his hands thrust in his pockets. After what looked like a brief conversation, the DI turned to come back in. A few seconds later, Abe followed.

'Abe, this is Hannah.' DI Collins was holding the door open, as Abe walked into the kitchen.

'Hello.' I shivered in the blast of cold air that hit me and then, as I looked at him, an extraordinary sensation came over me. I'd thought about this moment. Abe was my link to Nina. I knew I should be showing warmth, sympathy, but as I registered his hunched figure and lack of eye contact, there was a hostility about him. Suddenly I felt less sure. 'I'm so sorry . . . about your mum.' When he didn't look up, I glanced at DI Collins, not at all sure I'd said the right thing.

Abe continued to stare at the floor, moving around a screwed-up piece of paper with one of his feet. Everything about him was tight. His pinched face, and the clothes that looked too small for him. The jacket he wore that barely stretched across his shoulders.

'Why don't you go and pack a few things?' DI Collins spoke gently to him.

'Can he do that?' I'd blurted it out before I could stop myself, thinking of the crime series I'd watched on television, where nothing could be taken from the scene before Forensics had been through everything with a fine-toothed comb.

'We're not treating this as a crime scene.' DI Collins looked at Abe, who hadn't moved. This time she spoke more firmly. 'Abe, can you go and pack what you need to take to your aunt's?'

As he turned silently and walked slowly towards the stairs, DI Collins looked back at me.

'We've no reason to believe this is anything other than a tragic accident. We'll have to notify the coroner, and they may decide to carry out a post-mortem, but from everything I've seen, I think it's unlikely. As soon as we have the death certificate, you can arrange the funeral.'

'Funeral?' This was all happening too fast. I hadn't even thought about a funeral.

Nina's funeral. My sister's body in a coffin.

'Don't worry about that just now. It's possible Jude will want to get involved, once he knows what's happened. Would you object to our passing on your contact details? He may well want to see Abe.'

I nodded. 'Of course.'

'Also . . .' Breaking off, she glanced upstairs, but there was still no sign of Abe. 'It might be a good idea for Abe to talk to a counsellor. It's something to think about – and it's up to him, of course. But he's been through a significantly traumatic experience. Once he's settled in a new school, they may be able to suggest someone.'

School? Was that down to me, too? 'What happens about school?' I looked at the DI, hoping she was about to tell me that he'd stay at the same one, but the realization sank in that he wouldn't be able to. Not if he was going to be living with me.

DI Collins nodded towards the stairs, where Abe was making his way down. 'There's no need to worry about that for now. Why don't we talk about it tomorrow?' Her air of calm did nothing to quiet the thoughts rampaging through my head. 'He's had a long, difficult day. Take him home and we can speak in the morning.' As he came into the kitchen, she paused, frowning. 'Just one thing before you go, Abe. Could I ask you if you've seen Jude recently? Your brother?'

Abe looked at the floor again, then shook his head.

She turned to me. 'We'll try to contact him. He should know what's happened. If you have any questions, or if you remember anything you think we should know, you can always call me.' DI Collins reached into her pocket, then handed us each a card.

As I stood there, the sense of panic was back. Was that it? Were we just supposed to leave? What would happen about the house? To Nina's stuff?

'I'll lock up,' DI Collins said, just as the doorbell rang. 'It might be easier for Abe if you give it a few days before you come back to collect the rest of his things. But there's not really anything else to do tonight. We'll take care of everything here, and I'll be in touch tomorrow.'

Carrying his bag, Abe followed me out in silence. In the car he continued to remain quiet while I tried, and failed, to draw him out.

'I'm sorry, the car's a mess.' I glanced across at him, but he didn't respond. After a few moments, I tried again. 'Do you like dogs? I have a terrier. He's called Gibson – after my guitar. I used to play in a band . . .' Trailing off when yet again there was no response.

He clearly wasn't interested. *But he wouldn't be*, I berated myself. *How could he think about anything else when he's just lost his mother?* We had that much in common: having lost someone. But it wasn't Nina I was thinking of. It was Matt, the memory sharper for its brief absence. The lights around me blurred as tears suddenly filled my eyes. Wiping them away, I wished more than ever that he was still in my life. *Oh, Matt . . . why couldn't you have stayed?*

In the silence, as I did my best to push thoughts of him from my head, the knot in my stomach was growing tighter. All the time that there'd been a distance between Nina and me, I'd convinced myself there was no other way. But seeing Abe after so long had deeply unsettled me. I tried to put myself into the mind of a fifteen-year-old boy, one who'd come home from school and found his mother's body; who was driving away from everything he knew, with someone who was effectively a stranger. I didn't know how to interpret the silence that felt almost like animosity towards me, but then I reminded myself: after what Abe had been through today, I should forgive him anything.

As we left London behind us, it seemed symbolic that its soft glow had faded to the same steely-grey as my life. Now that I had time to think, the ghosts were back, spectres of self-pity and loathing, the dark abyss of hopelessness. At my bleakest after Matt left, I'd given them form, acid-pitting holes in any pleasure that might have existed; the hopelessness a dark mist from which no corner of my life would ever be safe.

And I was supposed to help a bereaved teenager. I'd no idea how I was going to do that. I drove automatically, not registering the miles passing until a car suddenly pulled out in front of us. Slamming on the brakes, I narrowly avoiding hitting it. 'Shit! Sorry. Are you all right?' I asked Abe, but, hunched in the seat next to me, he didn't react. Biting back my frustration, I wondered if this was how it was going to be: his refusal to speak, while I floundered, unsure how to deal with this stranger of a nephew.

It wasn't until an hour later, when I turned off the motorway onto the quiet road on the edge of the New Forest, that Abe spoke. 'I have to go back.' He started to reach for his rucksack, pulling it off the floor onto his lap as he unfastened his seat belt.

'What are you doing?' I panicked. He looked as though he was about to open the door. Whether I wanted it or not, I had a responsibility to look after him. 'You can't go back there, Abe. You're too young to live on your own.'

'This is too far away.' He made no attempt to disguise his anger. 'You have to stop. I need to get out.'

'Abe, *no* . . .' I put my foot on the accelerator. We'd crossed a cattle grid, marking the part of the Forest where ponies and cattle wandered freely. I was driving much faster than I usually would through there, but I couldn't risk him getting out and disappearing into the darkness. 'You can't get out here. There's nothing for miles.' I paused, then carried on more gently. 'The police aren't going to allow you to live alone.'

'They don't have to know.' His voice was full of resentment.

'They'll check on you.' My voice was rising. 'DI Collins is calling tomorrow. She'll ask about you. If you're not with me, she'll want to know where you are . . .'

DI Collins had said she'd be in touch. But I knew what the reality was. There would be no police investigation. Nina's death was an accident. DI Collins might check up on us for a day or two, but beyond that, we were on our own.

'I don't care.' He sounded sullen, but I took it as a sign he'd given in when he let his rucksack slip onto the floor, then slumped back into his seat.

His outburst had unnerved me. I knew I was out of my depth. My experience of teenagers was limited to the few who came to my house for music lessons. They were bright, motivated, privileged. I had no idea how to deal with reticence and rudeness, let alone grief. But as I drove I was worrying that, once we were home and he was out of the car, if he decided to take off, I wouldn't be able to stop him.

'Why not give it tonight,' I said, trying to sound more in control. 'We'll talk to DI Collins tomorrow and see what she says.' It wasn't the time to repeat what she'd already told me – that, as things stood, with Jude's whereabouts unknown, Abe had nowhere else to go.

What were you thinking, Nina? You, of all people, would have known I'm not cut out to raise children.

Whether it was alcohol or drugs that had been her down-fall, suddenly I was angry with her: at her selfishness, her weakness. For letting her addiction get out of hand, when she had Abe to think of, for letting him down. We all had our battles. But I'd always known that her air of brightness and dazzling smile distracted from the blankness in her eyes, the empty pit deep inside her. Once, she'd confided in me her belief that she was different from other people. How worthless she felt. It had shaken me to the core, threatening the security I'd always known when I was with her. Later, when I asked her about it, she laughed it off. *I was pissed, Hannah. You know what I'm like. Look at my wonderful life* . . . And that was that. It was an episode that had faded, then vanished altogether. Looking around at her life, seeing what I wanted to see, I'd believed her, not thinking about it again. Until now.

Keep to the plan, Hannah. Nothing's changed . . . Even when things went wrong, we'd agreed what to say. No less, no more – it was in the script. *Sisters don't keep secrets from each other.*

As we drew closer to Burley, then turned onto the road I knew every inch of, which led towards Bransgore, I was driving on autopilot again, thinking back to a time of dated clothes and people whose names I'd forgotten, drifting around at one of Nina's parties. The idyllic cottage in the middle of nowhere, which for a while I'd shared with her, had been remote – I'd forgotten just how remote. Nina's children ran wild through the surrounding woods. At seventeen, having just left home, I'd been young and naive, impressed by how carefree her life seemed, unable to look beyond the facade she presented to the world. Wrapped up in my own life – the band, its success, and then its failure – I believed Nina's every word when, if I'd been watching more closely, I would have seen the first telltale signs of her downfall.

But everything was easy, with the exquisite torment of hindsight. The irresistible, pointless knowledge that things could have been different, when they weren't. There was no changing what had already happened, nothing to gain from dwelling on it. Like the broken hearts and shattered dreams that life was littered with, there were doors to the past that should forever remain firmly closed.

3

As I drove on, Abe's anger seemed to have given way to resignation – even if only temporarily. With the resentment and stubbornness he'd displayed, I was expecting it to be short-lived. He didn't seem like someone who would give up easily, but maybe he was beginning to see how limited his options were. With only a few more miles to go, I felt exhaustion kick in as I drove on. If it had been light, I could have pointed out the low, heather-clad hills and prickly gorse, the mist that often descended here; the ponies and cattle that roamed; the scent of sea air that drifted inland. The sense of space I loved. I felt myself filled with a fleeting optimism that just maybe, if Abe liked it, too, we had a chance.

'We're nearly there.'

There was no traffic as we came to the narrow lane with a scattering of houses on either side on the outskirts of the village. After passing the small shop, I slowed down and, a few yards further on, turned into a rough, unmade track that meandered between fields until it eventually came to an end in front of a small farmhouse.

'We're here.' I switched off the engine and turned to Abe, who hadn't moved. I hesitated for a moment, then opened the car door. 'Shall we go in?'

As I got out of the car, I glanced up at the sky. It had the rain-washed clarity that only existed after a weather front had blown through. There was no moon tonight, just an intense, indigo blackness that glittered with stars.

After London and the hours of driving, I savoured the silence, feeling it soak into me. It was a silence that had a sound all of its own – the faintest whisper of the air moving; the hoot of a distant owl; of my own breath, then my footsteps on the path as I walked towards the front door, followed by the sound of a dog barking as the security light switched on. As I opened it, a small terrier rushed past me, then ran down the path towards Abe. He backed away.

'He's friendly, I promise.' I whistled to Gibson. 'Here, Gibson . . . Good dog.'

Abe watched him, a look of suspicion on his face, as Gibson ran back to me, then followed me in.

The door led into a small boot room, which housed the boiler and had a row of hooks, on which hung an assortment of jackets and coats. I switched on a light and hung up my jacket, then went through into the kitchen, where I was greeted by the sight of the pile of mail I was saving for Matt, and the bottle of wine I'd been about to open before I'd taken the call from DI Collins. As I put my bag on the table, I heard Abe come in behind me. I turned to look at him, but after briefly glancing around, he just stood there, staring at the floor.

'Would you like something to eat? A sandwich or something? A drink? Tea? Coffee?' I was gabbling, the way I always did when I didn't know what to do.

Abe shook his head.

'You must be tired. Shall I show you your room?'

As I spoke, I silently cursed myself. I didn't want him thinking I was rushing him out of the way, which was what it sounded like; reminding myself that, after everything he'd been through, he needed reassuring, comforting. He didn't respond, but just stood there, his arms folded, looking awkward.

I took a deep breath. 'You should have something to eat,' I said, more calmly. 'Why don't you sit down?' As I turned my back to put a couple of slices of bread in the toaster, I heard him pull out one of the chairs. Wishing he'd say something, I tried to keep my patience. He wasn't making this easy.

It seemed pointless to ask more questions that he'd refuse to answer. After placing a plate of buttered toast in front of him, I put the kettle on and made two mugs of tea. After handing one of them to him, I passed him a bowl of sugar. 'Help yourself.'

Again, he didn't respond. He'd been through hell, I had to remind myself once more. *But he isn't the only one . . .* As I picked up my mug, I was thinking of Matt, here in this kitchen one evening not that long ago, before he left, out of the blue. We'd cooked a meal and we'd been talking about Italy, one country on a whole wish list we'd planned to explore together. I remembered his hands in my hair, twisting it up on top of my head, before letting it fall again; the touch of his lips on mine. Feelings I'd never known before, that I'd never feel again. Quickly I tried to push them from my mind, focusing instead on Abe, as he ate the toast and drank his tea.

After he'd finished, I looked at him. 'Would you like me to show you where your room is?'

Without answering, he stood up and walked over to get his

rucksack, then followed me through the door into the small snug, which was one of my favourite parts of the house. It was cosy, its main feature a wood-burner set in the old brick fireplace. I'd stacked logs on either side of it and had pulled up a couple of armchairs close by. For the short time he was here, Matt and I had spent the long winter evenings here, drinking wine and putting the world to rights. I was struggling now. It was impossible not to think of him. Matt was everywhere in this house, in every room, round every corner. *Like now.* I swallowed the lump in my throat.

Two doors led off the snug. 'The sitting room's through there.' I pointed to the one on the left. As well as a pair of sofas, it housed my piano and the three guitars which were all that remained of the much larger collection I'd had when we first moved here. These days, apart from when I was teaching, it was a room I rarely used. 'There's a TV in there – just make yourself at home.' I turned towards the other door, glancing at Abe. 'The stairs are through here.'

I led the way through to the staircase, and then at the top, instead of turning left towards my bedroom, turned right, opening one of the three doors further along the passageway. Switching the light on, I went over to the window and pulled the curtains closed, then fetched an extra blanket from the wardrobe. 'I hope this is OK for you? The bathroom's opposite. There are clean towels on the towel rail. Help yourself.' I unfolded the blanket and laid it on the bed, pausing for a moment. 'I'm so sorry about your mum.' I watched him for a response of some kind, but apart from the slightest movement of his shoulders, there was nothing. Clearly he didn't want to talk. Maybe he needed to be alone. 'Is there anything else you need?'

He shook his head.

'OK . . .' Stepping past him into the doorway, I hesitated again. 'I'll leave you to it. I hope you sleep well, Abe. I'll see you in the morning.' Closing the door, I paused on the other side for a moment, listening for any sounds of movement, but there were none. Quietly I walked away.

Downstairs in the kitchen I cleared the mugs and plates, then sat down. It was after midnight, but my mind refused to wind down. What was I going to do? My life had become unrecognizable. In a matter of hours, I'd discovered that my sister had died and I'd become the guardian of her teenage son. All just a week or so after Matt had walked out. *Matt*. Without Abe's presence to distract me, the reality of Matt's absence hit me anew and, now that I was alone, sadness overwhelmed me.

After meeting, it hadn't taken long for a closeness to develop between us. Matt and I had shared many interests; he'd loved the same music I did, had the same sense of humour. His wife had called constantly, insisting on meeting him. She'd become obsessed, he'd told me, but I had no reason to worry. And I hadn't. I'd trusted him. It made it harder to understand how, after all his promises – his declaration that I was the only woman in the world for him – he'd simply walked away, without properly explaining why. Something had changed; almost overnight, it seemed. After he'd told me he was leaving, I'd tried to talk to him, but he'd been silent, closed off from me. Numb with shock, I'd waited downstairs while he packed a suitcase. The worst moment had come when he said goodbye. When it was his choice, I couldn't make sense of the pain I'd seen in his eyes as they held mine briefly, before he looked away.

I'd stood there, watching him close the door behind him, fighting an urge to run after him as he walked down the path, not moving, just listening until the sound of his car had faded away. He hadn't told me where he was going, just that he'd come back sometime for the rest of his stuff. Ever since, I'd been waiting to catch him, wanting to talk to him, holding on to the hope that, after a few days apart, he'd have changed his mind. But he hadn't answered my calls or texts. I'd heard nothing.

Now, sitting at my kitchen table, I was engulfed by a pain that was physical, leaving me gasping for breath. Then I slumped forward, my body shaking with sobs, as I gave in to grief. Not just grief for Matt, but for the life I'd believed lay ahead of us, for the future we'd planned to share, all of it gone.

The house was quiet the following morning. In the weak March sunlight filtering through the kitchen window, I sat at the table and made a few calls to cancel the pupils who had lessons booked the following day. There were too many matters needing my attention, all related to Nina and Abe. As I put my phone down, I thought briefly of Abe, upstairs in the small bedroom that was now his, with the window that looked across the fields.

I'd found last night impossible. If I was honest, I was wishing I'd been more assertive – I was already dealing with enough. I should have told DI Collins straight off that this arrangement wasn't going to work and that I hadn't thought it through; but I hadn't been prepared for the disruption, and the emotions Abe's presence had unleashed.

This morning I felt the presence of Nina's ghost around

me, as long-forgotten memories flooded back. Guilt, too, because I should have been able to help her, as she had me. *I'll always be here for you. Sisters help each other, Hannah* . . . If only I had, Abe would still be living with Nina, instead of here, against his will, with me.

Finding my bag, I hunted for the piece of paper DI Collins had given me, then called the Chapel of Rest to arrange an appointment, pushing out of my mind the thought of viewing my sister's body, thinking instead about Nina's London house. It had felt impersonal, impermanent, as though its occupants were passing through. Had it been deliberate on her part? A constant reminder to herself not to get too used to it, that there were better ways to live? I preferred that to the alternative: that she'd given up and hadn't cared. That wasn't how I remembered her. Even when things hadn't been easy, she'd somehow always made the best of it.

It seemed unbelievable, impossible that ten years had passed. Not when we were sisters; when it didn't matter what had happened between us. How had so much time gone by without me finding her?

I let my mind wander back to when I was seventeen. Nina had referred to her cottage as borrowed. I'd never thought about it before, only realizing now that I'd never known who owned it. It had been miles from the nearest village, up a long track and with a dilapidated charm that perfectly suited her bohemian lifestyle.

When I turned up there, she'd taken me in without hesitation, but then Nina had a generosity of spirit that had drawn people to her: weak, good-looking men, creative types, waifs and strays was how I'd thought of her eclectic, ever-changing household.

They were carefree days, which had stretched seamlessly ahead of me, without reason to suspect anything would change; holding no suggestion of what was to come. Summer had been ten and Jude five, both of them used to people coming and going, happily doing their own thing while the chaos of Nina's life happened around them.

Sometimes, they'd disappeared for hours. They must have ranged far enough to have met the nearest neighbours. The name Nell came to mind. I could dimly remember Summer telling me about picking strawberries from Nell's garden; how one day they'd baked a cake. Then Summer had come running back, telling Nina about it.

Neither of the children had gone to school. Nina had enthused about them having the carefree kind of childhood that was light-years from the upbringing she and I had known. Proudly, I remember her telling me how she'd elected to home-school them. *Children need space, Hannah. Freedom . . . Remember how we hated school? Look how happy they are! It's what matters most, isn't it?* I'd watched a wistful look come over her face. I knew she was thinking of our own childhoods; the rules and restrictions, the cruel, controlling ways of our parents and the violent consequences of disobeying them. It had been worse for Nina, her only escape to run somewhere no one knew where she was.

Maybe it was a desire to leave the past behind. To believe that life could be different. Either way, we should have known: you couldn't trust people. Even in the cocoon she'd woven around them, Nina couldn't protect her children. Nowhere was ever safe.

The last time I went back to the cottage, just before she moved, I'd seen Jude only fleetingly, on his way out to meet friends. It was after Summer had gone. Abe had been sleeping. None of Nina's hangers-on had been around, but everything had changed by then. Most of them had drifted away, so that it had just been the two of us. Nina had opened a bottle of wine, but even though it was mid-morning, I knew from her overly bright eyes and the way she slurred her words that she was on something. There was a telltale half-drunk glass on the side, which she ignored and I pretended not to see.

Taking in the mess inside the cottage, as well as the state Nina was in, I couldn't help but worry about the children. I tried to broach my concerns, but she was past listening to me. As she got angry, I weakly allowed myself to be diverted, but I was preoccupied with my own problems. My life had shrunk since the band had broken up, and my brief marriage to Nathan was on the rocks. Nina hadn't liked Nathan, proclaiming him shallow and vain. I'd defended him, turning a blind eye to his unexplained absences and secretive phone calls, until the day came when he told me he'd met someone else.

History was repeating itself: she was another singer, in another up-and-coming rock band, and would inevitably last as long as the band was successful, I told myself. *As I had* . . . But she was welcome to him. I hadn't really loved Nathan, I knew that. I'd missed the buzz and excitement of being in the Cry Babies more than I missed Nathan. My pride had been dented, that was all. He belonged in a world I no longer had a part in.

For a while I'd had the idea of teaching music to private students. After the divorce, the house was mine and I had some money, but not a huge amount, and I needed to keep it coming in. I'll never forget how Nina hated that when success had been in my hands, I'd given up, as she saw it. She refused to let it go. *This is your chance, Hannah. When you've come so far, I don't understand how you can do this. People still know who you are. Most of us never get chances like this.* She hadn't understood that people knew me as part of a band that had glimpsed the sunshine briefly, before our moment had passed. I remembered how twitchy she was that morning, how quickly she drank her glass of wine and refilled it.

Abe would have been four years old at that point. In the years since, I'd often stopped to think about what his life had been like, but assured myself that Nina would have done her best to take care of him, the way she had the others – not perfect, I knew that, but no one was ever perfect.

But with my own problems at the forefront of my life, the presence of Nina and her children had become like a photograph: there in the background, being slowly bleached by the sun, blurring their faces until I could read what I wanted into them – choosing happiness, freedom, love, instead of the struggle and isolation that really lay there.

Then I thought of Abe's face when I first saw him last night, when he'd followed DI Collins into the kitchen. There'd been no misreading how unemotional and switched off he'd seemed. It was as though he hadn't heard anything I said to him. Maybe he'd learned to do that in order to cope with life. If it had been dominated by Nina's drinking, it couldn't have been at all easy for him.

However impossible the differences between Nina and me, I couldn't deny the guilt that was weighing ever more heavily on me. Nor could I get rid of the feeling that I'd turned my back on them all, even though it was Nina who'd taken things into her own hands, moving and making the decision not to tell me where she'd gone. *But I had tried.* I'd gone back to her cottage that last time, only to find the windows closed and the front door ajar, creaking slightly as the wind caught it. Pushing it open, I'd ventured inside, moving from room to room, my agitation increasing as I found each of them empty. Apart from a mural she'd painted on her bedroom wall and the garden that she'd planted, which, since she'd left, clearly hadn't been tended to, there was no trace of her ever living there. I'd felt cold as the reality sank in. She'd effectively cut me out of her life.

Standing there for a moment, I thought of all the people who had fleetingly passed through these rooms; of Nina's children. Of Summer, who had been more vital than any of them. A whisper of that fateful evening came back to me before, just as quickly, I blocked it out.

Going outside, I'd sat on the doorstep, aware of a mixture of emotions. Sadness and loneliness, but I couldn't hide the fact that I felt relief, too, that I no longer had to answer to my sister, or justify my choices to her. By leaving in this way, she'd granted me freedom – to make my own decisions; to be myself.

'Jesus!' A movement startled me, jolting me back to the present. I hadn't heard Abe's feet on the creaky floorboards, just caught sight of his still figure framed in the doorway. 'Sorry. I didn't know you were there. You made me jump.'

He stared at me, not moving, then after a few seconds looked away.

'Would you like some breakfast?' I tried to sound bright, as I got up and pulled out one of the chairs from under the table. 'Take a pew.'

He did as I suggested and I wondered if he'd slept. There were grey circles under his eyes and his skin looked paler than yesterday, if that was possible. Compared to the teenagers who came here for music lessons, he looked younger than his fifteen years – and vulnerable. After putting the kettle on, I pulled out the chair opposite and sat down.

'I've never been in a situation like this,' I said, studying his face. 'I'd really like you to feel at home. Can you tell me what kind of thing you usually eat? Whether you like tea or coffee, that sort of thing?'

Abe just shrugged.

I tried again, puzzled. 'I could make tea? Scrambled eggs?' Searching his face for clues and taking the slight jerk of his head as a nod, I got up again and went to the fridge to get some eggs, relieved there was no sign of yesterday's hostility, but unsure if his silence made things easier or harder.

After he'd finished eating, he got up and walked outside, slamming the door behind him before Gibson could join him. Troubled, I was watching him walk across the garden when my mobile rang.

'Ms Roscoe? It's DI Collins. How's Abe?'

'He's OK – I think. He's just had breakfast.' I hesitated, not wanting to sound unsympathetic, but I needed her to know how difficult this was. 'But it's hard to know. He's hardly spoken. I'm not sure this is going to work, to be honest. On the way here last night he made it clear he wanted to go back to London.'

'Has he mentioned it again today?'

'No. He's just gone out. I assume just for a walk. Unless . . . Oh God. I hope he hasn't taken off.' I started to panic. 'Maybe I should go and look for him.'

'You're not going to be able to keep him in your sight all the time.' Her voice was reassuring. 'He'll probably come back soon enough. It's a major change for him. He needs time to get used to things. Just see how it goes.' She paused. 'Actually, I wanted to talk to you about your sister. The coroner wants to carry out a post-mortem. We couldn't be sure when we moved her, but it's been confirmed that there was a second injury to her head.'

'God!' Horrified, I imagined Nina falling and getting up, drunk and in pain, then falling again. 'That's awful. She must have fallen twice.'

'It's possible. We'll know more when we get the pathologist's report.' DI Collins was quiet for a moment.

I was thinking suddenly. Did this change anything? 'I've arranged to visit the Chapel of Rest later today. Is that still appropriate?'

'If you could, it would be helpful.' She paused. 'I'm not suggesting he starts school right away, but having a routine might be good for him. And it may be a good idea just to check out what the options are. It might be useful to speak to Abe's school in London first. I've a phone number here. Do you have a pen?'

'Hold on a moment . . .' I went to get my bag, rooting in the bottom until I found one, pulling out an old shopping list to write on. 'OK.'

As I wrote it down, the back door opened and Abe came in. 'He's just come back.'

'Good.' The DI sounded unsurprised. 'I have to go, Ms Roscoe, but I'll be in touch as soon as I have any more to tell you.'

Turning off my phone, I looked up. Abe was still standing there.

'That was DI Collins,' I told him, not sure whether I should mention what the police officer had said about the second injury to Nina's head. I decided against it. 'She asked how you were. I did tell her that you weren't happy to be moving so far from home.'

I watched Abe apprehensively, wondering if it would trigger another outburst, but he just shrugged.

'Did you go for a walk? If you like, I could show you some of the footpaths.'

'Can I take your dog?' He said it without meeting my eyes.

'Yes.' I was flabbergasted. It was the first time he'd shown interest in anything. 'Of course. Gibson would like that. Maybe later? I thought this morning we'd go into town and get you a few things.'

After that briefest of interactions between us, I was optimistic, hoping it was the beginning of some sort of relationship between us, but by the time we'd driven to the shops, he'd defaulted. Everything I said was greeted with the same indifference. I wanted to buy Abe some clothes, but ended up making decisions for him, picking out a couple of shirts, jumpers, a pair of jeans, trainers that were sturdy enough to walk across the Forest in, my enthusiasm dwindling as he stood there, his hands in his pockets, saying nothing. I bit back my irritation when he didn't utter so much as a *thank you*, but there were a million excuses for his behaviour. I had to remember that.

I left him alone while I made the trip to London to the Chapel of Rest, driving home later that afternoon in silence, filled with a sense of shock at what I'd seen; unable to shake the image of the inert body that bore only a passing resemblance to my sister.

I was in my kitchen that evening, the light fading, when I heard the latch on the back door click, but as I spun round, I found the room empty. Getting up, I walked over to the window, where through the almost-darkness I could just about make out Abe walking across the garden, stopping where the trees thinned out, apparently watching the sunset, his figure silhouetted against the pink-streaked sky.

An hour later, when he hadn't come back, I started to get worried. Pulling on my jacket and getting my torch, I went to look for him, Gibson trotting along beside me. Away from the house, it was completely dark. Making my way towards where I'd last seen Abe, I switched on my torch, shining the beam around, picking up the eyes of a startled rabbit for a split second before it bounded into the hedge.

'Abe?' I called out quietly, not wanting to startle him, but there was no reply.

Without the sun, the air had rapidly cooled, the grass already damp underfoot. Ahead of me, I picked out his shape in the beam of my torch, his hands in his pockets as he stared up at the night sky.

'Abe?' I called again more loudly, pulling my jacket around myself. 'It's cold. Are you coming in?'

He didn't move. Suddenly I was angry – at his rudeness, his unresponsiveness. At Nina, for putting me in this situation. At his invasion of my home.

I didn't try to hide it. '*Abe!*' I knew I should have had more control, but it was as though he was ignoring me. Marching up to him, I grabbed his arm. He spun round. 'The least you can do is answer when I talk to you, instead of being so bloody rude. You're in my house and I'm trying to help you, but you're making it impossible . . .' My voice had risen and I was shaking, with cold, with frustration, with rage.

I wanted a reaction of some kind. Anything. An apology; even an outburst about how I didn't care and I didn't want him there. Instead, he turned back and carried on staring at the sky. 'That's Mars,' he said at last.

'Which one?' Distracted, I followed his gaze.

'There. The bright one, high up.'

'You know about the stars?' In my surprise, I forgot my anger. Having stumbled across a topic he wanted to talk about, I wanted to keep the conversation going.

I felt him shift slightly beside me.

'That's a planet. Mercury.'

I looked in the direction he was pointing, to another star, which was just as bright, much lower in the sky.

'You could see Venus a few days ago.'

'Where is it now?'

'Gone.' He didn't elaborate.

Just like his mother, I couldn't help thinking. *Here yesterday. And now she's gone . . .*

'In London, it's not like this. There's too much light pollution. You can't see so much.'

It was the first insight he'd offered into his life, and I realized how little I knew about him. I felt my earlier anger dissipate, as my heart went out to him. I fumbled, looking for the right words. 'Abe, if you ever want to talk – about your mum . . .'

He was silent for a moment. 'Not really.' His voice was devoid of emotion.

'It must have been so hard for you,' I said gently. 'I know she had problems. Drinking, I mean.'

'Look . . .' He hesitated, as if fighting some kind of internal battle. When he went on, he sounded angry. 'You have no idea. Everyone thinks she had a problem, but she'd stopped drinking. She was going to AA meetings. Things were going to be different – she told me that. When I left school, I was going to get a job and we were going to move to a nice house.'

'But—' I broke off. He was right. How could I have known what went on between them? I didn't know what to say. But there was no point denying the obvious. He had to have seen it, when he found her. 'She had been drinking that day, Abe. You and I both saw the empty bottle.'

'I'm not lying.' His voice was filled with anger. 'Someone must have put it there.'

'But why would they do that?' I couldn't keep the incredulity out of my voice.

'Dunno.' He sounded stubborn. 'But someone did.'

'Oh, Abe . . .' As I reached out to touch his arm, he stepped away, and that was it. He clammed up. When we went inside, he looked at me once, briefly, resentfully, before going to bed.

Summer

Where did it all start, Mother?

Once upon a time, with the fairy tale about the princess with blue eyes and pretty hair, who lived hidden away in the woods with her three children? The pretty cottage guarded by tall trees, the deer that grazed in their shadow.

Magic. It was all around us. Your eyes sparkled as you told us.

I used to watch you fetch the bottle that made the magic brighter, then we'd dance on the soft grass, fill the air with the sounds of our laughter. You'd stop for a moment, closing your eyes, holding out your arms while the breeze caught your dress, and I'd hold my breath, wait for you to fly.

It was desperation that gave birth to your fairy tale, carving it from hopes and dreams you struggled to hold on to, when the world you'd grown up in had none; formed from the molten anger of your parents swirling around you, a fragility that was moulded by their cruelty; always hiding the truth, between your words, behind your smile; in your silences.

You wanted to give your children what you'd never had. One of your lies. You'd said it so often you believed yourself, but it was never about us. It was what your own damaged soul craved. The love, space and freedom you never had.

But magic fades, Mother. Love isn't about parties and music. Freedom has a price.

Nothing lasts – you, more than anyone, should know that.

And fairy tales get twisted, but you couldn't see the darkening, spiralling decline you were caught in, which was sucking us in with you. You escaped the only way you knew how: drinking away the ghosts that haunted your days and nights, that still loomed over you when you sobered up. We couldn't.

We used to watch you, Jude and I. Count the number of drinks. After two your frown would fade, after four you'd be laughing. Six, and you might lurch as you walked, but that was the floor, you told us. God, you really had to do something about that floor . . . Why don't you go and play? Your eyes would smile vacantly at us, then drift away.

Do you know that often Jude and I would start the hour-long walk to Nell's, hunger growling inside us? That was when things got bad. Do you know how young Jude was, Mother? How far that was for a small child to walk, for food and kindness? By the time we got there, he was exhausted. But Nell knew, disapproval written in her eyes, the way she nodded, as she silently opened her door and let us in.

Did you know you were starving us? That we lay awake at night, hoping Sam would bring a loaf of bread or one of your friends would bring something. But you wouldn't believe that, would you? There was enough food, wasn't there? And this life was for us, you really believed that. You'd done everything you could to give us what you'd never had, couldn't we see that? We had so much to be grateful for.

How far back did it start, Mother? A life that revolved around your next drink, then the one after and the one after that.

When you had young children who depended on you, couldn't you have stopped?

4

Hannah

In between the short, fractious exchanges with Abe, I allowed myself to grieve for Matt. Coming out of the blue, his departure had left me in denial, devastated. Fluctuating hope that he would come back had given way to a deeper inner knowing that it was over between us. I should have told him the truth, I knew that. But I hadn't – and now it was too late, but it was a sense I wanted to deny; a truth I wasn't ready for. Abe and I had that much in common. Both of us needing to lick our wounds, until enough time passed and the rawness of loss began to heal. Life went on, but under the shadow cast by grief, even spring's unseasonal warmth and the earliest spring flowers showing delicate buds above the earth failed to move me the way they usually did.

Over the next couple of days, when I could bring myself to, I packed what remained of Matt's possessions into boxes, then moved them outside into the shed, while Abe kept himself to himself, spending most of his time in his bedroom. When my pupils came for their music lessons, he was nowhere to be seen, but he had his laptop and his phone. I didn't know, but

I assumed it meant he was keeping in touch with his old school friends. I tried to ask him about them, but he just gave one of his habitual shrugs, before telling me there wasn't anyone. And all the time I was trying to find a way to talk to him about Nina. To draw him out, to get him to tell me about his life, or how he was feeling, but I got nowhere.

I'd been putting off calling his school, not sure exactly what to say to them, but Abe's continual indifference forced the issue. I couldn't go on letting him treat me this way. Maybe someone who knew him would be able to help. I waited until I was alone, before dialling the number DI Collins had given me. The voice that answered the call sounded disinterested.

'Hello? I don't know whether you can help me. I wondered if I could talk to someone about Abe Tyrell.'

'Are you family?'

'I'm his aunt—' I started, but she interrupted.

'Do we have your details on our system?' Her officious tone irritated me.

'I'm his guardian,' I said hotly. 'You have my name as next of kin. His mother died a few days ago. The police contacted you.'

'Oh.' She sounded surprised. 'Yes. Of course. Hold on a moment, please.' She was gone for about five minutes, and when she came back, she sounded more sympathetic. 'If you give me your number, I'll ask one of his teachers to call you at lunchtime.'

'Thank you.' The school already had it, but it was simpler to give it to her again. Then, after I'd hung up, almost immediately another call came through.

'Ms Roscoe? It's DI Collins. Do you have a moment?'

'Of course.'

She sounded as though she was in a hurry. 'There's been a development. In fact there have been several. In short, I need to talk to Abe. Today, if possible. Are you both there this afternoon?'

'Yes . . .' I was frowning. 'Can you tell me what this is about?'

'I'll fill you in later. We'll be with you soon after two, traffic permitting, if that's OK with you?' I wondered who was coming with her. The 'we' clearly indicated she wasn't coming alone.

'I'll be here.' Other than one pupil at five o'clock for a piano lesson, I had no plans for the rest of the day.

'And Abe?' DI Collins added. 'It's important that we talk to him, I can't stress that enough.'

'I'll tell him.' But I couldn't promise. It was up to Abe whether or not he was there.

It was nearly midday by the time he came downstairs, wearing the same old school trousers with one of the new shirts, still sharply creased, fresh from its packaging.

'Hi. Did you sleep well?'

'OK.' He looked exhausted.

'How about some breakfast? I could cook some eggs?' When he looked vaguely interested, I added, 'Fried? On toast?'

He gave a brief nod.

While I fetched a frying pan and placed it on the hob, I heard him pull out one of the chairs. After putting two slices of bread in the toaster, I cracked a couple of eggs into the pan and, while they were cooking, turned to face him. 'DI Collins called earlier. She wants to talk to us both – this afternoon. I said we'd be here.'

But he didn't respond.

'She didn't say what it was about,' I added, buttering the toast and placing the eggs on top, passing the plate to Abe just as my mobile buzzed. 'I need to take this,' I said apologetically, seeing the unknown number on the screen and guessing it was one of Abe's teachers. Quickly passing him a knife and fork, I slipped out through the back door, closing it behind me.

'Hello?'

'Is that Ms Roscoe? I'm Elizabeth Rainer, one of Abe's teachers. I understand you wanted to talk to me?'

'Yes. I do. Thank you for calling back.' Relief flooded through me as I walked down the path away from the house, not wanting Abe to overhear me. 'He's been with me since his mother died.'

'I'd heard about what happened. I'm so sorry. Poor Abe. How is he?'

'I don't know,' I told her, hoping she'd be able to give me some kind of insight. 'I can't seem to get through to him. He ignores everything I say – well, pretty much,' I added, thinking of the night we were looking at the stars.

'So how can I help?'

'I just wondered how well you know him . . .' I faltered. 'What's he like? With other people . . . Does he have friends? I'm supposed to try and find a school for him locally. I've no idea what to say to them.'

'He's a quiet boy,' she said thoughtfully. 'Clever, though. His strongest subject is maths. As for friends, I don't really know. He always seemed to keep himself to himself. But then—' She broke off.

'What?' My ears pricked up.

'I was only going to say that living with his mother's problems can't have been easy for him.'

I don't know why, but I was surprised. If the school had known, surely they'd have done something, like notify social services, or maybe even get Abe taken into care. 'You knew about her drinking?' As with DI Collins, deliberately I didn't mention drugs.

'I worked it out. It became obvious there was a problem with money. Abe missed out on school trips, and he'd outgrown his school uniform . . . His mother made it to a parents' evening – just once. In fact I met her. It was clear she was drunk – or on something. I spoke to her on the phone a couple of times, when letters weren't replied to, that sort of thing. Her speech was slurred and she didn't make much sense. It was always the same. I felt sorry for him. The problem is . . .'

'Please go on.'

'I was only going to say that the effect on Abe was considerable. Damaging. Addiction affects the whole family. And it's isolating. It wouldn't have been possible for Abe to have a social life. Imagine how embarrassing it would have been, taking a friend home and finding his mother drunk. He would never have known what he was going home to – whether she'd be drunk or sober; unconscious, even. Also, he would have been aware that his mother couldn't afford any of the extras other families managed. And there was nothing he could do about it. All he could do was wait, until he was old enough to become independent. I felt so sorry for him.' She paused for a moment. 'I don't know if that's any help.' She sounded doubtful.

'Thank you.' I hesitated. 'You're right. I hadn't thought of it like that. I haven't found him a new school yet.'

'School might be good for him. Good luck with everything. I really hope he settles in.'

As I ended the call, I was deep in thought. Everything she'd said made sense. I was wondering if Abe's anger was directed at his mother, rather than at me, and at a world that had made everything so tough for him. Walking back towards the house, I was trying to work out what to say to him. His resentful silence seemed to be thawing at last into more of a tolerance of my presence. I was sure it would help him to talk, but so far he seemed intent on internalizing everything. As I got to the back door, I heard his voice. My hand froze on the door handle.

'Here, Gibson. Come here.'

As I listened, I smiled to myself. Animals could be the best ice-breakers. I could hear Gibson whining for attention and imagined him sitting at Abe's feet, holding up a paw as he begged for treats. It was one of his party tricks. The whining was interrupted by a loud yelp of pain and I threw the door open, to see Gibson standing there, quivering, as he held up one of his paws.

'You've hurt him.' I couldn't stop myself as I rushed to my dog. He was shaking uncontrollably.

'It was an accident.' Abe looked sullen. 'He got under my feet. I didn't do it on purpose.'

'Well, be more careful,' I cried. 'For God's sake . . .' He had no idea how important Gibson was to me and how, since Matt had left, Gibson was my only constant, almost always at my side.

Without saying anything, Abe stormed out of the room. A few seconds later I heard his feet on the stairs, then the sound of his bedroom door slamming shut.

Crouched down next to my dog, I examined Gibson's leg,

relieved to see that he was gingerly putting it to the ground again. I was already regretting shouting at Abe the way I did. I knew my reaction had been over the top, but it was only much later that I was able to identify why. There was something about Abe I didn't trust.

DI Collins arrived promptly at two o'clock with another plain-clothes officer, a man, who looked somewhat older.

'Ms Roscoe, this is DCI Weller. He's in charge of your sister's case.'

A cold feeling came over me as I shook his hand. Last time I'd spoken to DI Collins, there was no case. They'd been treating Nina's death as an accident. 'Please, come in. Abe's upstairs. I'll go and tell him you're here.'

As they came inside, I closed the door, suddenly claustrophobic. It wasn't just their presence, it was the feeling of foreboding that swept over me. As they followed me into the kitchen, DI Collins spoke. 'Actually, before you get him, it might be good if we could talk alone.'

'Of course.'

She glanced at the door. 'Do you mind if I close it?'

'I'll get it.' Walking over, I quietly shut the door and then, turning to them, gestured towards the table. 'Please, have a seat. Would you like coffee? Or tea?'

'No. Thank you.'

As they sat down, my unease was growing. 'I thought you said there was no case?'

'As I mentioned earlier, there have been a couple of developments.' DI Collins got out her notebook. 'But before I go into them, can I ask you if Abe has told you much about his mother?'

'Not really.' I shrugged. 'In general, he says very little. The other night, though . . . He did say that Nina had stopped drinking and was going to AA meetings. He hasn't mentioned her taking drugs, but when I mentioned the empty bottle in her room, he got quite angry.'

'He would have been upset,' DI Collins said. 'If he believed she'd given up, he must have felt badly let down.'

I hadn't thought of it in those terms, but she was right. And hadn't everyone let Abe down – including me? I thought of how I'd shouted at him earlier. 'Another thing he said was that some-one must have put it there deliberately. The bottle, I mean.'

DI Collins glanced at the DCI, then back to me. 'You're sure he said that?'

I nodded. 'It seemed an odd thing to say, but he was adamant.'

After making a note of it, she looked up at me. 'We've spoken to one or two of your sister's neighbours. Mostly they had little to say about her. They mentioned that she didn't appear to have a job and that her behaviour was odd . . . One of them said that, more than once, they'd seen her with a younger man who used to hand her something – presumably drugs. They also knew her in the shop at the end of her road, where she used to buy vodka. Otherwise, it seems she was rarely seen. By all accounts, Abe was quite solitary. A couple of them said they'd seen him at night, outside, standing there for hours, as though he was looking at the sky.'

'He's been doing that here. He's interested in the stars.' I paused. 'I've called his school.'

'And?' DI Collins looked interested.

'I spoke to one of his teachers. I wanted to know her impression of him, because I'm not finding him at all easy.'

'Who did you speak to?'

'Elizabeth Rainer.' I watched as DI Collins wrote it down. 'She said that Abe was bright, especially at maths. Also that he kept himself to himself, but she thought that wasn't surprising, given his mother's problems.' I paused. 'Have you found Jude?'

This time it was the DCI who spoke. 'We have an address, but as yet we haven't spoken to him. I would imagine he doesn't feel too well disposed towards the police.' He glanced at DI Collins. 'He was found guilty of GBH. He was given three years. He got out a year early – a month ago.'

I heard myself gasp. I'd told DI Collins that she could give him my address, but I was having second thoughts. 'Maybe it's best he doesn't know where I live. But what if he wants to see Abe?' I was panicking, imagining an angry Jude taking matters into his own hands, taking it upon himself to find out where his brother was and just turning up here.

'I understand. Under the circumstances, it's probably best if we don't pass on your details for now – though he may well get in touch with Abe. Do you know if they've spoken?'

I shook my head, making a mental note to ask him. 'I've no idea.'

The DCI went on. 'If he does turn up here and you're worried, you can always call the local police. I think it's unlikely, though. From the little Abe's already told us, it doesn't look as though they were close. And Jude's going to have to be careful – if he doesn't want to end up back inside.'

'Is this what you came to tell me?' I looked from one to the other.

When DI Collins was silent for a moment, I knew there was more. 'After you and Abe left the other night, I did another search of Ms Tyrell's room. I found a suicide note.'

'But . . .' I shook my head, trying to make sense of what she'd just said. 'Nina hit her head. There was blood. It was an accident.'

'That was what we thought. We're waiting for the post-mortem results, because at first it looked as though Ms Tyrell had taken an overdose. There was an empty bottle of sleeping pills, which I missed the first time I searched her room. And the note, of course.'

'What did it say?'

'That she'd tried to sort out her problems, but she'd ruined too many lives. She was sorry to do this, but Abe was better off without her . . . That was about it.' She frowned. 'It's likely she was suffering from depression. She'd been prescribed anti-depressants in the past – we've spoken to the GP practice she's registered with, though they hadn't seen her for two years.' She paused. 'Were you aware of your sister's history of depression?'

'No.' I was silent for a moment. There'd been moments of bleakness, but no more than that. There wasn't anything more I could tell her. 'Is there anything else I don't know?'

It was the brief hesitation before she spoke. There was something – something they didn't want to tell me. I was filled with alarm.

DI Collins looked carefully at me. 'Can you think of any reason why someone would have wanted to harm Ms Tyrell?'

I stared at her. 'I've already told you that I hadn't seen Nina for ten years. I've no idea who was in her life, or what she did. We'd completely lost touch.' I paused, frowning at them. 'But you just said she committed suicide.'

'That's how it appears. But we haven't ruled out the possibility that someone else was involved.'

'You think someone killed her?' I stared at her, horrified.

'We're not sure. There are several things that don't fit.' She glanced at DCI Weller. 'As I told you before, there was another contusion to the back of her head. Again, we need the full pathologist's report before we know for sure, but we're not convinced it was an accidental blow.'

'What about the suicide note?' I looked at her.

But my question went unanswered as DCI Weller leaned forward, his elbows on the table. 'I don't know whether you noticed, but there were a couple of CCTV cameras rigged up near where she lived. A year ago there was a spate of break-ins and a few people who lived in the street clubbed together and had them put in. We've been through the footage – it looks as though, earlier that day, Ms Tyrell had a visit. We're not sure who from. We haven't been able to identify the person.'

'I don't understand.' I was having trouble grasping what he was telling me. 'Are you saying that she took an overdose, but someone came in and killed her before it had taken effect?'

'Or perhaps her killer tried to make it look like a suicide.' DCI Weller looked at me.

Her killer. I was still struggling to take it in. 'But the note – her handwriting . . .'

'It's possible it was forged. We've taken it to analyse the handwriting – we found a letter she'd written recently, to compare it with. They look similar enough, but we'll know more when Forensics have looked at them.'

God, Nina . . . What happened that day? Who could have wanted to hurt you?

DI Collins spoke. 'Right now, we can't really tell you any more than that.' She glanced at her watch. 'Would you mind asking Abe to come in?'

My head was buzzing. In the short space of time since the police had arrived here, Nina's death had gone from an accident to a suicide, to suspected murder. I got up. 'Of course.' As I went upstairs, I was still reeling. I knocked softly on Abe's door. 'Abe? Are you in there? DI Collins is here. She asked if you'd mind coming to talk to her.'

There was quiet for a few moments, then I heard the floor creak, just before the door opened. Without saying a word, he pushed past me.

I followed him back downstairs and into the kitchen, where DI Collins was getting to her feet. 'Hello, Abe. How are you?'

He shrugged, only half looking at her. 'OK.'

DI Collins nodded. 'Abe, this is Detective Chief Inspector Weller. We'd like to ask you one or two things about your mum, if you're all right with that?'

Glancing at the DCI, he gave a nod.

'Why don't you sit down.' DI Collins waited as Abe drifted over and pulled out one of the chairs, slumping onto it.

I stood there, uncertain as to whether or not I should stay. 'Do you want me to go?'

'That's up to Abe.' She turned to him. 'Do you mind if your aunt stays while we talk to you?'

He shrugged again. 'If she wants.'

I glanced across at DI Collins, who nodded. I pulled out another chair.

'How are you settling in?' she asked him gently.

'OK.' His face gave nothing away.

'Abe, we wanted to find out more about your mother.' The DI watched his face the whole time she was speaking. 'Did she see many people?'

'No,' he muttered, his face expressionless.

'Had she fallen out with anyone?'

He shook his head. Then he looked up at her. 'Why d'you want to know?'

DI Collins hesitated. 'Do you know how often she used to drink, Abe? Was it every day?'

Abe's eyes flickered towards me. 'I already told *her*.' He nodded in my direction. 'She'd stopped drinking. She was going to AA.' He said it angrily, daring anyone to challenge him.

'Abe, it's best you just tell us the truth. Some of your neighbours have told us about her drinking.' DI Collins spoke gently.

'They're lying.' Abe glared at her, his face red with anger. 'How would they know anything about her, when they hardly saw her?'

The police officers exchanged glances. It was a fair point. When she was rarely seen, how was anyone supposed to know how Nina spent her days? But there was enough evidence to suggest that Abe was understandably in denial.

'We're just trying to work out exactly what happened,' DI Collins said diplomatically. 'Do you know which AA group she went to?'

He looked down again. 'It was in some church place. Down the road — on Tuesdays.'

'Do you know which church?'

He shook his head and DI Collins glanced at the DCI. 'It shouldn't be hard to find out.'

'Why are you asking all this?' His eyes blazed into hers. 'There was an accident. She hit her head—' He broke off.

'The thing is,' DI Collins glanced at me, then back to Abe,

'we're not sure that's what happened. We found a suicide note.'

'NO!' He stood up, his face furious. 'She wouldn't do that.'

'I agree. We don't think she did.' DI Collins spoke slowly and calmly. Abe sat down again. 'You see, the thing is, there was another injury to the back of her head. We're not sure yet, but we don't think it was accidental.'

Part of me wanted to reach out to Abe, to protect him from the brutality of what she was saying to him. I watched as he clasped his hands together, but he'd closed down again. His face gave nothing away as he spoke. 'So why was there a suicide note?'

'We don't know.' There was a moment of silence. 'A lot of things don't make sense right now. But please be assured, we'll find out what happened. Was there anyone she used to meet? Or who used to come to the house? Friends of hers? Or family?'

He shrugged. 'Not really. She used to have this friend called Lisa, but they hadn't seen each other for ages. Mostly she was on her own.'

'Do you know where Lisa lives?'

Abe shook his head. 'I think she moved.'

The DCI leaned forward. 'Did your mother have a laptop?'

Abe shook his head again. 'Sometimes she used mine. But hardly ever. Why?' Suddenly he looked alarmed. 'You can't take it. I'll need it for school.'

'I'm sorry. I'm going to have to ask you to hand it over. You'll get it back. But there could be something on there that's important.'

Abe stood up. 'There isn't.'

'We still need it, Abe.' DI Collins spoke firmly. 'Can you get it for us, please?'

He paused, then fled from the room and up the stairs, where I could hear him crashing around, before he reappeared carrying his laptop. He slammed it on the table and stormed out.

'I'm sorry.' DI Collins looked unhappy. 'He's not coping too well, is he?'

'No. He really isn't. It isn't easy for either of us.'

'Give it time.' She hesitated. 'We'll talk to your sister's AA group. She might have made a friend there who can tell us something.' Pausing, she got up. 'We'll be in touch.'

5

The weather had been unseasonably warm for March, with clear pale-blue skies and a warmth that was almost summer-like, rapidly changing at sunset when the temperature plummeted. I got used to Abe slipping outside as the day came to an end, standing there while the last of the light faded, watching the sun slip behind the trees, the outline of their branches stark against the pink- and lilac-hued sky. I wondered if he found the same solace out there that I found – it seemed to calm him in some way.

That evening, the wind picked up. I heard it gusting through the trees and buffeting against the windows as something outside got blown over, so that I almost missed the knock on my back door. The leap of my heart was involuntary, illogical, but I couldn't help hoping. Had Matt come back?

But as I opened the door, hope turned to disappointment when I was greeted by the sight of a familiar face.

'Curtis. This is a surprise.' Before Matt and I met, Curtis and I had been on a few dates until I broke it off. He was a nice enough guy, just not really my type. I hadn't seen him for a while. I was guessing he'd got wind of the fact that Matt had gone. I was right.

'Hi.' He paused. 'How are you? I heard—' He broke off.

'About Matt.' Needled, I finished the sentence for him, wondering who he'd heard it from, as the wind caught the door.

'Looks like we're in for a storm.' He was hunched, his collar turned up around his neck as he stood there on the doorstep.

Resigned, I stepped back. 'Do you want to come in?'

'Thanks.'

Closing the door behind him, I wandered back through to the kitchen. He stood in the doorway watching me. 'How are you doing?'

I didn't answer his question. Instead, I turned round to face him. 'How did you hear?'

He shrugged. 'One of Matt's friends – in the pub.'

'What did he say?' I glared at him, hating that I'd been talked about behind my back.

'Hey, take it easy, Hannah. No one was gossiping. All he said was that he hadn't seen Matt since he'd moved out. Nothing else. Then we changed the subject.'

'Sorry.' I sighed. 'You know I hate the way people gossip round here. Would you like a drink?'

'A coffee would be good.' His face was sympathetic as he stood there.

Curtis meant well, I knew that. Not for the first time, I wished I was more attracted to him, but it just wasn't there. I filled the kettle and switched it on, then went to the fridge for the bottle of wine, aware of him watching as I topped up my glass. Just then Abe burst in through the back door. Without so much as glancing at me, he kicked off his boots and disappeared through to the snug. Seconds later I heard his feet on the stairs.

'My nephew,' I said by way of explanation, taking in Curtis's look of astonishment. I took a gulp of wine and then, passing Curtis his mug of coffee, pulled out one of the chairs and sat down.

Curtis looked at me questioningly.

'My sister died. And please don't say you didn't know I had a sister.' I was already on the defensive. 'It's a long story. I didn't talk about her because we weren't in each other's lives. OK?'

'Cool.' He looked unfazed. 'How long's he staying with you?'

Leaning forward, I fixed my eyes on his. 'How about forever?'

He frowned. 'Really? You're OK with that?'

I shook my head. 'I don't really have a choice. There isn't anyone else.' Drinking my wine, I was silent.

'You're going through it, aren't you?' He said it gently, as I got up and went to fetch the bottle.

I blinked away the tears suddenly filling my eyes. 'A bit.'

'Can I help at all?'

Sitting down again, I looked at him. I wasn't sure what he meant. Given our past, Curtis getting involved in my life could be complicated.

It was as if he read my mind. 'Look, I'm offering as a friend, no more. I know you've just split with Matt. It occurred to me that your nephew might like some male company. I could take him fishing – or something else . . . I don't know. Just an idea.'

I tried to imagine Abe in his school trousers sitting on a river bank with Curtis, and couldn't. 'I'll think about it . . . but thanks.'

Just then, Abe came back into the kitchen. After Curtis's offer, it seemed a good idea to introduce them.

'Abe? This is a friend of mine. Curtis.'

'Hi.' Curtis looked at him. 'Hannah was just telling me you've moved here. Hope you're settling in?'

Abe frowned at him. 'Thanks.' He walked over to the fridge and got out a carton of milk. After pouring a glass, he went back upstairs.

I looked at Curtis's questioning face. 'This is what it's like. All the time.' I was speaking quietly, not wanting Abe to hear me. 'I've tried, but there's no conversation – well, hardly any. The only thing he talks about is the stars.'

'Really?' Curtis looked up sharply. 'It just happens that I have an old telescope. It was a passion of mine, too – a few years back. If you like, I could bring it over and show him how to use it.'

I was restless after Curtis left. Maybe he was right. Maybe Abe would relate better to a man. The way things were between us, anything was worth a try. Wandering through to the sitting room, I sat at my piano, my fingers wandering up and down the keys for a few brief moments, before I got up again and collapsed onto the sofa.

As I sat there, drowsiness hit me, the combination of a difficult day after other difficult days. Trying to keep my eyes open, I focused on the few pictures that were hanging on the walls.

They were nothing special – the small landscape painted by

a local artist, which I liked because it captured the emptiness of the open pastureland. Then there were a couple of larger abstract paintings on either side of the fireplace, which Nathan had bought and hadn't wanted to take with him. I'd never particularly liked them, but the room needed something of their size and I'd never got round to replacing them.

They were striking rather than attractive. Then, as I looked at them, I frowned suddenly. I was sure they'd been moved. The one on the right of the fireplace had been on the left. I was sure it had. Or maybe not – when had I last looked at them closely? As I tried to think, a feeling of unease came over me. They had been swapped. I distinctly remembered the darker of the two being hung closer to the window, where the light would catch it. And now it wasn't. Had I moved them and simply forgotten?

I was still puzzling over the pictures when I went to bed. It was later than usual, and I lay there, floating in and out of consciousness, lulled by the rain beating against the windows, listening as it gradually grew heavier, drowning out my thoughts. As I drifted off to sleep, I was dimly aware as my bedroom door creaked open.

Drowsily, imagining it could only be Abe, I tried to call out. *Abe? Is that you?*

But no sound came from me. As my eyes flickered open, slowly they adjusted to the darkness, making out the gap where the curtains didn't quite meet, while all the time I was aware of the rain beating against the window, heavier than earlier on, I vaguely registered. Then, from somewhere out of sight, I heard what sounded like slow footsteps.

I was suddenly wide awake, my heart thumping as I tried to turn and see who was there. Then the realization slowly sank in. I couldn't move. My body was completely frozen, paralysed, as though a heavy weight was pressing on me.

Another sound sent a rush of fear flooding through my veins. Panicking, I fought to lift my body off the bed, but my only movement was the involuntary racing of my heart, as pure terror rose in me. Someone was there. I could sense their presence, hear the sound of their breathing, slower than mine as they edged closer.

Overwhelmed with the need to escape, I was powerless. Then a pair of eyes loomed out of the darkness, too close, as they stared into mine.

Before I could scream, there was a loud bang. I sat up, petrified, relief flooding through me that I could move again. My hand shook when I reached for the bedside lamp and switched it on. In its dim glow, the room was empty.

I was convinced someone had been in my room. Collapsing back onto my pillows, my heart still racing wildly, I found the sound of the rain against the windows oddly reassuring as I contemplated what had just happened. My heart slowed, and logic gradually crept in. It had been terrifyingly, vividly real, leaving my body coated in sweat, but it had been a dream. It had to have been. Then I thought of those eyes that had stared into mine, as a crash of thunder made me jump and the room lit up in the electric glare of a lightning flash.

It must have been the thunder that woke me. Then I heard another noise – the sound of a door slamming somewhere downstairs. I leapt out of bed and crossed the room to the window, as another flash of lightning lit the garden, briefly illuminating a dark figure crossing the grass.

As I watched, I couldn't be sure if it was Abe or not. Pulling on my slippers, I ran along to his room and knocked. When there was no answer, I pushed open the door. A draught of cold air reached me. 'Abe? Are you there?'

When he didn't respond, I switched on the light. The covers were thrown back and his bed was empty, rain blowing in through the wide-open window. Going over there, I pulled it shut and closed the curtains, then went downstairs.

Quickly I searched each room, but there was no sign of him. *Should I call the police?* I remembered DI Collins's reassurance that first day when Abe went off, that he would come back, and he had. But I was panicking. I'd no idea why he'd gone out at this time of night, in this storm. What if he didn't come back? What if something happened to him? Glancing at the time, I decided I'd give him an hour. If he wasn't back by then, I'd call the police.

From his bed, Gibson opened his eyes briefly, then ignored me. Pulling out a chair, I sat down at the table, listening to the storm outside, uneasy as I remembered the dream again. The fear, my racing heart, the eyes staring into mine still seemed so real. Had they been his eyes? Could Abe have been in my room?

Then I remembered the paintings. I still wasn't sure if I'd moved them or not. Right now I didn't know what to think. Leaning forward onto the kitchen table, I rested my head on my arms, closing my eyes for a moment, thinking of my earlier conversation with DI Collins. It was possible someone had killed Nina and tried to make it look like a suicide attempt. If that was the case, who would do it – and why? The police hadn't mentioned any sign of a break-in. And there would have been nothing worth stealing. Nina had never been interested in possessions. I couldn't remember her ever owning anything of any value. My sister may have been weak, but weakness wasn't a crime. I couldn't imagine why someone would want to harm her.

As the memory of the dream faded, I must have dozed. I was woken abruptly as a door slammed shut. Drowsily I looked up, to see Abe standing there, water dripping off him.

'Where've you been? I was worried.' My voice was husky from sleep.

'Out.' He glared at me furiously, as if I had no right to be there.

I pulled myself together. 'What were you doing out there?'

'Does it matter?' Hands thrust in his pockets, he hunched his shoulders. 'I can go outside, can't I?'

'Of course,' I said weakly. I didn't want to start a fight with him. 'I was worried, that's all.'

'Yeah.' He stood there. 'So worried you fell asleep.'

I flinched at the sarcasm in his words. 'I was giving you time to come back. If you didn't, I was going to call the police.'

'The police?' He stared at me, utterly incredulous. 'For fuck's sake, I was watching the storm.'

'I didn't know that, did I? And you're soaked. You better change your . . .' I started.

He backed away. 'Don't fucking tell me what to do,' he said aggressively, fleetingly meeting my eyes with a look that chilled me, before disappearing out of the kitchen. I heard his footsteps on the stairs, then along the landing, before another door shut loudly as he went into his bedroom.

As I sat there, I was overcome with frustration. I didn't understand his rudeness, his contempt towards me. I'd never have imagined he'd simply been watching the storm. I was too exhausted to think about it now. But on top of everything else, his behaviour had unnerved me. I knew that, at some point, I had to confront him.

6

Back in bed, I listened to the storm rumbling in the distance, aware of the faintest glimmer of daylight creeping through the curtains before I finally drifted off to sleep. It was only a couple of hours later that I woke up. As I lay there, I was still thinking about Abe.

It wasn't the first time I'd felt intimidated by him. Suddenly I was angry. I was trying to do the right thing by him, yet I got nothing in return. I made up my mind. I'd had enough of him hanging around the house. It was time I got him into a local school. Then I was going to take Curtis up on his offer, if Abe would go for it. After getting dressed, I made a couple of phone calls to the two closest schools to arrange to visit them, surprised at how easy it was, once they knew the circumstances. Then I went upstairs and knocked on Abe's bedroom door.

'We're going to look at a couple of schools. We need to leave in half an hour.' My tone was no-nonsense. I didn't wait for a reply. I wasn't going to give him the opportunity to be rude again.

To my surprise, he was ready to leave on time. Not just

that, but he was wearing clean clothes and he'd combed his hair. I'd steeled myself, expecting more rudeness and resentment, rather than the indifference he displayed as we were shown around the two schools. In the end, the decision was made based on distance. We went home with a uniform tie and jumper and the following day, even though I'd offered to take him, Abe walked down to the village and caught the bus.

I was hoping that the routine would bring much-needed normality back to my life. What I hadn't expected was the sense of relief I felt once Abe had left the house. Suddenly I had it to myself for a few hours – and, with it, the space to reflect. But maybe too much space wasn't necessarily good; it wasn't long before my head filled with thoughts of Matt.

For the first time in days I tried to call him, but he didn't pick up. Hating how powerless I felt, I got up and started pacing around the kitchen. Then, unable to settle, I whistled to Gibson and, pulling on my jacket, took him out.

I hadn't been out walking since Abe had arrived. Taking the path that led across the fields, I headed in the direction of the village, breathing in the earthy scent of the cool air. The sky was a clear blue and the ground waterlogged after the storm, the short grass spongy underfoot. Gibson kept running off, following trails known only to him, while in the peace and stillness I felt at last as though I could breathe.

In the distance, I could hear the rumble of a tractor coming from one of the nearby farms, then as I got closer to Burley, through the trees ahead, a scattering of houses came into view. Listening to the chatter of birdsong, I was beginning to believe I had my life back. That, after losing Matt, I could start to imagine moving forward. In the fleeting moment of optimism, I felt the heaviness that had weighed on me lift slightly.

Across the field I noticed a couple of other people out walking. At this time of year I rarely met anyone, but as we drew closer, my heart sank. The Denhams had lived here for thirty years and prided themselves on knowing everything about everybody.

'Hannah.' Colin Denham's customary greeting, as he stopped a few feet away. 'How are you?' Then, without waiting for an answer, he added, 'I haven't seen that young man of yours for a while.'

I felt myself tense. 'He's been busy.' I could feel his wife's eyes boring into me, rooting for details. I forced a smile that hid my irritation with them. 'Beautiful day, isn't it? How are you both?'

'That boy we've seen around . . . Is he staying with you?' Colin's manner was overly jovial.

I stiffened. I had no time for their blatant intrusiveness. All they wanted was gossip. I should have guessed they'd have noticed Abe – I wondered where they'd seen him. But they didn't need to know about Nina. 'Yes. He's my nephew.'

Mary Denham stared a little too long at me, clearly wanting to know more. 'I thought there was a family resemblance.'

'I hope he hasn't been making a nuisance of himself?' I kept my voice breezy.

'No, no . . . We just couldn't help noticing him. A new face, you know how it is round here.'

Only too well, I wanted to say. People like the Denhams, who liked prying into other people's lives, were the reason I kept away from them. 'Of course,' I said politely. 'Well, if you'll excuse me, I really should be getting along.'

'Yes, quite . . .' They both stood back and let me pass. Feeling their eyes on me as I walked away, I was sure I could hear them muttering to each other. But my personal life was nothing to do with them and I wanted to keep it that way. I was reminded of something Nina had always said. *The more you tell people, the more they want to know.* She'd been right. It was far simpler not to tell them anything.

That afternoon, I was about to put on some washing when I remembered the clothes Abe had been wearing, the night he was out in the storm. Going upstairs, I went along to his bedroom. It was untidy in there, his clothes and possessions strewn everywhere, the damp clothes in a pile on the floor where he'd left them. But as I bent down to pick them up, something else caught my eye, under his bed.

It was a laptop. But I'd distinctly remembered him handing one over to DI Collins, and the irritation he'd made no attempt to hide. I'd no idea where this one had come from. As I stood there, I heard the kitchen door slam. It had to be Abe, just back from school.

Quickly gathering up the damp clothes, I went downstairs. Abe was at the bottom. When he saw what I was carrying, he frowned.

'I was about to put some washing on,' I said brightly. 'Then I remembered these. They got soaked when you were out in the storm.' I nodded towards the armful of clothes. 'How was school?'

'OK.'

'That's good . . . Was it much different to your old school? Were they friendly?'

'It was just school. Can I get past?'

I wanted to ask him about the laptop, but his hostility stopped me. 'Of course.' I stood to the side and let him go upstairs, then went to put the washing on, but I was still thinking about the laptop. I was in a quandary. As far as the police investigation went, I wasn't sure if Abe was withholding evidence – and if I knew about it and kept silent, then I, too, was guilty of doing the same.

I could imagine what Abe's reaction would be if I mentioned it, but I knew I had to. In my head, I rehearsed what I was going to say. *Abe, when I went to get your clothes, I couldn't help noticing another laptop. Don't you think you should have handed it over to the police?* But I knew that, however I worded it, he'd be angry with me. I decided in the end to leave it – at least for now. It didn't resolve anything, but we had to live together. Another confrontation was hardly going to help build trust between us.

I was distracted by the front doorbell ringing. Looking at the time, I realized it was my first student. Piling the washing into the machine and switching it on, I went to let them in.

For the next couple of hours, I was focused on teaching, pushing thoughts of Abe from my head until the last of my pupils had gone. Then as I went through to the kitchen, I found him already in there, pulling on his jacket.

'Do you like Indian food? I thought I'd cook a chicken curry.'

Loitering in the doorway, he nodded briefly. 'I was going to take Gibson out.' His sideways glance was brief, without making eye contact.

'Of course. Good idea. It'll be about an hour.' As Abe called him, Gibson trotted over, then followed him outside.

When they came back, Abe was the most relaxed I'd seen him since he'd got here. As we ate, I told him what Curtis had said about bringing his telescope over. If not exactly enthusiastic, he didn't dismiss the idea.

Again, I thought of the laptop, but couldn't bring myself to lower the mood, putting it off, justifying the delay to myself. If Abe had thought it would help the police enquiries, he'd have handed it over, surely. Out of all of us, it would be Abe who'd want Nina's death resolved more than anyone.

Where did it start, Hannah? Was it with the band falling apart? Your teenage years? Your childhood? I'm curious. What was it that turned you into what you are?

The past is heavy, isn't it? A weight on you. Did it lift briefly when Matt was with you? Before the twist of fate that wrenched him away for good? So that you didn't walk, head down, hunched, loneliness clouding your eyes, as you do now; nervy, in your leather jacket and skinny jeans, your eyes flitting around, never settling on anything for long.

It doesn't seem fair, does it? That however hard you've tried – no matter how much time passes – you can't escape the past. Bad things always happen to you, don't they, Hannah? As if there's some kind of agenda against you. But, if you're honest, there's a part of you that knows it's what you deserve.

Your past is a book slammed shut, buried at the back of a dark cupboard, because it's not your fault, but there's one chapter that you – and you alone – are accountable for. A decision you made that altered lives.

Do you think about that time? About Abe, Jude and Summer? Are you haunted by the fallout of your actions? Or are you too selfish, too preoccupied? Don't turn away, Hannah. Even you can't pretend it didn't happen. You know only too well what I'm talking about.

And now there's Abe. People have noticed him, but people in villages notice most things. They're already talking about you both, wanting to know more. Why has he come here? Who is he? Why is he living with the music teacher that her students are slightly in awe of; the same woman that Matt left and that Curtis is still in love with, whose sister was an addict and killed herself? They may not know that yet, but when the press get hold of what happened, they will.

But she didn't kill herself. You killed her, Hannah; you caused her slow, steady suffocation from the abandonment and loneliness you could have prevented; the bleeding from the problems that you could have helped her with, which started as a scratch and, unchecked, became a severed artery. You could have cured her pain with love.

But you chose not to. You had your reasons – a hundred of them, why you had to do what you did, all of which make perfect sense to you – but you're still guilty, Hannah. And somewhere, deep inside, you know.

7

Hannah

More than anything, I yearned for the return of peace to my world. Peace that had been ruptured, first when Matt left, then again – even before I'd salvaged it – when Abe came to live here. Even when he was at school the house felt different, as if it held the echo of his presence. My home, my life, seemed to have shifted.

I managed a brief interlude of tranquillity when I walked Gibson the next morning, driving a few miles out of the village to walk the stony paths that crossed acres of open heathland, losing myself in a drab landscape that was only just struggling back to life after the winter, the brown of the heather lit now and then by bright-yellow flashes of common gorse, the air laced with salt.

At this time of year, when it rained, it could be bleak out here. Today there was weak sunlight, but I didn't mind that. It was the emptiness of the heathland I craved, to feel the solace it offered. It was too early in the year for the tourists who flocked here in summer and so, apart from the ponies and cattle that wandered freely, Gibson and I met no one.

I walked for a couple of miles, feeling the stillness soak into me, the air cool on my skin as my mind started to calm. It was a timeless landscape, which was transformed each year from the bleakness of winter to the lush green of the summer months, before turning into the reds and golds of autumn again. Today held the promise of spring, in tiny leaf buds and brightening shades of green, the first wild flowers appearing in more sheltered places, reminding me that life went on; that, no matter what happened, there was always hope.

But it was a false, short-lived sense of peace I found. Peace that stayed with me only until I turned up the track to my house, and which was cruelly shattered when I saw Matt's car parked on the gravel outside.

Parking next to him, I got out of my car, my heart racing. Out of nowhere, I was filled with hope. He was here. Maybe we still had a chance. Suddenly aware of my clothes, I was wishing he'd called to warn me, so that I could have put on some make-up and worn something other than the ripped jeans and ancient sweater I'd pulled on this morning.

Tentatively I was walking up the path towards the house, trying to think about what I wanted to say, when the door was opened from the inside.

Matt stood there. He looked tired, thinner than when he'd left. As I took in the serious look in his eyes, my hopes vanished. I knew instantly he hadn't come back for a reconciliation. I'd always been able to read his face. Gibson was at his feet, dancing around, his tail wagging furiously. Matt bent down to stroke him.

'How are you?' His eyes were solemn as they looked up and met mine.

Swallowing, I held his gaze. 'I've been better. You?'

'I'm OK. I hope you don't mind. I still had my key. I let myself in. I thought it might be easier . . .'

I stood there. I didn't know what to say.

He went on. 'I came to pick up the rest of my stuff, but I can't find it.' He was abrupt, his voice lacking the warmth I remembered.

'I packed most of it in boxes. They're in the shed. I'll get the key.'

He stood back and let me inside. The key was on a hook in the kitchen and, as I came back with it, I stopped in front of him. If I didn't say anything now, he'd be gone before I knew it, and it would be too late.

'Couldn't we talk, Matt?' I tried to sound calm.

As his eyes met mine again, I felt the familiar flicker of connection between us. But he looked away.

'There's no point, Hannah. I'm sorry.' His voice was hard.

'I don't understand.' Hearing the desperation in my voice, I stopped myself.

He shook his head. 'I know you don't. That's the problem.' He looked at me again. 'You should talk to someone. Get help.' Then his eyes narrowed as he looked at Abe's boots on the floor. 'You have someone here?'

I stared at him. It had been his decision to leave. It was none of his business who was here now. 'My sister died. Her son's staying with me. He didn't have anywhere else to go.'

His face took on a look of incredulity. 'You had a sister? Jesus, Hannah!' He shook his head. 'I've known you all this time. We were living together. You never thought to tell me you had a sister?'

'We were estranged.' I felt cold all of a sudden.

'What else don't I know about you?' Matt was silent for a

moment. 'Relationships are supposed to be based on honesty. And trust. I've had time to think about this – and, you know, the one thing I still can't get my head around is how, after all this time, I've no idea who you really are. Oh, I know, you're Hannah Roscoe and you live in the house your husband left you. You used to be in a band, and you teach music to private pupils – but other than that, behind those blue eyes and that smile, I really don't know who's in there.' He shook his head sadly. 'But you know what's even worse? I'm not sure you do, either.'

I pushed past him and walked back out, heading for the shed. Unlocking the door, I went in and pulled out the suitcase, then got each of the boxes I'd packed up, dropping them on the ground before locking the shed again, aware of Matt standing behind me.

'Your stuff.' I nodded at the boxes, not meeting his eyes.

He didn't move. 'You may not want to acknowledge what happened, but it doesn't change it, Hannah. It won't go away. The past will always be there.'

I clamped my hands over my ears. 'Shut up, Matt. You don't know what you're talking about.'

I felt his hand grasp one of my arms, too tightly. 'I know far more than you think.' His voice was icy.

Twisting my arm out of his grasp, I backed away. 'Fuck off, Matt! I've nothing to say to you.'

'Yeah, right.' His eyes glittered. 'That's how it is with you, isn't it? A minute ago you wanted to talk. But as soon as I say something you don't want to hear, you tell me to fuck off. And you wonder why I left.'

I couldn't understand why he was twisting everything. Whatever he thought he'd found out about me, it was hardly fair of him not to tell me what it was, give me a chance to tell my side of events. Nothing he was saying was making sense. It felt like he'd gone a step too far for us to go back, to try and fix things. My eyes filled with tears as I realized. 'It's like you said. There's no point trying, is there? Just take your stuff, Matt. I'm going inside.' Just then I heard my phone buzz. I fished it out of my pocket. It was DI Collins. 'I have to take this.' Answering it, I turned and started walking back to the house.

'Ms Roscoe? I thought you'd want to know where we are with the investigation.'

'Yes. Of course . . .' Clearing my throat, I tried to concentrate on what she was saying, aware of Matt standing there, watching me, as I walked back towards the house.

'It looks as though your sister had been drinking the day she died, but her blood-alcohol level wasn't high enough to kill her. There wasn't any evidence she'd taken pills, either.'

'But . . .' I was trying to think straight. 'What about the empty bottle – and the suicide note? What was the point of that?'

'It looks like someone attempted to make it look as though she'd taken her own life – but they didn't think it through.'

I was shaking my head as I went inside and closed the door behind me. 'They could never have imagined they'd get away with it!' It was yet another bizarre incident that didn't fit.

'I agree – unless they didn't expect the police to get involved, with blood tests carried out and so forth. We've also examined the CCTV footage. I told you before, it showed a figure walking along the street, then across the road towards your sister's house. About fifteen minutes later the same figure appears again, walking back in the opposite direction. We've also confirmed the timing is consistent with your sister's death.'

My heart missed a beat. 'Can you see who it was?'

'Not yet, but we're still working on the footage. All we know is that they were of average height, wearing loose-fitting jeans and a bulky hoody, which entirely obscured their face.'

'So you don't even know if it was a man or a woman?'

'Right now, it's impossible to tell. But we're looking at other CCTV in nearby shops and Tube stations, to see if whoever it was shows up anywhere else.'

But there were dozens of shops, and several Tube stations that could be reached on foot, not to mention the thousands of people using them daily, no doubt a proportion of them wearing loose-fitting jeans and hoodies. I began to grasp the scale of the investigation.

DI Collins went on. 'Forensics have finished in your sister's house. You can go in whenever you like. The key's been left with her neighbour.'

As I switched off my phone, I suddenly realized that although I knew the house needed clearing, I'd given no thought to going back to Nina's. Looking up, I saw Matt standing in the doorway. I hadn't heard him come in. I wondered how long he'd been there. Reaching into his pocket, he held out something. 'Your key.'

'Is that it?' My earlier anger had faded. 'You're going?' Hope flickered, briefly, faintly. How had it come to this?

'I'm sorry . . .' He hesitated.

'Matt, couldn't we work this out?' I kept my voice calm. I had to ask, even though I could see the answer on his face.

'God, Hannah! After everything you haven't told me, how could I ever trust you? It's too late, can't you see that?'

'It's not too late, Matt. I can change.' I couldn't keep the desperation out of my voice. And it was true. Surely he could see that?

He stood there for a moment, then sighed. 'Hannah, we're way past ever working this out. I'm sorry. I should go.' He turned and walked away, closing the door behind him.

Completely numb, I watched from the window as he walked down the path and loaded the last few things into his car, then stood there for a moment, looking towards the house. I shrank behind the curtains, not wanting him to know I was watching him. Then he got in his car and, seconds later, drove away.

Only when his car was out of sight did I slump onto the floor, leaning against the wall, aware of the tears streaming down my face, feeling overwhelmed by the hurt, betrayal and hopelessness I'd suppressed while Matt was here. All made worse because I didn't understand.

I would have stayed where I was, watching the light slowly ebb away, if I hadn't remembered Abe would soon be home. Getting up, I dried my face, not wanting him to see me in this state. Shaken to the core by Matt's appearance, I went to the fridge, getting out a bottle of white wine, my hand shaking as I poured a glass. I drank it quickly, welcoming the numbness that started to creep over me, blunting the edge of my pain, as I felt a flicker of strength return. Maybe it was as well he'd gone, because today I'd seen a completely different side to him. The kind, gentle Matt I remembered had become cold and vicious, stabbing at me with his harsh words and his lies.

His reaction when I told him about Nina had been unnecessary. I'd had reasons for not telling him about her. It would have meant opening the lid on that part of my past I'd tried my hardest to leave behind. There was nothing wrong with that. There were chapters in everyone's lives they'd rather forget. I was no different from anyone else.

I felt my resolve strengthen. As far as Matt was concerned, I was better off without him. My tears were already forgotten when, just minutes later, I heard Abe at the back door. Putting my glass in the sink, I pulled myself together and turned to face him.

'How was your day?' I tried to sound bright, noticing the look of suspicion on his face. 'DI Collins called a little while ago.' I spoke quietly, wanting to break it gently to him, but there was no way to take the brutality out of what I had to tell him. 'Abe, they're fairly sure that whoever killed your mum wanted it to look like a suicide attempt.' I watched him, expecting anger, tears, a reaction of some kind. But he showed nothing. 'Also, they've picked up someone on CCTV who they think may be a suspect.'

Staring at the floor, his face was blank as he nodded slowly.

'She said that Forensics have finished in the house. If you like, we could go up there on Saturday.'

Abe looked at me oddly.

'To London,' I added. 'Only if you want to, but I thought you'd want to pick up the rest of your things – and anything from the house you want to keep. I suppose we'll have to think about house-clearance for the rest.' I wasn't sure how he'd feel about going back there, but I'd been sure that at some point he'd want the rest of his stuff.

'So . . .' he frowned. 'I'm staying here?' Only he didn't frame it as a question.

I paused. 'It looks that way.'

He said nothing. Then suddenly he stormed out. As I heard

him go upstairs, I thought of the second laptop again. I'd completely forgotten about it when I was talking to DI Collins earlier. Since the police were now looking at a murder investigation, I knew the time had come to talk to Abe, however difficult it was going to be.

I went upstairs and knocked on his bedroom door. 'Abe? Can I come in for a minute?'

It was so quiet that for a moment I wondered if he was in there, but then I heard footsteps from inside, before the door was flung open. 'What do you want?'

'I need to ask you something. But first I want you to know that I wasn't prying into your things, because I'd hate you to think that. But when I came in to get your washing the other day, I couldn't help noticing you had another laptop. I'm only mentioning it because of what DI Collins said. Maybe you should give it to the—'

He interrupted me, looking furious. 'What are you talking about?'

'It was there, Abe. Under your bed.' I pointed to where I'd seen it.

'There's nothing there,' he said rudely.

I was shaking my head. 'But, Abe, I know what I saw.'

He opened the door wide. 'Why don't you look for yourself.' With an exaggerated sweep of his arm, he gestured towards the bed.

I hesitated. 'I'll show you where I saw it.' I went over and moved the bedclothes slightly and pointed to where I'd seen the laptop. 'It was there.' Looking under the bed, I frowned. The only thing under there was a thick sketchbook in a black cover.

'Believe me now?' His voice was full of contempt.

'Sorry . . .' I started backing out. 'I'm so sorry, Abe. I was obviously mistaken.'

'Yeah.'

As soon as I was out of the room, he slammed the door behind me. Already I was regretting not standing up to him. He was lying, there was no doubt. I knew what I'd seen, but – faced with his denial, and in the absence of any proof – there was nothing I could say. All I'd managed to do was damage our relationship even further.

Going back downstairs, I found my phone and texted Curtis. *Yes please to the telescope. H.*

I needed his help.

8

I was consumed with wanting to know why Abe had lied about the laptop. I knew enough about teenagers to know that phones and tablets were how they stayed connected, so I could understand him wanting to hang on to it. Maybe I was reading too much into it. He knew what was on it and whether there would be anything of any use to the police. What bothered me most was why he'd lied.

But communication was non-existent between us. For the rest of the evening Abe refused to speak to me, while I bit back my frustration, knowing another confrontation would achieve nothing. Unless I found the laptop, there was little I could do. But since seeing Matt, something else was nagging at me. It was his comment – about relationships being based on honesty. It had struck a chord. It wouldn't be easy, but when the time was right, there was a conversation I needed to have with Abe.

I'd already decided to thoroughly search his room and, while he was at school the next day, I let myself in. Taking care to leave everything as I'd found it, I looked everywhere I could think of, but there was no sign of the laptop.

The black-bound sketchbook was still under his bed. As I stared at it, I was starting to doubt myself. Could I have been mistaken?

I was distracted by the sound of Gibson's barking, alerting me to the arrival of someone. Going to my room, I looked out of the window, but there was no car outside. I called down to him, but after a few seconds his barking became more agitated.

As I reached the bottom of the stairs, I heard what sounded like knocking on the back door.

'Gibson . . .' Hearing me, Gibson barked louder and then, as I walked into the kitchen, he jumped up at the back door. 'It's OK. You want to go out?'

The door wasn't locked. I opened it and Gibson took off across the garden, still barking frantically. I was puzzled. I could have sworn someone had been knocking and I knew Gibson didn't usually bark at nothing, but as I stood outside and looked around, there was no sign of anyone.

I was already uncomfortable and, when I pulled on my boots and started walking around the house, my uneasiness grew. I knew I'd heard something. Then as I reached the back of the house, across the fields a slight movement in the distance caught my eye, in the shadows under a group of trees. Was someone there? Frowning, I watched for any further movement, until Gibson came running over, wagging his tail.

Seeing nothing more, I gave up. If anyone had been hanging around, they'd clearly gone. But as I went back inside, it crossed my mind: could it have been Jude? As far as I knew, the police were still trying to track him down, but I couldn't help thinking, it wouldn't be surprising if, at some point, he turned up here.

It happened again later that evening. As usual, Abe had disappeared outside into the darkness. I was sitting in one of the armchairs in the snug, with a drink and a book. I'd felt cold earlier on and I'd already lit the wood-burner. Now I piled on more logs, listening to the crackle of burning wood, starting to feel drowsy in the heat it was throwing out.

After a while, I put my book down and closed my eyes for a moment, until I was startled awake by what sounded like someone knocking on the window. In my haste to get up, I knocked my drink over. Even as I told myself it was a stem of the rose that climbed up the back of the house, caught by the wind, I knew it wasn't. I'd pruned that rose not long ago and carefully tied the stems back; not only that, but there was no wind.

As I stood there, I heard it again. Then the back door opened and slammed shut, followed by silence. I froze, feeling my heart thudding, straining my ears to listen. Was someone in the house?

'God!' I jumped as Abe came through the doorway.

'What?' He glowered at me.

'I think I heard someone. Outside. They were knocking on the window. It wasn't you, was it?' Was he trying to put me on edge for some reason? But it couldn't have been him, I realized. The sound had barely stopped when he'd opened the door.

He looked at me as if I was mad. 'No.'

'Someone was there,' I told him urgently. 'I'm sure they were. Just now. We need to lock the back door.' As I hurried towards the kitchen, Abe followed.

'I'll go and look. If you want.' It was the first time he'd volunteered to do anything.

I gasped, as relief filled me. 'Would you? Be careful, though. We don't know who's out there. Take Gibson.'

As he pulled his jacket back on, I watched him go outside, Gibson following at his heels. Suddenly I was overcome with guilt that I wasn't going with him, but the noise had unnerved me and I felt too shaky.

I was relieved when, less than five minutes later, he came back in. 'There's no one there.'

I hurried to lock the back door behind him. 'You are sure, aren't you? It's just that I know I heard something.'

He frowned at me. 'I'm sure. It's stopped, hasn't it?'

'It seems to have . . .' I hesitated.

'Maybe it was a bird or something.' *Or maybe you imagined it*, I could almost hear him thinking as he turned and started walking towards the stairs.

'Thank you,' I called after him, but he didn't respond. It was as if he hadn't heard me.

Still on edge when I went to bed, I didn't sleep well, waking earlier than usual, thinking of the tapping on the window again, as I realized it could only have come from one of the shrubs planted along the back of the house. Most likely one of the long, arched stems of the rose had come untied. Suddenly wanting to know, I got dressed and went downstairs, then pulled on my boots and went outside.

Breathing in the earthy scent of the cool air, I walked across the grass, taking in the dew glistening in the early-morning sunlight, pausing for a moment to watch a blackbird perched on a branch, in full song.

Around me, nothing moved. Apart from the bird, it was silent. I carried on walking, the sun briefly dazzling me as I reached the back of the house, continuing towards the window that looked out from the snug. As I looked at the plants, it was just as I'd thought. The climbing rose was firmly tied back and there were no loose stems that could have reached the window. Studying it, I was puzzled. I knew I hadn't imagined the noise. Then, as I looked around, I saw something lying in the grass under the window. Walking closer and bending down, I picked up a stick.

Uneasily, I turned towards the window, tentatively tapped the stick against the glass, then let go of it as if I'd been burned. It was no accident that the stick was there. Someone had obviously dropped it. It was the same noise I'd heard last night, I was sure of it.

The rest of the day I was on edge, locking the door after Abe left for school, listening out for unusual noises, constantly glancing outside. I wasn't sure what was happening, or why, but I knew something wasn't right.

That evening, when Curtis turned up with the telescope, disappearing into the garden with Abe, I didn't join them. I knew Abe wouldn't want me there. Instead I waited inside until, an hour later, Curtis came back in.

'I've shown him how to use it.' His eyes were bright as he walked into the kitchen. 'He's still out there. I asked him if you'd mind, but he said you wouldn't.'

I shook my head. 'It's fine. It's where he spends most evenings. Did he say much to you?'

Curtis frowned. 'Not really. But then he has just lost his mother. It's a difficult time for him.'

'Yes.' I was silent for a moment. It was what everyone was saying to me. 'But what I find difficult is that most of the time he doesn't react to anything. It's like he's switched off.'

Curtis shrugged. 'It could just be that it's early days.' He paused. 'You haven't told me what happened to your sister.'

'No.' I sighed, aware that if he was getting to know Abe, even slightly, I should tell him. 'The police think someone killed her.' I glanced at Curtis, taking in the look of shock fleetingly crossing his face. 'But I can't imagine who would have done that to her. She was a gentle person, who would never knowingly have hurt anyone. At first the police thought she'd been drinking or had taken something, then fell and hit her head. But now they think someone killed her.'

Curtis shook his head, a look of sympathy on his face. 'Did she drink a lot?'

'She drank, but not that much. Nina's thing was drugs.' I frowned, watching him nodding. 'What?'

'It might explain why Abe is so detached – switched off, as you put it. He's had to find a way to protect himself. If your only parent is permanently out of it, it rather leaves you on your own, I'd imagine.'

I frowned. Since when did Curtis know about these things? Before I could ask, the back door opened and Abe came in. 'How was the telescope?' I called out.

Closing the door, he came through to the kitchen, his cheeks pink from the cold. 'Good.' He looked at Curtis. 'Thanks.'

'You're welcome. It's good to see it being used. Here, I'll give you my mobile number, then you can text me if you have any problems with it.'

Abe's expression became more guarded. 'The police took my phone.'

'Oh.' Curtis looked surprised. 'OK. Well, I'll write it down for you.'

I'd been about to interrupt, telling Abe I already had Curtis's number, but Curtis caught my eye and I stayed silent. Abe nodded, watching as he wrote it on a piece of paper, while I went over to the fridge and got a beer out for Curtis. The exchange between them was positive, but it was needling me. If Abe was open towards Curtis, why was he so different with me? I could only think he had something against me, but I had no idea what it was.

After Abe went upstairs, I told Curtis about the noise I'd heard last night, mortified by his apparent amusement.

'Hannah, it could have been anything!' He was trying not to laugh at me.

I was irritated. 'Actually, the next morning I went and had a look in daylight and found a stick that had been dropped there. And the other morning, something else happened. There was this knocking on the door. It went on for a few minutes – I was upstairs. Gibson was barking. But by the time I went downstairs to open it, there was no one there.'

'Probably kids,' Curtis said briefly. 'Out here, with no neighbours, you're a bit of an easy target. There are a lot of places to hide out there.' He must have seen the expression on my face. 'I wasn't entirely serious, Hannah. I'm sure it was nothing.'

In all the years I'd lived here, the neighbourhood kids had never done that kind of thing. Somewhat guardedly, I decided to tell him about the pictures. 'There's something else. You know those two pictures in my sitting room?'

'I think so – the ones Nathan left behind?'

Even though I didn't particularly like them, the paintings

somehow symbolized my old life, when the band was success-ful. My marriage to Nathan may have been brief, but the paintings had been here almost as long as I had. Remembering how drawn Curtis had been to them when he first saw them, I nodded. 'The other night, when I went in there, someone had moved them.'

'What do you mean?'

'I've always hung the darker one by the window, because of the light, but when I went in there the other night, they'd been swapped.'

He shrugged. 'You could have moved them and forgotten.'

I spoke quietly. 'I could have. But, Curtis, don't you think I'd have remembered? And I don't move paintings. The only thing I've changed since Nathan left was when I cleared out some stuff before Matt moved in.'

He was frowning as he got up. 'Show me.'

I knew he'd notice straight away that they weren't where they'd always been. Going through to the sitting room, I turned on the light and led him over to the paintings. 'There.' I stood there, frowning, gazing at the paintings in silence. 'I don't understand,' I said at last.

His arms were folded as he stared at them. 'So, tell me what's wrong.'

But I wasn't listening to him. Someone had been in here again. 'They're back where they used to be. But it definitely wasn't me who moved them. It has to be Abe.' Suddenly I wanted to have this out with him. I started marching towards the door, prepared to go upstairs and challenge him, but Curtis stopped me.

'Hey, not so fast. What exactly are you going to say to him?'

'I'm going to tell him to stop fucking with my stuff.' I was furious. 'If this is his idea of a joke, it's really not funny.'

Just then I heard Abe's footsteps on the stairs.

'Abe?' I called sharply. 'Can you come here, please?'

There was silence, then he appeared in the doorway. 'What?'

Glancing at Curtis, I took a breath. 'Have you by any chance moved my paintings?'

His face was blank. 'What?'

'Those two.' I pointed to the two abstracts on the wall behind me.

'That's where they always are, isn't it?' Suddenly he sounded less sure.

'They are now.' I was impatient. 'But they weren't.'

Abe shrugged. 'I hadn't noticed.'

As I stood there, a sense of helplessness came over me. It was clear that neither of them believed me, but I knew what I'd seen. 'Never mind. I probably imagined it.' But I didn't mean it. I knew someone had been in here and moved them, and if not Abe, then who? I started walking back towards the kitchen, trying to cover up what I was really thinking. 'It doesn't matter.'

After pouring another glass of wine, I sat down, still thinking. Neither of us spoke until Abe had gone back upstairs. 'He's a strange one,' Curtis said quietly.

My skin prickled. 'He's had a tough time. Cut him some slack.' After all the problems I had with Abe, I couldn't believe I was defending him.

Curtis looked at me oddly. 'I don't know. It's probably nothing. He's just completely different from other kids I've met. But how many kids have had a life like the one he's had? It's hardly surprising.'

'Would you like another beer?' I got up, wanting to change the subject. For reasons I didn't want to think about, dwelling on the hardships Abe had endured was too uncomfortable.

'Thanks, but I'd better not. I've got an early start in the morning. I'd better go.'

There was something else strange that I hadn't told Curtis about. A couple of things were missing. One was a small bronze statue of a naked woman, which Nathan had brought back from his travels. I'd liked it even less than the abstracts. After he left, I'd moved it, and for years it had sat tucked away on a windowsill, almost out of sight. Before Matt moved in, I'd carried some of Nathan's collection out to the shed, making space for Matt and singling out the pieces I wouldn't miss. Maybe the statue had been among them – I couldn't remember. I'd have to check.

The other was a framed photo of the Cry Babies, which again I'd hidden, but only because of the memories it evoked. Maybe I'd put it in the chest with everything else that reminded me of those days, hidden, so that I didn't have to look at them.

Just before I went to bed, on impulse I went into the sitting room again and switched on the light. Collapsing on the sofa, I stared at the pictures – in the same places they'd always been. Curtis was right. The most likely explanation was that I'd imagined it. I frowned. It was easier to believe him, and yet I'd been so sure.

On Saturday morning Abe and I set off for Nina's house, Abe sitting next to me in typical silence. Every so often I glanced across at him, but each time his expression was blank, his eyes, as he stared ahead, not moving.

It was early enough that the roads were quiet. As we drove through the miles of open countryside, more signs of spring were appearing, hints of colour breaking through. I loved it most out here when the heather flowered, its dusky mauve stretching in every direction as far as the eye could see. This morning we disturbed a small herd of deer, which froze, watching my car for a few seconds, before suddenly taking flight. It was a habitat that belonged to wildlife. It never failed to amaze me how many animals it supported and, even more, how they managed to survive the winter.

'Have you heard from Jude since you've been here?' It was a reasonable question. I was still convinced someone had been hanging around, and the only possibility I could think of was Jude.

'No.' Abe muttered the word.

'I'm surprised. I thought he'd want to see you.' Was he lying? Why was I questioning everything he said to me?

Out of the corner of my eye I caught the diffident shrug that was his reply. I gave up at that point, driving in silence, watching as the fields and trees that flanked the motorway were replaced by industrial estates and vast warehouses. The closer we got to London, the heavier the traffic got. At some point I lapsed into thoughts of Matt. In the short time since I'd seen him, hurt had turned to anger. All I wanted was to bury the chapter of my life that contained him alongside other lost chapters. Whatever had changed between us, he wasn't the man I'd fallen in love with, that much was clear. But it didn't stop the aching sense of loss I felt. It would take more than one difficult exchange for me to move on. But I had to start. Love didn't always endure. It could end brutally, leaving you bruised and broken; abandoned, somehow lessened. Maybe it was better not to love. It wasn't worth the pain.

As I turned into Nina's street, it felt as if months had passed, instead of the two weeks it had been since I'd come here that evening to collect Abe. I managed to park in the street and then, with Abe's help, gathered up the boxes we'd brought, from the back of the car. Leaving them on Nina's doorstep, I went next door to get the key.

I knocked, then stood there waiting, listening to the backdrop of traffic noise and the blare of music from further down the street. I wondered if any of the neighbours had got to know Nina, remembering what DI Collins had said. Then I saw the curtain move, just before a woman opened the door.

'Yes?' She had a hardness about her, not just in her eyes, and in the way she stood there, but in her unsmiling face, her hair dyed the wrong shade for her skin tone.

'I understand you have the key for next door? I'm Nina's sister.'

She peered past me to look at Abe, clearly recognizing him. 'You've got the boy, then?'

I nodded. 'He's staying with me.'

Then she frowned. 'There was shouting that day. You know . . . When it happened.'

'Really?' My ears pricked up. 'Have you told the police?'

She shook her head. 'I wasn't here when she dropped the key in.'

'You should tell them. Speaking of the key,' I paused, then asked again, 'could I have it, please?'

As she turned and walked down the passageway, I made a mental note to tell DI Collins what the woman had said about the shouting. Seconds later she reappeared and handed me the key.

'Thanks.' As I started walking away, I was aware of her watching me.

'You bringing it back?' She sounded suspicious.

I paused, turning briefly. 'Should I?'

She shrugged. 'Police asked me to keep it. Makes no difference to me.'

The woman made no attempt to hide the fact that she was still watching us, as I unlocked Nina's door and opened it, pushing against the volume of mail lying just inside, which made it clear that no one had been in for a while. Relieved to be inside, I closed the door behind us, bending down to pick up the post.

Unlike last time, the house felt damp as well as cold – I shivered. The heating had clearly been turned off. I glanced at Abe. 'Can you put some lights on?'

I almost wished I hadn't asked him to. The harsh overhead light only accentuated the state of the house, which even in a short period of time had deteriorated still more. I passed Abe a couple of boxes. 'Why don't you make a start on your room?'

As I went through to the sitting room, I heard his footsteps going upstairs. Opening the curtains, I looked around the room. I hadn't been in here that night I came to get Abe. Like the kitchen, it was unloved, with dated wallpaper and a faded sofa that I was amazed I recognized from the cottage. As I stood there, I scanned the room for photos or anything personal that Abe might like in the future. But apart from the sofa and a dilapidated armchair, there was only a pile of magazines under a cheap coffee table and a small TV, which Abe might want for his bedroom, but little else worth taking.

Going through to the kitchen, I opened cupboards and drawers, but apart from one drawer that was stuffed with utility bills and envelopes, some of which were unopened, there was little of interest. Collecting the paperwork together, I piled it into a carrier bag, then looked under the sink, slightly shocked when I saw the empty vodka bottles crammed in there. Looking more closely, I saw more bottles, the kind that would have contained pills, but unlabelled. I thought of Abe's denial of his mother's problems, his insistence that she'd stopped drinking. Whatever she'd been on, she must have tried to hide it from him.

I paused for a moment, hit by a pang of sadness that this was how my sister's life had been. Being in such rundown surroundings could only have made matters worse for her.

Oh, Nina . . . All this time, was it really so unbearable? But you went through so much; took the brunt of everything. Now it's my turn to protect you.

Upstairs, I knocked on Abe's door, before pushing it open. 'Are you OK?'

He nodded.

I glanced around the room, taking in how sparsely furnished it was, how grim. 'If you want to bring your own bedding back, we can roll it up and take it with us,' I offered. 'Or anything that will make your room more homely.' But looking around again, I could see there wasn't anything. No pictures or photos. He'd piled a few books in one of the boxes and some clothes in another. 'What about your bedside lamp?'

It was a cheap anglepoise desk lamp, but that wasn't the point. 'S'pose.' He went over and unplugged it.

Leaving him to it, I went along to Nina's bedroom. The first thing I noticed was the bloodstain on the carpet, now dried to a dull brown. Trying not to think about how she died, I hunted around for the photos that I knew had to be here.

As I opened it, her wardrobe exuded an unwashed smell. It was crammed with clothes I could remember her wearing at the cottage, and slowly I went through them, their fabric seeming to hold an echo of the music, people and parties of that time. Glimpsing a brightly patterned Pucci-esque dress that I'd always loved, I pulled it out. The last time I'd seen her wear it, she'd twirled round so that its skirt had flared out. She'd been hiding tears behind her brightest smile, but only I had known that. A whisper of her voice came to me. *Hey, Hannah . . . Get dressed up! The show must go on, never forget that.*

Blotting it out, I pulled out one or two other dresses. Then, in the bottom of the wardrobe, buried at the back behind her shoes, I found what I was looking for.

My hands were shaking as I pulled out the old shoebox, which years ago she'd covered in pink paper. The colour had faded, but it was still tied with the green ribbon I remembered. Sitting on the floor, I untied the knot and opened it.

Inside, she'd laid a neatly folded scarf on top, but underneath it was as I'd known it would be: full of letters and photos that dated back to her teens. As I started leafing through them, a wave of nostalgia swept over me. My life was in there, too – the part that had existed alongside Nina's, but here and now there was too much to take in. Putting the lid back on and tying it up, I placed it on her bed to take home.

Next, I started on the chest of drawers, finding underwear and T-shirts in one drawer, Nina's collection of costume jewellery in another. A necklace caught my eye, of multicoloured crystal flowers. Carefully I untangled it from the others and lifted it out to take with me. It had no monetary value, but to me it symbolized a time when life had been so much simpler.

In the bottom drawer I found her tenancy agreement, and then my heart missed a beat as I discovered a diary from 2007. I was shocked.

Why, Nina? After everything that happened, why couldn't you let it go?

Amazed the police hadn't taken it, I picked it up and started reading, feeling ghosts around me, as the events of that year came flooding back. Closing it, I placed it on her bed next to the shoebox. I couldn't risk leaving it here for anyone else to find. But what I'd read had rattled me. Then the guilt was back, rearing up and flooding over me, that Nina and Abe had been living like this while I'd lived so differently.

It was too much. I had to get away. Getting up and quickly collecting everything together in the box I'd brought up here, I called to Abe, 'Are you done? Can we go?'

It was premature. I'd planned to go through more of Nina's stuff, bagging up what needed to be thrown out and salvaging anything worth sending to charity shops, so that there was no need for us to come back, but I couldn't bear to stay here a minute longer. Hurrying downstairs, I called him again. 'Abe? You ready to go?'

'Yeah.' He was ahead of me, his voice from the bottom of the stairs making me jump.

'Great.' I found myself breathless. 'Are you sure there's nothing else you want? What about the TV? I thought you might like it for your bedroom.'

But he shook his head. 'It doesn't work.'

'Right. Let's load the car up.' I marched towards the front

door, still carrying the box of Nina's things, fumbling to open it and stumbling outside, breathing in gasps of air.

There are too many ghosts, Nina. Even after all this time, they never left you. They haunted you, didn't they? Until you escaped into your stoned world, where they couldn't follow. And now they've come for me.

After ten years of trying to blot out what was too painful to think about, I couldn't shake the sense of the past catching up with me. Outside, my legs felt unsteady as I walked towards the car, resting the box on the bonnet as I reached into my pocket for my keys. Images of Nina and her children flashed through my head, followed by more – of that awful night I wish had never happened. *I'm sorry, Summer. You'll never know how sorry.* Glancing around, my eyes searched the street as I desperately tried to distract myself. Silently counting my breaths, I felt myself calm slightly as I put the box on the back seat and Abe appeared, carrying another box.

'I'll help you with the rest.' Closing the car door, I followed him back to the house. After we'd finished loading everything, relief filled me as I locked the door. It was only when we were halfway home that I realized I still had Nina's key. My heart sank. It meant I'd have to go back.

9

Now that I had Nina's tenancy agreement, I had no excuse not to notify the council that she rented from. Then, I supposed, I'd have to arrange house-clearance, and probably cleaning. I'd forgotten to ask DI Collins if she'd managed to contact Jude.

It couldn't be that hard to find him, surely. Preoccupied with Abe, I'd given only a passing thought to Jude. He'd be about twenty now. A man, rather than the boy I thought of him as. A man for whom life had been hard, I had no doubt. Not least because he was the son of an addict.

In the ten years since I'd seen Nina, the ghosts of the past had left me alone. But the sight of her diary had brought them back in full force. Not for the first time, I was wondering how much Abe knew. Jude, too, for that matter. But I couldn't ask. Before we fell out, Nina had insisted that we make a pact. She'd called it the script. *Nothing will change what happened, Hannah . . . No one must ever know.*

She was talking about the secrets we shared, which were buried in the passing of time, in silence. It was where they should stay. It was why it made no sense that she'd kept the diary.

I helped Abe carry the boxes upstairs and then, whistling to Gibson, I pulled on my boots and jacket, needing to walk, wanting space to clear my head, to be alone. At the back of the house I climbed over the fence and headed for a footpath that skirted the edge of a ploughed field. After London, the peacefulness was all the more noticeable, broken only by the cries of birds and the wind rustling through the trees, sounds that soothed me. Slowly I felt a tentative optimism filter in. I had to believe it would get easier, surely, for both me and Abe. It couldn't get much worse.

Now that Abe had collected his things and I could deal with Nina's affairs, I was hoping that life would settle down, that Abe would become more communicative. I considered going through some of Nina's old photos with him, or other keepsakes she'd collected over the years, thinking it might open the door to conversation between us – if he was interested. I wasn't sure he would be, but it was worth trying. As things stood, I had little to lose.

The shoebox was still in my bedroom on the floor, where I'd left it. I'd guessed Forensics would have found it and would either have taken anything relevant or dismissed the contents as of no interest to them. Until now I hadn't looked inside, since bringing it here, but that evening I sat on the floor and started to go through it, not at all sure what I'd find. Slowly leafing through photos of Nina, taking in how young, pretty and carefree she looked, I remembered just how young she'd actually been when she moved out of our parents' house. Just sixteen, and pregnant with Summer.

Before that . . . I shuddered. They were years I didn't want to think about, which held memories that were better off forgotten. Younger than Nina, I hadn't realized for years what she was going through. When you grew up with the brutality and cruelty we'd been exposed to, it became normalized, and ceased to shock. Now, looking back, I knew differently. I remembered how Nina had fought back against him as he dragged her up the stairs; how strong he was, how rough; how she always lost. My sister locked in her bedroom, hammering on the door, screaming to be let out, her cries hours later giving way to sobbing, then dying out. The silence that seemed to last forever, so that I lay in bed unable to sleep, wondering if she was dead. Her pale, blank face when he let her out, sometimes three, four days later. How afterwards, when I crept into her bed in the middle of the night, it was as though Nina had been anaesthetized.

Although Nina had tried her hardest to hide her pregnancy, he'd found out, but then he'd never missed anything. I remembered him screaming at her, calling her the most vile names, telling her that unless she had an abortion, she was to get out and never come back. How he never wanted to see her again.

As I thought of my sister creeping into my bedroom one night, telling me she was leaving, tears were rolling down my cheeks. Questioning whether she knew what she was leaving me to, when of course she did. She'd lived with it for years, but couldn't take any more.

It didn't take long before I was treated to the same abuse, triggered by the smallest detail. A mark for a piece of school work; the defiant way I met his eyes, as he put it. They were years that had been unbearable, the most painful of memories. After being buried all this time, I was unnerved by the intensity of the emotions they unleashed.

Trying to push them from my head, I pulled out another

photo: of me, aged seventeen, in the early days of the band, when I'd first come to live with Nina, with my hair bleached and eyes rimmed with black. Away from my parents, I looked alive, happy and confident. For a while, that's how I'd felt. For the first time in as long as I could remember, I'd been happy. I lived with my sister. The future had looked incredible. The Cry Babies were one of the fastest-growing success stories of that time. I'd been living the dream.

There were more photos taken around the same time, of Nina's friends at one of her impromptu gatherings. When I first went to live there, she'd had a large circle of friends and, with the nearest neighbours two or three miles away, her cottage was the venue for many parties. I remembered loud music drifting through the woods, all afternoon into the evening, stopping only at sunrise the next morning; cooking on fires at the edge of Nina's garden; the old water trough she used to chill drinks; the vast awning someone had rigged up at one side of the cottage, so that whatever the weather, there was always somewhere for everyone to crash.

In my naivety, I'd never stopped to think where the food had come from. Nina had been off-grid. There'd been no child support, no benefit payments of any kind. Her friends had sometimes brought food with them, and I had a vague memory of boxes of groceries being left at the back door, but I had no idea who by.

I picked up another photo, of myself and Nina together, when we were children. As I looked at it, a shiver ran down my spine. To anyone who didn't know us, we looked like normal, happy children, smiling at the camera. Smiles perfected from years of practice. There was no indication of the fear that lay hidden underneath.

Not surprisingly, she hadn't any photos of our parents. Then I picked up another, of Jude and Summer, taken before I lived with them, when Jude was a chunky toddler, unsmiling as he stood next to his sister. Summer. She looked about eight, with honey-brown skin and long hair lightened at the ends by the sun. She was wearing a yellow checked sundress, her feet were bare and her eyes bright, laughing as she looked into the camera.

I pulled out more photos of the two of them; some of them with Nina, too, studying them, feeling myself frown. I hadn't noticed before, but it had seemed that as Summer blossomed, Nina had faded, almost as though Nina's own vitality had been drip-feeding into her daughter's veins. I could remember the terrible rows that grew progressively worse as Summer got older, lashing out at her mother, venting her frustrations at their way of life. And then, that terrible night.

Summer's death had left Nina heartbroken. It had to be the reason she'd kept the diary. Apart from the photos, it was the only other reminder she had of that time, of Summer, her guilt over what happened making her punish herself, reliving the pain as she reread, over and over, what she'd written. But when it could so easily have been avoided, how could she not?

Part of me wasn't ready to face the diary – not just yet. The past seemed too real around me, and it was as though the ground under my feet was shifting. But I couldn't put it out of my mind and the following evening, after a couple of glasses of wine, I steeled myself to read it.

In 2007 Summer would have been fourteen, Jude nine and Abe just four. I flicked through the first few pages, which were empty, then found the next page scrawled unmistakeably in Nina's handwriting:

27th January: I'm going mad – Summer argues, Jude's angry and Abe says nothing, I don't know what to do any more. It gets worse, not better, trying to keep the house warm, the children fed, when I have no money, when all I want is another pill to make it go away. Am I being punished? I wish you were here, Hannah. Why, just for once, can't someone help me?

The anguish in her words shocked me. Nina hadn't told me how she was feeling. But at that time I'd been dealing with my own problems. 2007 was the year that began for me with optimism. The Cry Babies had burst into the year, playing all over the country, about to sign with a major record label, success within our grasp. By year's end, it was a dim and distant memory. And in between . . . I remembered hope, turning to disbelief, then devastation, when after our single hit record, everything changed and the band fell apart. None of us could believe what had happened.

Rumours circulated as to why we'd broken up – how we'd fallen out, how we weren't reliable – none of them true. At the time I'd been distraught, unable to think about anything else. It was a time when, if Nina had been struggling, I wouldn't have noticed. But neither had she told me, instead welcoming me as she always did, whenever I turned up there, desperate. But Nina knew what it was like to have nowhere to go. She never turned anyone away.

A week or so later there was another entry:

4th February: Summer, Summer, Summer . . . Why is she always so angry with me? All I wanted was to give my children freedom, love, peace, the sky, the stars. Everything I never had.

What else matters? But it's not enough for her. Nothing's ever enough. Whatever I give her, she wants more.

Jude just glares. Glares and stares and swears. Then he goes out and doesn't tell me where. Will Abe be the same? Do I deserve this from my children? But I can't change anything. This is our life. We don't have anywhere else to go.

Had she been drinking when she wrote that? I couldn't help but wonder if she was exaggerating. But there was no denying the arguments; Summer's strong will and loudly voiced opinions; Jude's bolshiness. Naively, I'd seen their behaviour as indicative of strength of character. Nina's words on paper were impassioned, but then drinking put a different slant on everything. I imagined her pouring her thoughts onto the pages while she finished a bottle of wine. It's what diaries were: a place to exorcize your darkest emotions, leaving them behind, then moving on.

And no two people saw things the same way. I thought of Matt. How our two worlds, which had been so similar, were suddenly poles apart, for reasons I didn't understand. Maybe that's how it had been for Nina and Summer. I read on:

14th February: Fucking Valentine's fucking Day, my life a fucking hell. I have no money, my children fight all the time, there's no food in the house . . . My sister is as fucked-up as I am, but after the childhood we both had, is it any wonder? There is no one to turn to. I can't bear to ask Sam again, but I have no choice. Other than him, I have no one.

Summer has another chest infection. I have the last of the anti-biotics Lucy left us. Sweet, lovely Lucy, who taught Summer to read, when her fucking useless mother failed. Who brought her books. What happens when Summer has her next chest infection? When she's finished the books? When they're hungry? When I tell them: there is no food? What do I do then?

The happy house that used to be full of people and life, is empty; holds only anger and darkness. No one comes here any more, there's no reason for them to. No parties or laughter. Just anger, tears, struggle. If it wasn't for the children, I'd end it now. But I can't, so I take my pills, craving the feeling as it spreads through my body and numbs the pain, as the problems I have no answers for magically fade away, as my thoughts stop tormenting me. Or drink until I pass out. Maybe one day, I'll never wake up. Maybe that would be best for everyone.

28th February: Where are you, Hannah? Please come back. I need you. You're the only person who understands.

It was as though she was sitting next to me, her voice clear in my head. Slamming the diary shut, I put it down, shocked. Not moving, I sat there for a moment, but there was nothing I could do; no point in letting it get to me. The time had passed. It was too late.

But I couldn't get Nina's words out of my head. The more I thought about her anguish, the more my discomfort grew. This had been the backdrop to Abe's life. He was the innocent in all this. None of it could have been easy for him. Suddenly I was compelled to talk to him, even if only a few words.

Getting up, I walked along the landing towards his room; as I got closer, I watched the blue tinge under his door give way to an orange glow. I paused outside. 'Abe? I just came to say goodnight. I'm going to bed.'

The muttered 'G'night' took me by surprise. I hadn't expected it. But as I started walking away, I stopped suddenly, halted by the return of the blue strip of light under his door – the kind of blue that came from an electronic screen, such as the laptop he'd denied all knowledge of.

I've seen you in your garden, Hannah. Watched you come through your back door, your eyes flickering around before closing it behind you; pulling on your jacket as you walk down the path, glancing at the sky briefly, then walking towards the footpath across the fields.

You and your sister, you're really not so different. Each of you with your own version of what happened, your own spider's web of lies, but you've been lying to yourself for so long, you've forgotten what's true and what isn't. And there are things you don't know about the boy, just as there are things you should know about Nina. You've hidden yourself away for too long. It's time you found out the truth.

How would you feel if you knew the boy met Matt, the other day? It happened as Matt drove away from here, his face shut down, closed. You were devastated, weren't you? I saw your tear-stained face, your shaky hands. They talked for a while – did you know that? Matt would have been good for Abe, wouldn't he? But, as you always do, you managed to cock that up, too.

The other morning, remember your dog stopped for a moment, staring across the garden towards the trees? It was me he was look-ing at – he'd seen me move slightly in the shadows. But he won't bark at me, Hannah. I've made sure of that. He wags his tail when he sees me. Oh, and I know his name, by the way. Gibson and I are old friends.

You haven't noticed my footprints in your flower beds, have you? My fingerprints on your windowsills, my eyes on the other side of the glass. When it's dark outside, you can't see me looking in. Your cottage windows are the perfect height so that I can glimpse you through the cracks of light where the curtains don't quite meet, as you wander from room to room. Restless, aren't you, Hannah? Why is that? Is your conscience stirring into life? Are the ghosts of your past right behind you?

You should think about what the boy does at night, getting his telescope out, watching the stars; remind yourself how small the human race is, with its petty, overblown rules and politics; the fighting for control in a world where no one has any, not really, when you think of weather systems and tides and orbiting planets and solar flares. The boy gets it – how, on the timeline of the universe, a human life is undetectable. You're insignificant, Hannah. We all are.

Do you know about the window that doesn't latch properly? You should be more careful. Someone might break in. Someone you really don't want in your house, who knows your secrets – like me.

Watch out, Hannah . . . Time is running out. I'm getting closer.

10

Hannah

The existence of the second laptop preoccupied me, obsessed me even. After Abe had left for school the following morning, I was about to search his room again when a text flashed up on the screen of my mobile.

Walk? 10? Usual place? E x

Erin lived a few miles away and shared my aversion to local gossip, which meant we'd struck up a friendship of sorts. Her job meant she was often away, but when she wasn't, we'd occasionally walk our dogs together. I hesitated, but knew I'd have time later to search Abe's room.

Sure. x

I glanced at the clock. It gave me enough time to shower and drive to the car park she was referring to. The laptop would have to wait.

I was late leaving the house, driving too fast along the narrow road that wove between the trees, glimpsing flashes of sky through their branches, the sun obscured by high cloud that lowered, darkening, towards the horizon. It wouldn't be for a while, but I was guessing rain was on its way.

Turning off the main road, I drove up the stony track, heading towards the car park where Erin and I always met, on the edge of an ancient stretch of woodland. Her car was already there, but if she'd been waiting long, as I went to join her she didn't say so.

While our dogs bounded around, we set off through the woods, along a straight path beneath towering beech trees.

'Sorry I haven't been in touch, Hannah. I've been in Madrid for the last fortnight. Wonderful for tapas and Spanish wine, but meetings every day. I'm bloody glad to be back, I can tell you. You need to fill me in. How's the lovely Matt?'

Erin had some high-powered marketing job, which took her away from time to time. The wind caught my hair as I shook my head. 'He's gone.'

'What?' Erin stopped walking and pulled me round to face her. 'You're kidding me. What do you mean, gone?'

'He left. About three weeks ago.' I tried to swallow the lump in my throat. 'He said he was sorry, but it wasn't working . . . His words.'

'Jeez. Did he give you an explanation?' She looked shocked.

'No.' I was silent for a moment. 'I guess I messed up.'

'Really?' Her eyes stared into mine. 'What do you mean?'

I started walking again, not wanting to tell her how Matt had discovered something I'd kept hidden from him. 'I mean he must have had a reason,' I said evasively.

She was silent for a moment. 'I thought you were really happy together.'

'So did I.'

I was aware of an edge between us. Erin knew me well

enough to sense that I was keeping something from her. We carried on walking, neither of us speaking, until we reached the other side of the woods where the trees thinned out and the sparse landscape stretched for miles in front of us. Away from the shelter of the trees, I pulled my collar up, suddenly cold.

Erin broke the silence. 'Oh, Hannah . . . I'm so sorry. I thought you two were really good. Have you talked – since?'

I shook my head. 'I tried to, but Matt wouldn't. He came back to get the rest of his stuff. He seemed angry with me, but he didn't say why.' I thought about explaining why I hadn't told Matt about Nina, but something stopped me.

She enveloped me in a hug. 'I would never have believed it. You should have called me.'

Suddenly awkward, I pulled away and we carried on walking. 'It wouldn't have changed anything. And other things have been going on.'

'Such as?'

'My sister died suddenly.'

'Jeez. Hannah, I'm so sorry. You've really been going through it. How did you find out? Does she have kids?'

'The police called me. I'm next of kin. Her youngest son is living with me.' I didn't mention Jude.

Erin was silent for a moment. 'Hang on, you said the police? Was it suspicious? How long's he staying for?' Questions were tumbling out of her.

'At first they thought it was an accident, now they're not so sure.' I was deliberately cagey. I didn't want her jumping to conclusions about Nina. 'He's staying indefinitely. There isn't anywhere else for him to go.'

I turned to meet Erin's shocked gaze.

'How old is he?'

'Abe's fifteen.'

'Cute name.' She was silent. 'God! This is too much to take in. I mean, no disrespect, but nothing like this ever happens to you.'

As we walked in silence, suddenly I needed to confide in her. 'I'm finding him really difficult. He can be quite aggressive.'

'He's a teenage boy, probably raging with angst and testosterone.' Erin was matter-of-fact. 'And don't forget, his life has just been turned upside down. Being a teenager can be hideous at the best of times. My sister has two. Does he talk to you?' We stopped to watch a buzzard, circling high above us. 'I can never believe the size of those birds. Look at its wingspan.'

I stared at the bird. She was right. Its wings outstretched, it appeared to soar effortlessly on the wind. It was a breathtaking sight, but my mind was on other things. 'Abe? Since staying with me, he's hardly said a word.'

'Is he usually like that?' Erin continued to stare at the bird.

'I don't know. I hadn't seen him for ten years.'

'What?' She sounded shocked. 'That long? Whatever happened between you and your sister?'

It was my turn to stare at the bird. 'I don't know. I suppose Nina and I had a bit of a falling-out. She moved away and didn't tell me where she'd gone. Then, before you know it, all this time had passed.'

She was silent for a moment. 'I had no idea you had a sister.'

I stiffened. It was like Matt, all over again. What was this obsession with needing to know about other people's private lives? I stopped looking at the bird and stared at her. 'What was I supposed to say to you? Hey, Erin. I have this sister but we haven't spoken for ten years, because guess what – she didn't want me in her life.' I didn't mean to sound bitter, but it really wasn't anything to do with her.

'OK, Hannah . . .' There was a puzzled look on Erin's face. 'I didn't mean to pry. I'm just surprised you hadn't mentioned her. That's all.'

Just then I felt the first drop of rain, sooner than I'd expected. I glanced up at the sky. 'We should go back.'

As we walked back to our cars, conversation between us was strained, despite both of us trying to restore it to its usual, more superficial level. Erin hugged me again, before getting into her car and driving away, but there was still the sense of a distance between us.

By the time I got home, the rain had turned to a steady drizzle. Still put out by my exchange with Erin, I tried to busy myself tidying the house, then going through some of my teaching notes. A couple of my pupils had exams coming up, and I had one particularly gifted pupil who I knew would go far, if I could maintain his interest. It became more difficult as they got older. Even the most talented pupils reached a point where they'd rather have a social life than do their music practice.

I was interrupted by the arrival of a delivery for Abe, which I signed for. But my concentration had been broken and I was restless. Outside, the rain had almost stopped. Pulling on my jacket, I called to Gibson. I needed to get out of the house.

As I set off briskly across the fields towards the village, I glanced at the clouds. Still heavily overcast, it looked as though this was only a brief respite from the rain. The wind had swung round to the north since earlier and I could feel its bite, so I walked faster as I tried to keep warm, taking the path that avoided the lowest-lying areas that were still waterlogged, listening to the shrill call of a blackbird perched high in a nearby tree.

As we came to the village, I clipped on Gibson's lead and climbed over the stile onto the lane. Turning left along the pavement, I walked past the few houses set back from the road, then a terrace of smaller cottages as I headed for the village shop. A couple of heavily pregnant ponies loitered on the other side of the road. Apart from their distended bellies, they were skinny after a long winter without enough grazing, and hungry, drawn into the village in search of food.

I used the shop infrequently. Often enough that Joe, the owner, knew who I was, but then he made it his business to know who everyone was. The shop sold a small amount of local produce and a few overpriced basics, serving more as a hub for the locals and a hotbed for gossip. Tying Gibson to the rail outside, I went in.

'Hello, young Hannah. Haven't seen you in a while.' It had been months, but Joe's memory for names never failed him.

'Hi, Joe . . . I've been busy.' It was deliberately evasive, even if it happened to be true. 'Could I have some stamps, please?'

'First do? They're all I've got.'

'First is good. Thanks.' I glanced around at the shelves while he rummaged behind the counter.

'Had a friend of yours in earlier.' He didn't look up.

'Sorry?' I frowned, thinking of Erin. 'When was that?'

'About an hour ago. She said you go way back. She was hoping to catch you while she was here. Nice lass. I'd say she was about your age. With long, dark hair.'

I frowned. 'Are you sure it was me she was looking for?' I

was trawling through my mind for someone who met his description. Erin's hair was mousy and shoulder-length. I'd no idea who he was talking about.

'Oh, it was you all right. She knew all about you and that chap of yours – sorry, by the way. I heard you weren't together any more.' He looked slightly sheepish as he held out the stamps.

I handed over the money. 'No,' I said shortly, hating how he knew about my personal life.

'She knew, too.' He looked at me expectantly.

'What?' I stared at him, horrified. 'You mean the woman?'

'Your friend, that's right. At least, I think that's what she said . . .' He looked less sure.

Thoughts raced through my head. Who was she? 'I can't think of anyone. What was her name?'

He shook his head. 'She didn't say.'

Suddenly I was uncomfortable. How did she know about Matt and me? Unless it was Matt she knew. Maybe she had something to do with why he left so suddenly. Then a worse thought struck me. Maybe they'd been having an affair. Matt meeting someone else would explain everything.

Unless she was Matt's ex-wife . . . Olivia had long, dark hair, but just as quickly I dismissed the thought. Now that we'd split up, Matt's ex would have no interest in me. In a hurry to get out of there, I swung round to leave.

'Hey, don't forget your change,' Joe called after me, but I was already through the door, letting it close behind me.

Untying Gibson's lead, I hurried away along the pavement, thinking about the woman, wanting to know why she was looking for me. Why would she have told Joe she was a friend of mine? It was obviously a lie. Unless she was fishing for information about me, for some reason. Then another thought occurred to me. Maybe she was a reporter, who'd got wind of Nina's death and thought she had a story. She might even have found out I used to be in a band. Maybe she was talking to other people in the village. That would account for how she knew about Matt.

There was no way of knowing. Or maybe Joe had volunteered more information than he'd told me and, being a journalist, she'd latched on to his every word. Joe wasn't discreet. From what he'd said to me, it was impossible to know.

It was odd, but I wasn't going to obsess about it. Head down, I walked into the wind, feeling it gust around me. If she was a journalist, I was wondering if she'd turn up at my house. What would I say to her? Reporters were persistent, weren't they? If she refused to leave, how would I get rid of her?

Halfway across the field, I felt a few drops of rain. When I glanced up at the sky, it looked as though this time it was settling in. I walked faster, my shoulders hunched and my head down into the wind, looking up only when I noticed a figure in the distance, walking towards me. I squinted, wondering if it was the woman Joe had talked to, but it was too far away to see who it was. I carried on walking, aware of the rain steadily increasing, and then, as the distance between us closed, I saw it was a man.

He was tall with short, dark hair, wearing faded jeans and a nondescript brown jacket, but as he approached, I noticed his shoes were too polished, out of place walking across a marshy field. Briefly I met his gaze, before glancing away.

As he drew closer, I became aware of his eyes, staring intently at me, as beside me Gibson growled. It was out of character for him to do that. Without knowing why, I felt my skin prickle, my uneasiness mount as I met the man's eyes for a second time. Stepping to one side to let him pass, I felt myself flinch as his arm brushed against mine, and then at the sheer impact of his presence as he swept past, as though a wall of air had hit me.

'Hello, Hannah . . .'

I gasped, but he was already walking away. How did he know my name? I knew it wasn't logical, but suddenly fear was running through my veins. Under the darkening sky I marched faster, not daring to turn round. Had I imagined him speaking to me? But as the wind started to howl, I knew I hadn't. I broke into a run, slowing only when another dog-walker came into view. When eventually I dared to turn round, there was no sign of him.

By the time I got back to the house, my hands were shaking. Closing the back door behind me, I pulled the bolt across, then went to the front door and checked that was locked, too. If he knew who I was, there was every chance he knew where I lived. Hadn't he been walking from this direction? Maybe he'd come to the house while I was out. Feeling myself start to panic, I went from room to room, checking the windows were closed, struggling with one halfway up the stairs, which refused to shut properly. There was no way anyone could reach it from outside, I knew that. But even then, as I stood in my kitchen, I didn't feel safe.

Summer

When did it change, Mother? When did you stop wanting to live?

Or did the lies get too much for you?

I know the story, about the grandparents you didn't really get along with. But they loved us, you always said. And we had Hannah. Weren't we lucky? Your aunt's in a famous rock band!

Hannah, with her white-blonde hair and wild eyes rimmed with black; sweeping into our lives, a perfect storm, leaving a chaos of turned heads and broken hearts in her wake. Hannah, who had her own dream, who danced for longer, partied harder than anyone, whose demons were louder than yours, Mother.

You didn't know I heard you both that night. Hannah had come to the cottage unexpectedly, her skin paler, quieter than I'd ever seen her. Late that night, woken by her shouting, I'd crept outside, then sat underneath the open window. Listened to Hannah's voice, distraught, as it floated out into the night; heard yours, lower, saying calming words I couldn't make out, which failed to comfort her, stop her wailing. Felt Hannah's turmoil drift out through the window, a dark shadow that settled over me.

The first of your secrets I discovered. Your gift to me. A burden I couldn't share, which didn't belong to a child. One that was there forever, to be followed by others.

Hannah wasn't well, you lied, when I asked you why she was upset.

She'd let you down, Mother, couldn't you see that? Why lie to me? Can't you tell, by looking at me, that I know?

She needed your help, you told us, hiding the truth behind your blank smile. Even though she didn't deserve it. But you didn't hear me say that. I swallowed the words before they exploded out of me. You could never say no. Not to Hannah.

Your children had everything they needed, after all. A roof over their heads, space to run free in. No one was ever cruel to them. So, sometimes they were hungry. Their mother was fucked-up and they didn't have a father, but what an idyllic life they were blessed with. What else could they possibly want?

Out of the corner of my eye, I caught sight of your lies breeding exponentially. Everything was fine, you told us. Another lie. Life was wonderful. Yet another.

How could it possibly not be?

11

Hannah

I couldn't stop thinking about the two strangers – the man who'd known my name, the woman in the village who was asking about me. At one time my life had been full of strangers, the context of Nina's cottage making them seem anything but. Closing my eyes, images drifted past, of figures that now seemed shadowy, drugged, drunk. In my mind, Nina's cottage was no longer the idyllic hideaway, set amongst drifts of wild flowers and trees strung with lanterns; instead it had become dark, dingy, unloved. And her children . . . I heard my sharp intake of breath, as Summer's face danced before me, her skin dirty and her hair tangled, as she shouted at her mother, not because she was being difficult. Nina had been out of it, high on drugs, while all three of her children had been hungry.

Shaking the thoughts from my mind, I cast my mind back to the strangers in the village. Who were these people who seemed to know me? I was beginning to imagine a conspiracy against me. Feeling another rush of fear, I went back through every room, rechecking all the windows, pulling the curtains closed. Shivering, realizing how cold I was, I went to the snug and lit the wood-burner, packing it with logs.

I don't know how much time passed, but the next thing I was aware of was being woken from a deep sleep by the sound of Gibson barking and a banging sound outside, first on the back door, then on the front. It was followed by a male voice shouting. Disorientated, I imagined the man I'd seen earlier. Just as I'd dreaded, he'd come here. Stumbling through to the kitchen, I searched for my phone to call the police, but then the voice called out again.

'I can't get in.'

Abe. Thank God. Relieved, I hurried to the back door, trying to pull myself together as I unbolted it. 'I'm so sorry. I lost track of time – I think I must have fallen asleep.' Trying to sound calmer than I felt.

As he came in, I closed the door behind him and slid the bolt across, then noticed the frown on his face as he watched me.

'Did you notice anyone hanging around, on your way back? Only there was a man earlier. He freaked me out. I'm sorry . . .' I shook my head, realizing how lame I sounded. 'It's why the door was locked.' I looked at him expectantly.

He stared at me, clearly irritated, then I noticed rain dripping from his hair. 'Oh no, it's raining again . . . I'm so sorry. You're soaked, Abe. You should get changed. And bring me your wet clothes. I'll dry them for you.'

'It's OK.' He pushed past and I heard his footsteps on the stairs. If he'd noticed that I'd closed all the curtains, he didn't say anything. I glanced at my watch. I needed to get myself together for my first student.

*

Teaching took my mind off the events of earlier and, by the time my last student left, I was the calmest I'd felt all day, until a phone call early that evening took me by surprise. It was the mother of one of my longest-standing students, Laura, very apologetically telling me that, as of now, Laura wouldn't be continuing her lessons with me.

I was dumbfounded. Laura had been coming here for five years and I'd taught her to play both the piano and the guitar. 'I'm sorry to hear that. She was getting on so well and has so much talent . . .' It was so sudden. Just last week we'd been discussing the next pieces she wanted to learn. She'd given no indication that she was thinking of giving up.

As her mother told me that Laura needed to devote all her time to her school work, I had a churning feeling in my stomach. From what she'd told me, Laura had always been an A-star student. Something about her mother's words didn't ring true.

Over the next hour it was followed by two more similar calls from the parents of long-term students. As I hung up on the second, I knew something was going on. It wasn't coincidence. Over the years I was used to the natural wastage that occurred among the students who weren't gifted musically or simply lost interest, but never among the more talented, and nothing like what was happening now.

When my phone buzzed again, I knew that this time I needed to try and find out what was going on – only this time it wasn't about a student.

It was DI Collins. 'I'm sorry to call you so late, but we've had the pathologist's report and I thought you'd want to know. It confirms that your sister was killed by a blow to the back of her head. When she fell, she hit the side of her head on the chest of drawers in her room. That was the injury you would have seen when you identified her body. We're working on the assumption that her killer was someone she knew. There were no signs of a break-in and no sign, either, of a murder weapon. It's possible she'd been out and left the door open, but otherwise whoever killed her either had their own key or she let them in. The report also confirms that she had been drinking, though not heavily enough to be a factor.'

'Did anyone see who it was?' I was thinking of when Abe and I went back there, of the neighbour who'd had the key, whose sharp eyes had watched my every move.

'We've spoken to her closest neighbours and none of them saw anyone. We're still going through CCTV footage.' DI Collins paused. 'We also found the AA group she attended and I'm going along to their next meeting. It's in a couple of days' time.'

'What about Abe's laptop?' Guiltily I thought of the second one I believed I'd seen, but I could hardly tell her about it now. Not when Abe flatly denied its existence.

'I'll need to check, but I think we've nearly finished with it. I believe there were a few emails from Nina, possibly to other members of her AA group, but nothing more than that, as far as I know. Once Forensics have finished with it, I'll arrange to have it sent to Abe. I believe his phone is on its way to you.'

That must have been the delivery I took earlier. I'd forgotten to tell Abe. 'I think it arrived today.'

'How is he?'

'Much the same. Doesn't say much. Goes to school and comes home. There's not much more to say.'

'He's grieving,' she said simply. 'I'm afraid you won't be able to organize the funeral just yet, which won't help him.

The death certificate won't be issued until after the inquest, but the coroner may be able to issue an interim certificate so that you can deal with your sister's estate.'

'Right.' If Nina had made a will, I hadn't found it yet. It reminded me that I still hadn't looked into the paperwork in the folder I'd picked up. I'd been aware of utility bills, bank statements, but I hadn't been through them in detail. 'How long before the inquest?'

'It could be up to a couple of months, maybe longer. But the coroner's officer will keep in touch with you and let you know what's going on.'

I was silent for a moment. 'Do you think the press would be interested in the case?'

'Not especially.' DI Collins sounded surprised. 'Why do you ask?'

'There was a woman in the village this morning. Joe – in the local shop – said she'd been asking about me. She told him she was an old friend of mine. He described her, but I didn't recognize her – she didn't give him her name.'

'It could be the press.' DI Collins was thoughtful. 'Unless it's one of your sister's old friends. Maybe they'd heard she died and decided to track you down.'

I doubted it. Nina's friends had been short-lived acquaintances, rather than friends.

She went on. 'But whoever she is, if she knows where you live, it's odd she hasn't been to the house.' DI Collins sounded puzzled. 'If anyone does get in touch – anyone who knew your sister – could you let me know?'

That evening it wasn't long before the rain had blown through, leaving the kind of skies that drew Abe outside like a magnet.

It was later than usual, but it didn't surprise me when he came into the kitchen and pulled on a coat.

'I forgot. There was a delivery for you earlier. It's probably your phone.' I fetched the parcel from the windowsill and gave it to him, watching him tear it open, then turn the phone on and play around with it for a moment. 'OK?' I asked.

He nodded, putting it in his pocket.

'Are you sure you'll be warm enough?' I could feel a draught of cold air from the window that didn't close properly.

Nodding briefly, he went outside, as my phone buzzed again. Glancing at it, my heart sank, as I saw 'Natalie Barnes' flash up on the screen. Natalie was another parent of one of my pupils. I could guess what was coming.

'Hannah, I'm sorry. Is this a good time?' She sounded hesitant.

'Of course. How can I help?'

'I'm not sure how to say this—'

Impatiently I interrupted her. 'You're calling to cancel Lauren's lessons. Am I right?'

'Oh God . . .' She faltered. 'Actually no. I'm really not, I promise you.'

'Oh?' I was taken aback.

'It's a bit of a strange one, but I'm guessing, from what you've just said, that you've had a few phone calls this evening cancellations?'

'I've had a couple.' I didn't want to give too much away. 'Why do you ask?'

'There's no easy way to say this, Hannah, so I'll just come out with it. There was a Facebook post a couple of days ago. Some of the kids have got hold of it. It was about you.'

I felt my face grow hot. 'What did it say?'

She hesitated. Then, when she spoke, she sounded embarrassed. 'If you really want to know, it said you had a drink problem.'

'Jesus! Who said that?' I tried to sound indignant, but I was mortified.

'I know . . .' Natalie sounded sympathetic. 'I took a screenshot, just in case they removed it. It was posted by a girl called Cara Matlock.'

'I've never heard of a Cara Matlock.' I was baffled. 'Why would she post something like that about me?'

'You really don't know her? How bizarre.'

'Probably someone's idea of a joke.' I was trying to make light of it, but it was anything but funny. 'In case you're wondering, there isn't an ounce of truth in it.'

'Oh God, absolutely. I wasn't suggesting there was – far from it.'

'So, as far as Lauren's lessons . . .'

'I wouldn't dream of her going anywhere else,' Natalie said matter-of-factly. 'In fact I'll write a post that states exactly that. Maybe I'll tag Miss Matlock – if I can manage to . . . Whatever, I'll get Lauren to help me.'

'Thank you.' Self-pitying tears filled my eyes. 'I'm grateful you let me know.'

'Whoever she is, she clearly has an axe to grind. I reported the post, by the way, but I'll email you the screenshot. Just in case.'

Just in case of what? Did she think there'd be more?

'And I wouldn't respond, if I were you,' Natalie went on. 'Don't give this Cara Matlock the satisfaction of seeing it get to you.'

After Natalie's call, I was straight onto Facebook. As I

searched, I found a number of Cara Matlocks, none of whom looked familiar. I was still scanning through the profile photos as Natalie's email came through. When I opened the attachment, my stomach churned with anxiety as I zoomed in on the face of a girl I'd never seen before, astonished as I saw that she'd found an old photo of the Cry Babies from somewhere. As I read her post, I felt sickened: *The real reason former lead singer Hannah Roscoe is a music teacher!!*

There was a second photo, taken more recently, in the pub – I remembered the night in question. I'd been there with Matt and we'd had an argument; for the life of me, I couldn't remember what about. I studied the photo more closely. I couldn't blame anyone for assuming I'd been drinking. It wasn't flattering. Underneath, someone else had posted a photo of a half-full wine glass and a pile of empty bottles. The post had fifty-five likes and a number of comments that I couldn't bring myself to read. Why would a stranger spread lies? It made no sense. My pupils enjoyed their lessons with me, as far as I knew. And I hadn't upset anyone, not to my knowledge. I had no idea why anyone would do this – but someone had. Suddenly I felt suspicious of everyone.

My hands were shaking as I picked up my glass of wine, staring at it. I drank no more than most people. I put it down again, then got up, trying to busy myself tidying the kitchen, but my mind refused to settle. I was thinking about the woman in the village, telling Joe she was an old friend of mine. Then there was the man I'd met walking, who'd known my name. And now, tonight, the post on Facebook.

As I put it all together, I was convinced someone was trying to get to me. The question was who? And why? It had all started since Abe had moved here. An uneasiness came over me as I thought of the laptop he was hiding, then of his constant resentment towards me. Was there a reason for it? He was clearly hiding something from me. There was only one thing I could do. Tomorrow, when he went to school, I was going to search his room as I'd planned to. Then, when I found the laptop, I'd confront him.

Too much stress was taking its toll, I knew that. Suddenly I was anxious again. I had locked all the windows, hadn't I?

Getting up, I wandered from room to room, checking them, then went back into the kitchen, sitting down heavily at the table, thinking of Nina. I would never have imagined her being in danger. What about me? With everything that was going on, was I safe?

I had a glass of wine, and then another – until, at last, I stopped caring.

During the night I woke up at some point, my mouth dry and my head thumping. As I lay there, something that I couldn't place niggled at me. Drifting in and out of consciousness, at last I slept, waking the next morning to dazzling sun streaming through the open curtains, blinding me. Rolling over, I felt a stabbing pain in my arm.

Wide awake all of a sudden, I sat up. Then recoiled as I looked at my bed sheets, spattered with blood.

12

In a panic, I leapt out of bed, the sudden movement making my head throb. I realized the blood had come from an inch-long gash on my arm. Then it came to me exactly what had been niggling at me last night. Abe had gone outside as it was getting dark, but I couldn't remember him coming back.

Grabbing a handful of tissues to hold against the cut, I hurried along the landing to Abe's bedroom, where I knocked on his door.

'Abe?' When he didn't answer, I tried again, louder this time. 'Abe?'

There was no reply. I pushed the door open and went in. The window was open, the curtains blowing in the wind. His bed was empty.

'Oh God!' Still clutching the tissues against my arm, I ran downstairs, checking each room in turn, in case he'd crept in and fallen asleep somewhere. But there was no sign of him. His jacket was missing. With a sinking feeling, I realized he must still be out there.

With my arm as it was, I couldn't pull on my jacket, wearing it instead over my shoulders and slipping boots onto my bare feet, before I stumbled outside, Gibson at my heels, zipping up my jacket as I hurried across the garden. 'Abe?'

Breaking into a run, the thumping in my head slowed me down as I checked each part of the garden, stopping now and then to call his name. I hesitated, scanning the fields beyond. There was no sign of anyone. Should I call the police now? Before any more time passed?

I felt in my pocket for my phone, realizing that in my haste I'd forgotten to pick it up. Running back to the house, I rehearsed what I was going to say to them. I had an instinct that something was deeply wrong.

Calling the police had done nothing to allay my fears. The person I spoke to made a note of Abe's description, then my address. Afterwards I went upstairs, frowning, as for the first time, I realized I was still wearing yesterday's clothes. Peeling them off, I showered, rust-coloured water pooling around my feet as I washed the blood from my arm. I'd no recollection of it happening. After drying myself, I bandaged it, then quickly dressed, stripping the bloodstained sheets from my bed and taking them downstairs to wash them.

Now, waiting for the police to arrive, I was starting to panic. Out of the blue I thought of the laptop. What if they wanted to search Abe's room? How much trouble would he be in if they found it?

My mind was all over the place. I ran back upstairs, then along the passageway to Abe's bedroom. On my hands and knees I searched under his bed, but there was no sign of it. Flinging open the doors to his wardrobe, I searched in there too, but apart from spare blankets and the few clothes Abe had hung in there, I found nothing. In the corner of the room was the box he'd brought from Nina's house. I went through it and then, in desperation, peeled back his bedding and felt under the pillows.

Glancing out of the window, my heart leapt as I saw a police car making its way up the track towards the house. I was running out of time. Looking around the room, I quickly started rearranging everything so that it appeared as it had when I found it. Then, as I straightened the bed covers, out of the corner of my eye I saw something.

It was behind the wardrobe and only just visible and, as I got closer, I saw what looked like a bundle of envelopes. Curious, I picked them up, and as I looked more closely at the one on the top, my blood ran cold. It was addressed to Nina. Why did Abe have them?

I was desperate to know what they were about, but just then the doorbell rang. I did what anyone else would have done. I couldn't take any chances. Hurrying along to my bedroom, I hid them.

Back downstairs, I was out of breath and my arm was throbbing as I opened the front door. Two uniformed police officers stood there.

'Ms Roscoe? I'm Sergeant Levigne, Hampshire Police.' He held out his ID, then nodded towards his colleague, a younger woman. 'This is PC Marsh. May we come in?'

I held the door open. 'Of course.' Standing back as they came in, I closed the door behind them, then turned to look at them.

'Is there somewhere we could take a few details?' Sergeant Levigne was tall, with brown hair and piercing blue eyes.

'Of course. Come through.' I led them into the kitchen,

gesturing towards the table and chairs. 'Would you like to sit down?'

'Thank you.' They each pulled out a chair, while I hovered uncertainly. As Sergeant Levigne placed the notebook he was carrying on the table, I sat down opposite them, suddenly frustrated at their lack of urgency. 'Abe's my nephew. His mother – my sister – died three weeks ago. I'm really worried about him.'

PC Marsh had taken out a notebook. 'When did you last see him?'

'Last night.' I thought frantically. It had been before the phone calls started, before I'd spoken to Natalie Barnes about the Facebook post. 'It was about seven thirty – it was getting dark. Abe goes out to watch the stars.' I looked from one to the other, but their faces told me nothing.

'Can you tell us what he was wearing?'

I cast my mind back, trying to remember. 'Black trousers – the ones he wears to school. A black coat and probably trainers; they're what he usually wears.'

Sergeant Levigne was silent for a moment. 'Just to put your mind at rest, we've checked with local hospitals. No one meeting Abe's description has been admitted since yesterday. It's more than likely that he'll just make his way back here, but in the meantime we'll circulate his details. Can I ask you a bit more about him?'

'Of course.' I nodded.

'Where does he go to school?'

'Ringwood.'

'The secondary school?'

I nodded again.

'Have you called them to see if he's there today?'

I shook my head. 'I assumed . . . as he hadn't been back all night, he'd hardly have gone to school.'

'Has he taken his school bag?'

In my panic, I hadn't thought to check. 'I'm not sure. He has two bags. I think they're both in his room—' I broke off as Sergeant Levigne nodded towards his colleague. 'We'll call the school and see if he's registered this morning.'

I stared at them blankly. Why hadn't I thought to do that? I got up. 'I have the number somewhere.'

'There's no need, we have it. Please, sit down.'

I did as he said, watching PC Marsh walk outside, talking into her phone.

'Has your nephew made any friends since moving here? Or is there anyone in the village he might have gone to?'

'I don't think so . . . I don't know.' Was there anyone? Unable to give them any answers, I felt uncomfortable. 'To be honest, since coming here he's said very little, other than to make it clear he doesn't want to be here.'

Sergeant Levigne frowned. 'Do you think he might have tried to go back home?'

I was silent for a moment. 'I suppose it's possible.'

'And home was where, exactly?'

'London.' I gave him Nina's address. 'There's a neighbour who doesn't miss much. You could talk to her.'

'Would your nephew have a key?'

I shrugged. 'I don't know. He didn't say anything when we went back there to pick up his things.' Then I remembered. 'I picked up a key from a neighbour. I meant to return it to them when we left, but I forgot. It's over there.' I glanced across the kitchen to an old metal bowl where I dropped things like keys and loose change. Getting up, I went to look. 'It's still there.

It never occurred to me before, but he could have his own key.' It seemed obvious to assume that a fifteen-year-old would be able to let himself in.

Just then, PC Marsh came back in. 'The school has him down as absent. They said that since starting there he's missed a few days, but in the circumstances, they were giving him time to settle in. They've tried to call you, but I think they assumed you knew about it.'

I thought of the missed calls on my mobile that I'd dismissed, without considering they might have been important. 'I had no idea. He gets dressed in his school uniform and goes off to get the bus. He's done it every day since he started there. If he's not at school, where does he go?' I stared at Sergeant Levigne. As I spoke, he'd been making notes.

'That's a question for your nephew. I assume you've tried his mobile?'

Feeling both sets of eyes watching me, I swallowed. 'I don't have his number.' I couldn't believe that I hadn't taken Abe's mobile number. What had I been thinking?

'But he has yours?'

I shook my head. 'I don't know.' It seemed unbelievable that we hadn't exchanged numbers, but until now it wasn't something I'd even thought about. Then I remembered that I needed to explain that, until yesterday, Abe hadn't had his phone. 'The police investigating my sister's death kept his phone. He only got it back yesterday.'

PC Marsh leaned forward. 'Your sister's death is being treated as suspicious?'

'Yes.' I frowned. As I looked at them, suddenly I realized. I'd assumed that somehow they'd have known about Nina, but clearly neither of them had. 'It looks as though my sister –

Abe's mother – was murdered. I'm sorry, I don't know why, but I thought you'd have known.' As they glanced at each other, I added, 'DI Collins. She's working on the case.'

'We'll speak to the local police in London. They can send someone round there.' Then Sergeant Levigne glanced at his colleague. 'Maybe I'll give DI Collins a call—'

'I have her number,' I interrupted. 'In my mobile.' I reached for my phone, then stopped. 'But they won't be able to get in. I have the key.' This was turning into a nightmare.

'Can I have the number, please?' After I gave it to him, to my surprise, Sergeant Levigne called her immediately.

As he started talking, he got up and walked out of the kitchen. PC Marsh turned to me. 'Would you mind if I took a look in Abe's room?'

I nodded. 'I'll show you where it is.'

She followed me upstairs in silence and I led her along the passageway to Abe's room. 'Here. He doesn't have much stuff. Nina – my sister – wasn't well off.' For some reason I felt a need to make excuses. I stood in the doorway, watching, as PC Marsh looked briefly through Abe's possessions, before she turned to me.

'Would you know if he'd taken any clothes?'

'I don't think he has.' My eyes settled on the rucksack he'd packed the night Nina died. There was no sign of the other, smaller one I'd noticed him use for school. 'There's another bag, smaller than that one, which he takes to school. It isn't here.'

'Can you describe it?'

'Black. Plain.' I shrugged. 'Another rucksack.' I watched her write it down.

'You hadn't noticed anything strange about him recently?'

'Not really.' I shook my head. 'He keeps himself to himself, mostly. He goes outside most nights when the sky is clear. He's interested in the stars.' As I was speaking, I realized I should tell her. 'There have been a couple of strangers in the village. Maybe they have something to do with this.'

'Oh?' PC Marsh looked interested.

'Yesterday, Joe in the village shop told me that a woman had been asking about me. She told him she was an old friend of mine. He described her, but I've no idea who she was. Then, when I was walking home, there was this man.' I frowned.

'Go on.'

'There was something about him that wasn't right.' I hesitated. 'He looked out of place walking across the field.'

'In what way?'

I frowned. 'He was wearing jeans and a brown jacket, but his shoes weren't the kind you'd go walking in. They were polished. The kind of shoes you'd wear with a suit. But—' I broke off. I was sure I hadn't imagined it. 'He knew my name.'

PC Marsh looked at me sharply. 'I'm sorry?'

'As he walked past me, our arms brushed. And he said, "Hello, Hannah." But he didn't stop. He kept walking.'

'You're certain you didn't recognize him?'

I nodded. 'Completely. I've never seen him before in my life.'

She took a last look around the room. 'There's nothing much in here—' She broke off, frowning. 'Is your arm all right?'

I glanced at it. Blood had seeped through the bandage, staining the sleeve of my top. 'I cut it. I'd better go and dress it.'

She nodded. 'Shall I see you downstairs?'

Hastily I went along to my bedroom, where I managed to find a proper dressing and another bandage. By the time I went downstairs, Sergeant Levigne had finished his phone call. 'I've put DI Collins in the picture. Someone's going round to check the house. She also said they'd try and get in touch with Abe's brother, and see if he knew where Abe might have gone.'

'I'm surprised Jude hasn't been in touch with Abe.' It was true, although would Abe have told me if he had?

Sitting down again, PC Marsh addressed her colleague. 'Ms Roscoe was just telling me about a couple of strangers who have been hanging around.' Picking up her pen, she turned to me. 'Could you give me a description of the man?'

'Tall. With short, dark hair. His eyes were dark, too. He wore a brown jacket and polished shoes.'

'He was walking across the field yesterday. He knew Ms Roscoe's name,' PC Marsh added, as the sergeant looked at me.

He frowned. 'And you're quite sure you didn't recognize him?'

I nodded.

PC Marsh stopped writing for a moment. 'You have to admit, Sarge. It's pretty odd. If he'd known Ms Roscoe, you'd have expected him to stop and talk. Not just say her name and walk off like that . . .'

Sergeant Levigne looked at me. 'You said there were two strangers?'

'I didn't see the other one. I heard about her from Joe in the village shop. She had long, dark hair. Apparently she told him I was an old friend.' I frowned. 'She knew things about my life. He said that, too.'

'And you're quite sure she isn't anyone you know?'

I shook my head. 'I did think she might be a journalist who'd found out that Nina had been murdered.'

'Possibly.' But PC Marsh didn't sound convinced. 'Is this the shop we passed on the way here? Just a few minutes away?'

I nodded.

'On our way back we'll call in and have a word with Joe.'

'Do you think they have anything to do with Abe?' Nothing they said was making me any less anxious.

They exchanged glances. 'We've no way of knowing. But at this stage we need to check out every possibility.'

'You'll look for him?'

Sergeant Levigne nodded. 'We'll circulate his details and start asking around locally, straight away. Do you have a photograph?'

'Only a really old one. From about ten years ago.' Nina had stopped taking photos after Summer's accident.

He paused. 'It would be a good idea if you stay here today – in case Abe comes back. Let us know if you hear from him.' I nodded as he stood up, handing me a card. 'We'll be in touch as soon as we have any news.'

After they'd gone, I called Curtis. The more people looking out for Abe, the better. When it went to voicemail, I left a message: *Hello, Abe went missing last night. The police are looking for him. If you see him, can you let me know?*

After sending it, I sat there. All I could do now was wait.

13

The conversation with the police left me consumed with guilt. Last night I'd been too wrapped up in my own problems to think about Abe. *History repeating itself, Hannah . . .* I didn't want to think about how it had been the same, years ago, when Nina had needed me. If something happened to Abe, I'd never forgive myself. He had been let down by too many people. He deserved better.

But my uneasiness was about more than Abe's disappearance. There was the cut on my arm; I was thrown, too, by the interest the police had shown in the man on the footpath who'd known my name. Suddenly feeling cold as I thought about him again, I went to the back door and bolted it.

I picked up my phone again, checking it for messages. I was hoping that at any moment I'd get a call from the police, and the nightmare would be over. There was a text from Curtis asking me to let him know when Abe turned up. But that was all.

As I sat in the kitchen, I thought of the letters I'd found in Abe's room, wondering if they held a clue as to where he might have gone. I should have thought of them before. Getting up, I hurried upstairs.

In my bedroom I went to the chest of drawers where I'd hidden them, then sat on my bed. Untying them, I carefully removed the first from its envelope and unfolded it, curious:

6th August 2006
Dearest Mother
I suppose I should call you that, even though, even though, even though . . .

Don't give me that look and go silent on me. We both know what I mean. You don't mother. Don't nurture, protect, care, the way a mother should.

But it's one of those things you don't talk about, isn't it?

One of those blank spaces shared by hushed words and screamed obscenities, which you won't remember. You never do, when you're drunk. You never will.

Underneath was an illegible signature. I put it down for a moment, then took out the next, in the same handwriting, trying to work out who'd written them. Looking at the scrawled signature again, I tried once more to decipher it, then felt my blood run cold. It wasn't Jude's signature. It was Summer's.

Unsettled, I got out the next couple of letters and started reading:

20th May 2006
I remember running through the woods. Tall trees planted in rows. The deer that used to graze in the garden.

I used to believe everything you told me, about bluebell whispers and daisy-chain dances, wishing on stars, the spells you wove under the new moon. The magical childhood you wanted for me – my magical mother – of hazy days and long grass and freedom.

Until I wanted to learn to read and you told me: I'll teach you. Do you know how many hundreds of times you told me that, before the dream turned to dust? Before I stopped believing you? How I felt, when I realized you never would? But it was your perfect childhood you were giving me, without structure and challenge and learning and discipline and boundaries. That was what you meant by freedom. It was hiding from the world, safe in your magic cottage, in the woods.

When what I want is freedom to fly – away from here. I want to learn, get a job, have a career. I don't want your make-believe world, Mother. I want the real one.

30th August 2006
Dearest Mother
I wanted to share some memories with you.

I remember how pretty you looked in the long purple dress with your hair hanging in curls. There was food in the kitchen and the bluebells in a jug on the table. The patchwork quilt on my bed, which used to be yours. The ginger cat that used to sleep curled up with me. Marley, I called him. Do you remember him? The windows that were always open, so that Marley could come and go; so that I could hear the birds in the morning, you always told me; how, at night, I could lie in bed and see the stars.

Your eyes that were so blue, smiled at everyone – all the losers who came to stay, your drunk, stoned friends. The same blue eyes that didn't see your children.

You didn't know that while you were curling your hair, one of your drunk friends was touching me up. Did you know what happened to Marley? I did tell you, but you smiled blankly, then carried on talking to someone you barely knew.

Well, I'll tell you again.

Poor, soft, gentle Marley scratched one of your stupid druggie friends because they hurt him, so they took him outside and drowned him in the water butt behind the cottage. I screamed at him not to, but he just pushed me away. That's what your friends are really like.

Those windows that were always open let the rain in, so that I got cold and my bed got damp. Even when my chest hurt, you never took me to see a doctor. People were bad, the world was evil . . . You were hiding again, frightened, weren't you, Mother? That other people would see the truth.

Do you know how many of my birthdays you missed because you were drunk? Do you even know when my birthday is? Or Jude's? Or Abe's?

You're broken, Mother. Your smile hides a thousand splinters of your heart, your spirit, your soul, while your daughter writes letters to you, so that you can read them when you're sober. It's the only time you'll hear what she's trying to tell you, in those few minutes, before you reach for another pill and disappear again.

The menace in the voice from beyond the grave made me shiver. It was undeniably Summer. Her letters held the freshness and directness that had been so typical of her, as did the images she described. But there was no hiding her bitterness and anger at Nina's drinking. I sat back, thinking of Abe. On the occasions he'd talked about her, he'd always seemed fiercely protective of Nina. It didn't make sense that he would have kept letters that did nothing but attack her.

Then it dawned on me. Maybe it wasn't that he wanted to keep them. He was stopping them from being read by anyone else.

As I lay back on my bed, my head filled with memories of Summer when she was younger. Many times she'd been off somewhere in the woods when I visited Nina. I'd always thought of her as happy and carefree. When I lived there, she used to sit cross-legged at my feet, looking up at me, asking about the band, or she'd creep into my bedroom and experiment with my make-up. The arguments between her and Nina got worse as she got older, but I remembered far worse, violent rows between Nina and our own parents. What went on between her and Summer hadn't seemed out of the ordinary.

And yet the letters were an unleashing of bitterness. I was about to reach for the next, when I heard Gibson bark from somewhere downstairs. Was someone here? *Oh God, what if it is that man? Or the woman who's been asking about me?* Quickly gathering up the letters, I hid them again, then walked over to the window that looked out on the drive.

There was no sign of a car. As I went downstairs, my unease was growing. Gibson barked again, and this time I heard a hammering on the back door. Standing behind it, I hesitated.

'Who is it?' I called nervously.

'It's me.'

It was Abe. Thank God! Fumbling with the bolt, I opened the door. He stood there, a mutinous look on his face.

'God, Abe . . . where have you been? I've been worried sick. The police are looking for you.'

'Police?' He looked dumbfounded.

'I called them this morning. Where've you been?' I broke off. He seemed completely unmoved.

'I was at school.' He hung his head, staring at the floor.

'Don't lie,' I cried. 'The police called your school. They said you weren't there. They said you've missed a few days – why haven't you been there? What's been going on?'

'I was late for registration, that's all.' He paused for a moment. 'If you don't believe me, phone them again. I signed into all my classes.' He started walking towards the door and I lurched after him, grabbing one of his arms.

'Don't you dare walk off like that! I have to tell the police you're back. I hope you realize how much of their time you've wasted.'

Abe stopped walking, standing with his back to me. Then he turned round. 'Why did you call them?'

'Because you were gone all night.' I couldn't keep the anger out of my voice. 'I thought something terrible had happened to you.'

His eyes narrowed as he looked at me. 'What *are* you talking about?'

'Abe, you've been out since yesterday evening. Didn't you think I'd be worried?'

'I wasn't out. I came in late, that's all.' He looked at me, incredulous.

'What about this morning?' I stared at him. He had to be joking. 'You weren't here, Abe. I looked in your room. Your bed didn't look slept in.'

He folded his arms defensively. 'I went out early, to go to the library. Before you were up.'

I stared at him. He was lying. I was sure of it. 'But I didn't get up late.'

He shrugged. 'Whatever. But you must have been asleep when I went out or you would have heard me.' He sounded utterly convincing.

'I still need to let the police know you're back.' I turned away from him to look for my phone, hearing his footsteps on the stairs seconds later, then the sound of his bedroom door being slammed shut.

Too late, I thought of the letters that were still in my room. I hoped he wouldn't notice they were missing, but if he did, I knew what I'd tell him – that the police had searched his room, that maybe they'd moved them accidentally.

Fetching my phone, I called Sergeant Levigne, but he didn't answer and instead it went straight through to the police station. Having left a message there asking him to call me back, I was taken by surprise, twenty minutes later, when a police car drew up outside.

I watched from the kitchen window as Sergeant Levigne and PC Marsh walked up the path towards the house. I knew what I'd told them was the truth, but what if they chose to believe Abe? Opening the door, I went to meet them.

'Ms Roscoe . . . We were in the area when the station gave us your message, so we thought we'd call in. I gather your nephew's back?'

'Yes. And he's fine.' Nervously I tried to laugh it off. 'I owe you an apology. It seems there's been a misunderstanding. He says he's been at school. He just missed registration first thing. He's come home as usual. It's exactly as you said.' I looked from one to the other.

But neither of them responded to my attempted humour. Sergeant Levigne glanced towards the house. 'Has he given you an explanation as to where he was last night?'

I looked at him. 'He says he came in late, but he was definitely here. And this morning he went out earlier than usual.' As I spoke, I frowned. 'But I'm certain he wasn't here. I don't know why, but he refuses to admit it.'

PC Marsh spoke. 'Is your nephew here now?'

I nodded.

'Can we have a word with him?' Her eyes met mine.

I swallowed. 'Of course. Come in. I'll get him.'

Leaving them in the kitchen, I went upstairs and knocked on Abe's door. There was movement from inside. 'What?'

'The police are downstairs. They'd like to talk to you.'

As I finished speaking, the door was wrenched open. Abe stood there, his face like thunder. 'This is all your fault. I haven't done anything wrong.'

I shrank away from him. 'Can't you just come downstairs and tell them that there's been a misunderstanding?'

'What – you mean lie to them?' He looked outraged.

'It's not a lie, is it? You weren't here, Abe.'

He didn't answer. Then he glared at me for a moment, before shaking his head and pushing past me.

I followed hastily behind him, anxious to hear what he was going to say. As he walked into the kitchen, Sergeant Levigne looked up.

'I'm Sergeant Levigne. This is PC Marsh. You must be Abe.' He paused briefly. 'You've had us quite worried.' He spoke amicably, then glanced across at me. 'Would you mind giving us a moment?'

Taken aback, I nodded. 'Yes. Of course. I'll . . . I'll be outside.' I hesitated, looking at Abe, still worrying about what he was going to say to them.

'Thank you.' PC Marsh nodded towards the door.

Closing the back door behind me, I walked down the path, barely noticing the muted blue of a cluster of tiny grape hyacinths that stood above the clumps of primroses, strains of their scent reaching me. I waited for a few minutes until I heard the back door open, turning to see Sergeant Levigne and PC Marsh walking towards me.

'Abe explained what happened.' Sergeant Levigne stopped in front of me.

'What did he tell you?' I needed to know.

'Just that he was sure you'd heard him come in, but that you'd probably had a few drinks, which was why you didn't remember the next day. He found a broken wine glass on the floor and cleared it up. There was blood, too – he was worried you'd hurt yourself. Then this morning you slept in later than usual. It's why you didn't hear him leave to go to school.'

It was the first I'd heard about the broken wine glass. I looked at him, utterly incredulous. 'He said *what*?' It wasn't even remotely true. 'I can assure you that isn't what happened. I didn't sleep late. He didn't come back last night, as I told you before. For some reason, he's lying. Probably because he knows he shouldn't have done it.'

They glanced at each other. 'No one's judging you, Ms Roscoe.' PC Marsh spoke quietly. 'It isn't a crime to have a few drinks.'

'But I didn't.' I stared at her, knowing that whatever they said, they were judging me. I could see it on their faces. 'I honestly didn't. I've no idea why, but he's made this up. You can't believe that I wouldn't have known he was in the house?'

'He showed us the wine glass you broke.' Sergeant Levigne frowned.

PC Marsh looked at me. 'Is that how you cut your arm?'

I stared at her. Was it? I'd no idea. 'I don't think so.'

'You don't remember how it happened?' She seemed surprised.

Uncomfortable, I shook my head.

Sergeant Levigne continued. 'Look, he's safe, that's what's important. Whether he's lying or not isn't a police matter.' He paused. 'One more thing . . . Let us know if these strangers cause you any problems.'

I nodded, watching as they walked down the path and got in their car. I knew they hadn't believed me. Turning back towards the house, I realized it was time to have this out with Abe, but I was distracted momentarily as a small shape darted past me, then soared skywards, instantly recognizable from the way it flew and the distinctive shape of its forked tail against the sky. The first swallow.

I watched it for a few moments, as it was joined by another, feeling my anger with Abe start to dissipate. It meant that I was calmer by the time I walked into the kitchen. Abe was still there, almost as though he was waiting for me. My throat was suddenly dry. 'Why did you lie to the police?'

He frowned at me. 'I didn't.'

'You told them I was too drunk to remember you coming back in. And something about a broken glass – apparently you cleared it up. Why, Abe? It's nonsense, you know that as well as I do.'

He stared at the floor. 'All I said was that I was surprised you hadn't heard me come back in, that was all.' He glanced across

at the empty wine bottles I hadn't taken out to the bin yet.
'Maybe they just assumed.'

I shrank at the sarcasm in his voice. I opened my mouth to
say something else, then stopped myself. So many strange
things were going on, nothing was as it seemed. Was it possible Abe was right? Had I seen him and simply forgotten?

Wearily I shook my head, trying to change the subject.
'Earlier, the police asked me for your mobile number. I realized I didn't have it. It's probably a good idea for you to give
it to me, don't you think? And I'll give you mine.'

He nodded.

But I couldn't leave it alone. There was already all that talk
about how I drank too much. None of it was true. 'I wasn't
drunk, Abe.' My hands were sweating, but I kept my voice
icy-calm. 'We both know you weren't here last night.'

'I haven't lied.' His eyes held mine for a moment, defiantly,
then he looked at my arm. 'I suppose you don't remember
doing that, either?'

'What d'you mean?'

Abe frowned. 'Your arm. It was quite bad. You cut it when
you fell over. It was when you broke the glass.'

I gasped in disbelief. None of this rang true. Then, when I
glanced at my arm, blood was seeping through the bandage
again. He could be bluffing.

He shrugged. 'Whatever. I'm telling you I was here. You're
saying I wasn't. Which of us is right, Hannah?' He sounded
almost triumphant.

I didn't answer. He was so sure of his ground as he stood
there. And it was the way he used my name. A chill came over
me. Suddenly I was worried. Did he know I'd taken the letters? After what I'd read, God only knew what was in the rest

of them. I could hazard a guess – but if I was right, then Nina's secrets weren't safe at all.

After he'd gone upstairs, I walked over to the bin and opened it, a rushing sound filling my ears as I stared at the broken wine glass. Picking up a piece of it, I studied it closely. On it were what looked like traces of blood. I dropped it, shaking my head in an effort to clear it, trying to recall breaking it, but I was unable to trace the haziest glimmer of a memory.

Suddenly I wanted to scream. I felt as though I was losing my grasp on reality. There was no one I could talk to about any of this. Was I going mad? But then another, more sinister possibility flitted through my mind. The cut was real enough. But it didn't mean the rest of Abe's story was true. He could still have planted the glass. The traces of blood might not even be mine. It was the most likely explanation. But I'd no idea why.

Upstairs, I changed the bandage on my arm. Then, an hour later, Curtis turned up.

As I let him in, I realized I'd forgotten my promise to call him. 'I'm sorry, I meant to call you. Abe's back.'

'Is he OK?' Curtis came into the kitchen.

'Yes.' I stared at him. 'No. I don't know. Do you want a drink?'

'Thanks. A beer?'

I went to the fridge, consumed with guilt at the sight of the wine bottles after what the police had said. Getting a beer for Curtis, I rebelliously picked one of the bottles up. 'Here.'

I passed him the beer, then went to get a wine glass. After pouring some wine, I sat down.

'Abe says he was here last night. He went out early. He's been at school.' I stared at Curtis, needing him to believe me. 'But he wasn't, Curtis, I'm sure he wasn't.'

Curtis was frowning at me. 'Hold on . . . you're not making sense, Hannah. Why would he lie?'

'I don't know,' I said helplessly. 'He told the police that I'd had a couple of drinks and hadn't noticed him come in.'

Curtis sat back. 'Had you?'

I stared at him. 'No more than usual. By that, I mean I wasn't pissed, Curtis. If he was there, I would have seen him.'

He frowned. 'I don't get it. You're saying he lied to the police? But why would he do that?'

'Because he didn't want to end up in any trouble?' It was the only explanation I could think of. I rolled up my sleeve, then started to undo the bandage, carefully lifting off the dressing. 'See this?'

Curtis flinched as he gently took my arm and looked at it more closely. 'That looks deep, Hannah. Have you seen a doctor? You might need stitches.'

I was shaking my head. 'It doesn't matter. I woke up with it, Curtis. I've no idea how it happened.'

'There's no way you couldn't have felt that, Hannah.' He frowned. 'Unless . . .'

'What?' I could guess what he was about to say. 'You may as well say it.'

He shrugged. 'If you'd had a few drinks, you might not have noticed. Hard to believe, though.'

I couldn't argue with him. Remembering my resolve to cut back, I glanced at my glass, feeling guilty again. 'Abe says

I cut it when I fell over last night. I broke a glass at the same time.'

He looked relieved. 'That would account for it. So what's the problem?'

'I don't remember any of it. Not Abe being here or breaking the glass, not cutting my arm – none of it.'

'You know . . .' Curtis paused. 'I really don't want you to take this the wrong way. But there was that thing about your pictures, and the person you were convinced was tapping on the window—'

I interrupted him. 'I didn't convince myself. I know there was someone,' I said angrily. 'There's a difference.'

'OK. Don't get defensive; all I was going to say was that losing your sister has been stressful. Maybe you should see a doctor. There might be something you can take for a while, just to help you through the next few weeks, that's all I'm suggesting.'

'No bloody way, Curtis.' I was furious. 'You think it's me – that I'm making it up. You're like everyone else.' When no one believed me, it wasn't surprising I drank too much. Getting up, I went to top up my glass.

'Ease up, Hannah.' This time his voice was sharp. 'Every time I see you, you're drinking way too much.'

'It's none of your fucking business.' I spun round, spilling the contents of my glass. 'You know what? I'm really tired, Curtis. Maybe you should go.'

His eyes met mine for a moment, but I looked away. I knew he was right, but I hadn't expected him to talk to me like that. I'd had enough of everyone thinking they knew what was best for me. I'd just lost my sister, and I'd just lost Matt. It was enough to stress out the sanest person. It was small wonder I was struggling.

Picking up his jacket, he walked towards the door. When he got there, he paused for a moment. 'I'll call you.' He looked at me. 'Right?'

But I didn't answer. I had nothing to say to him.

Summer

You've never asked, Mother, but have you wondered how I learned to write? Of course! You taught me, didn't you? Sitting down at the table, lovingly showing me how to form letters, just as you patiently listened to my fumbling attempts to read . . . Remember? Blank smile in place, you conjure up the image I'm describing. The nurturing mother, tending her children. It was everything you wanted, wasn't it, Mother?

You almost believe me . . . But you don't remember, do you? Not really. Frowning for a moment, not sure if it's because you were off your face. But you can't recall teaching me because you didn't, Mother. Another lie, but who cares when your life is full of them?

Your idea of home-schooling was letting us fend for ourselves. It was Lucy Meadows who taught me. Lucy who saw through the lanterns, the music, the fairies in the garden, but you won't remember her, because instead of getting wasted with you, she sat in my room and taught me to read. It was because of Lucy that I learned to love books and the worlds contained in their pages. She's the reason you're reading these letters – she taught me to write, too. Then I taught Jude.

My own mother didn't think I needed to learn to read. It made me see how unimportant I was, how fucked-up you were. The fucked-up daughter of fucked-up parents. But I don't bear grudges. What goes around comes around. Nature has its own way of dealing with the weak, slowly blotting out their sunlight, strangling them with weeds.

But the strong only get stronger.

It's the same with people.

You'll see.

14

Hannah

I didn't sleep well that night. As well as being angry with Curtis, there were too many conflicting thoughts running through my head. Yet again, with everything else going on, I'd forgotten to ask Abe if he knew anything about Cara Matlock or the Facebook posts. Suspicious of everyone, after the incident with the police, I'd briefly considered whether it might have something to do with him, before dismissing the idea. But his account of the night I'd reported him missing, and how I'd cut my arm, had completely unnerved me.

My arm in particular had shocked me. As I lay in bed thinking about it, I knew I had to stop drinking so much. To suffer a cut of that severity, without any memory of how it happened, meant I must have been out of it. I could no longer ignore what everyone was saying to me. I'd reached a turning point. I had to change something. If not, who knew what would happen next.

The following morning I overslept and, by the time I woke up, Abe had already gone to school. I felt disorientated as I got up, my head all over the place. As well as everything else, the

160

letters were preoccupying me. I wanted to finish reading them – with luck, in time to put them back before Abe came home from school. The fact that he hadn't mentioned their absence made me hopeful that he hadn't noticed they'd gone.

My arm was throbbing this morning and, under the bandage, it was red and inflamed. No longer could I put off going to the doctor and, once I was dressed, I called the local surgery and made an appointment for later that morning.

After re-bandaging my arm, I sat on my bed, carefully untying the bundle of letters again and picking up where I'd left off yesterday, feeling myself carried back to that time in Nina's cottage where, with each letter, Summer's frustration became more apparent:

15th April 2007

How many falls until you fly, Mother? How many pills before you slip the chains of your tormented existence forever?

You were gone all day yesterday. You didn't tell us where you were going. Do you know how worried I was that something had happened to you? When you came back, I asked you where you'd been. You gazed into the distance and said, 'Look how the light catches the raindrops.'

You, the eternal dreamer, living in your fantasy world, shot my own dreams down in flames. I wasn't allowed them. I had everything I needed. Where did that come from, Mother? That need to control? To cut me down the moment I stepped beyond what you wanted for me? Is that what your parents did to you?

Dreams are lifeblood, Mother. You, more than anyone, should know that. How else do you get through the grittiest times to find the most brilliant moments? You had dreams, once, Mother, which went beyond the cracked walls of this cottage, the damaged souls you draw here. Tangible, so that you could feel them like snowflakes or a butterfly's wings, against your cheek. Aren't you terrified you've lost them forever?

I found a photo earlier, of you and me and Jude. In the photograph, I'm fine. You can't see the twisted thoughts running through my head, but I learned from the best. Smile, and the world smiles with you, you always said . . . People never question a smiling face, but then most people are blind to what they don't want to see, even when it's the truth.

Truth. Oh, that's long ago vanished from your little world of magic and parties, where the flowers sparkle and the everyday unfolds like some macabre, distorted fairy tale; where everyone smiles because smiling makes everything OK, even when the smile's a lie.

It's a world where there's an answer to all your problems. Mother's cure-all. Not talking – that would be far too uncomfortable. Who needs to talk, when there's a pill; when, in a few minutes, your problems are so far away you can't remember them.

But they wait for you, don't they, Mother? Those problems? In the cold light of day, they're back, aren't they, filling you with pain, haunting your every moment, until you take another pill, banish them again.

Your disappearing, ever-shrinking world. That's what I remember most.

I was shocked at Summer's depiction of her mother. It was unnecessarily harsh, I couldn't help thinking. I'd always admired the side of Nina that was able to smile in the face of adversity, but Summer clearly hadn't seen it like that.

Then, for the first time, I tried to imagine life through Summer's eyes, seeing the cottage, the garden, the miles of woods.

It had been wonderful for them in so many ways. Nina had tried so hard to do what was best for her children. But somewhere inside, I knew there were things that shouldn't have happened, things I could have prevented, if I'd tried.

There was no point going over it now. It was too late. Putting away the letter, I unfolded the next:

2nd June 2007

Dear Mother,

Do you know how much I want to talk to you? How much it would mean if you listened to me? But it's always the same, when it's about something you don't want to hear. You shut down and turn away, with a random observation about the persistence of the rain or the unseasonal migration of the birds, which makes you look past me at something I can't see. Do you know how it feels when your own mother won't listen to what you want to tell her? I wish I could let myself believe you were thinking of me, just once. But you don't think of anyone but yourself.

Mother, do you know how much I wish things could have been different and that you were happier? I'm not talking about the stupid, plastic smile you plaster on your face. I mean in the deepest part of you, where it counts. The kind of happiness that radiates out from there and reaches others.

I know you can't help what happened to you and Hannah. I know you're trying to do your best. But it sucks, Mother. I don't want to live under the radar forever. It's your dream. It isn't mine. It isn't freedom. There's no future.

Take away my chains, Mother.

Set me free.

Let me fly.

As I read, I could hear Nina's secrets unravelling, but I was compelled to read on, wondering what she had told Summer about our own childhoods. My heart sank as I realized the likelihood was that Abe had read these, too. He must have. Why else would he have kept them? Putting the letter down, I picked up the next. This time as I read, I felt my skin prickle:

23rd June 2007

When are you going to tell the truth, Mother? You want to take your secrets to your grave, don't you? But it won't work. I won't let you. Don't you think people deserve to know what happened all those years back? That blood is thicker than blood? Oh, but of course, that won't have crossed your mind. As always, you're thinking about you or Hannah, not about Abe.

It's too late for me and Jude. We're only nine and fourteen, the fucked-up children of a fucked-up mother with fucked-up parents. Polluted with your fucked-upness running through our veins. If there's a shred of decency left in you, don't do it to Abe. Give him what you didn't give us. Freedom to have a life, Mother, not to run wild as we did, but the kind that begins with an education, so that he can be part of the world, not forever hiding from it.

One day you'll have to tell him what you've been keeping from him. Can you do that? Be brutally, heartbreakingly, self-sabotagingly honest? Take the hit yourself, in the name of truth? But this time you won't be able to run from it, the way you always run from things; pretend it didn't happen.

Bury the lie.

Because here's the thing. If you don't tell him, I will.

It was dated a week before Summer died. As I put the letter down, I felt sick. In the wrong hands, it could be made to look as though Nina wanted her daughter out of the way.

I needed to know exactly what Summer had found out. It was possible she'd been bluffing, desperate to get her mother to listen to her, but that last letter had an almost threatening tone to it. *What had she known?* The next was dated earlier in the year:

16 April 2007
Dear Mother
You are your own devil, and you make this world your own hell.

Now, Mother, let's talk about THAT NIGHT.

The biggest lie of all the lies.

But you don't remember, do you?

You don't remember me coming to you, telling you that Lenny had come into my room and got into bed with me. You liked Lenny, didn't you? Gazed at me blankly when I told you. I remember your reply: But Lenny wouldn't do that.

But Lenny didn't like mad old, sad old addicts like you. Lenny liked girls, Mother. I was the only reason he was in your cottage.

Three questions:

Why would I lie to you?

Why did you believe Lenny?

When Sam heard what happened to me, why did you lie to him, too?

Sam, who wanted to call the police, put an end to what Lenny had done more than once. You didn't want the police called, did you? I know what you told Sam, because he told me: Summer lied.

But a lie isn't always a lie, is it, Mother? For so many reasons – remember?

THAT NIGHT . . . Lenny didn't mean it, you told me. Of course he didn't!! Your outrage, when I told you what he'd done to me.

It was a misunderstanding, wasn't it, Mother? That was all. Sexual abuse trivialized; swept away under the carpet, with everything else you can't bear to live with.

Here's a fact for you, Mother.

Lenny raped me. And you didn't believe me.

Your daughter

Summer

I was shocked. How hadn't I known about this? I had a faint memory of Lenny, a skinny man who'd hung around Nina's for a while. He'd been odd, but I found it hard to believe he'd done that to Summer, yet I couldn't imagine why she'd have made it up.

Not wanting to risk Abe knowing I'd had the letters, I was carefully keeping them in exactly the same order I'd found them in, as I carried on reading. But it was later than I thought. I glanced at my watch, suddenly remembering the doctor's appointment, reluctantly reassembling the letters, torn between keeping them and returning them to where I'd taken them from, in Abe's room.

In the end I decided to put them back, hoping Abe still didn't know I'd found them. There were a couple I had yet to read and I was aware that I needed to know what else was in them, what Abe knew. I had a suspicion I knew what they were leading towards. If I didn't have to wait at the surgery, I'd have time to carry on when I got home.

Locking the house, I walked down the path towards my car. Starting it, I was still deep in thought as I drove along the track towards the village, when things started to happen all at once.

It began when I saw the dark-haired man who'd known my name, walking up the track towards me. Fear shot through me. Then, as he saw me, he stepped into the middle of the road, holding out his arms as if flagging me down.

On top of everything else in my mind, logic had long deserted me as, without knowing where it had come from, I was overwhelmed by a sense of danger. I considered reversing, then running for the safety of the house, where I'd call the police. But what if he caught up with me before I got there? I braked for a moment, while he slowly walked up the track towards me, his eyes not leaving my face. It was involuntary rather than conscious, but I knew I had to get away from him.

Slamming my foot hard down on the accelerator, I drove at him, holding my course, waiting for him to move, but he stood his ground. At the last minute he stepped aside, but I'd already swerved round him, onto the verge and into the hedge.

Almost losing control, I managed to pull away. Then somehow I was past him, my hands clammy on the steering wheel, my heart hammering in my chest. As I glanced in my rearview mirror, I could see him standing there, watching me drive away. For a moment I even thought he was laughing at me. Putting my foot down, I felt the rear wheels slide out of control, only just managing to straighten them, still driving too fast when I reached the road. Without stopping, I turned right, completely misjudging the speed of the van coming towards me.

Braking hard, I was horrified as I felt my wheels lock, then heard a sickening crunch at the same time as my head hit something and pain shot through my body. It was the last thing I remembered.

*

I had no way of knowing how much time had passed when I came round, to the muffled sound of voices all around me. Slowly I became aware that I was in my car. I tried to move, but I felt a hand pressing me down, holding me still, and heard an unfamiliar voice. 'Don't move. You've been in an accident. An ambulance is on its way.'

Accident? Then it came back to me. I'd been driving away from that man. Oh God, what if he found me? I turned my head, trying to talk. '*Someone was after me . . .*' But my words were lost in the noise around me.

'Try not to talk. You mustn't worry. You're going to be fine.' This time I registered it was a woman's voice.

I tried again. '*The man . . .*' I knew what I wanted to say, but I couldn't form the words. In the distance, I heard a siren. Then, opening my eyes, an impossible face swam into focus – a face that I knew couldn't be here. It was the face of a ghost, staring into mine. That was when I knew I was losing it. I tried to scream, but my voice was mute, silent. Then I felt myself drifting away, as everything around me faded to nothing.

15

Afterwards I had no memory of the paramedics arriving, or of being lifted into the ambulance and driven at speed to the hospital. I don't know how many hours passed before I regained consciousness. Left alone in my hospital bed, I tried to piece together the disjointed fragments of what I remembered. I'd been driving. Too fast, I knew that. I recalled a sense of fear. I'd been trying to get away from someone. Suddenly I saw a replay of the dark-haired stranger, standing in the middle of the track, blocking it; of him laughing at me as I scraped past him in the hedge; of driving away too fast onto the main road, straight into the oncoming traffic. Then I thought of the man again, and it was as if I was caught in a nightmare. What if he'd gone to the house? What if Abe was there alone? A sense of panic rose in me. Reaching for the buzzer, I pressed it, again and again, until a nurse came hurrying in.

'My nephew,' I said weakly. 'He lives with me. He's alone. I need my phone.'

'Don't worry, it's locked in your cupboard.' She fished in

her pocket for a set of keys, then unlocked the drawer. 'How old is he?'

'He's fifteen. The police know he's there.' Would anyone have thought about Abe? I had no way of knowing if either Sergeant Levigne or PC Marsh knew about my accident. My only other hope was that, knowing the village, word would have got around and maybe someone might have thought to check on him.

She passed me the phone and I scrolled through the numbers until I found his, filled with relief as it started to ring. But it went to voicemail.

I looked at the nurse. I'd no idea what to do. 'He isn't answering.'

'Is there someone you can call? To go round there and check on him?'

I nodded, thinking of Curtis, finding his number and willing him to answer, but it went to voicemail too. I looked at the nurse. 'He's not there.'

'Is there anyone else?'

'Erin.' I sank back weakly. 'My friend.'

The nurse nodded. 'Why don't you try her? I'll come back in a minute.'

I waited until she was out of earshot, then called Erin. 'Erin, it's Hannah.'

'Hannah! How are you?' Any trace of the awkwardness between us last time we met seemed to have vanished.

'I've had an accident. I'm in the hospital.' My voice wobbled.

'God, Hannah! What happened? Are you OK?' Erin sounded shocked.

'Yes. They're keeping me in overnight. I'm hoping to go

home tomorrow.' Tears pricked my eyes. 'Erin? This is really important. I don't know where Abe is. I've tried calling him, but he isn't answering. He should be at the house, but I've no way of knowing. Could you go and see if he's OK? There's been this man hanging around. He was there this morning, before my accident—' I stopped. Suddenly I was shaking.

'Hannah? Of course I will. But this man . . . if you're worried about him hanging around, you should call the police. Get someone to go round there, OK?'

I nodded. 'Yes.'

'Call them, now. As soon as we've finished talking. Then call me back.'

Ending the call, I scrolled down the list of recent numbers, finding one I didn't recognize. Relief filled me as my call went through to the police station.

'Hello? Could I speak to Sergeant Levigne?'

'He's not here just at the moment. Can I ask who's calling?'

'Hannah Roscoe. He came out to see me when my nephew went missing.'

'One moment.' The phone went silent for a couple of minutes. Then a different voice spoke.

'Ms Roscoe? This is PC Marsh. How can I help you?'

'I'm worried about my nephew. Abe,' I reminded her. 'You know the man I told you about? The one who knew my name?'

'Yes . . .' She sounded hesitant. 'Why are you worried, Ms Roscoe?'

'I was in an accident. I'm in hospital. Just before it happened, I saw that man again, on the track that leads to my house. I'm worried that Abe's there alone. I've asked my friend to go and check on him. But if that man's come back

. . . Can you send someone round? *Please?*' I could hear myself getting hysterical.

'Calm down, Ms Roscoe. I'll go over there now. What's your friend's name?'

'Erin,' I said desperately. 'Erin Bailey. But Abe doesn't know her . . .'

'Have you tried calling your nephew?' PC Marsh's voice was calm; calming.

'Yes. It went to voicemail. I'll try him again. But I need to know you're going there.'

'Call your nephew, Ms Roscoe. I'll call you back once I've seen him.'

'Thank you,' I said breathlessly, ending the call and immediately trying Abe again. 'Abe? Is that you? It's Hannah.'

'Yeah. Where are you?'

'I'm in the hospital. I was in an accident. I'm OK – it's a long story . . . Abe, this is important. Have you noticed anyone hanging around? There was a man earlier. Tall, with dark hair. I've told the police. They're coming over.'

'Not the police again.' He sounded angry.

'I had to, Abe. I called my friend Erin, too. She's coming over. She's nice. Maybe you can stay with her for a night? Until I'm home?' In the background I could hear Gibson barking. 'Can you feed Gibson?'

'Yeah. Someone's at the door.'

'Make sure it isn't the man,' I said anxiously. 'Don't let anyone in, Abe. Not unless it's Erin or the police.'

'Yeah.' He hung up.

Forgetting I'd told Erin that I'd call her back, I lay in the bed, my eyes drifting upwards as the ceiling swam out of focus, a sick feeling in the pit of my stomach. Nothing felt real. Not the events of earlier, that man, the way he'd been blocking the track; being here in the hospital. My car . . . There was only one thing I could do. Pulling myself upright in bed, I pushed the sheet back and moved my legs to one side, then stood up tentatively. I hadn't thought how I was going to do it, but I needed to get out of there.

I was still wearing my clothes. Glancing around, I saw my shoes under the cupboard beside my bed. Pulling them on, I picked up my jacket, slipping my phone into my pocket and making it as far as the door before the nurse came in. She shook her head.

'You shouldn't be on your feet, Ms Roscoe. You had a nasty knock to your head and you were unconscious for quite a while. The doctor wants to see how you are in the morning. Come on, I'll help you back to your bed.'

I stood there, shaking my head. 'I'm all right. I want to go home.'

'How were you planning to get there? Is someone coming for you?'

I frowned at her. I hadn't thought that far, but it was hardly a problem. I could try Curtis again. Or I'd get a taxi, if necessary. 'It isn't far. I'll get someone to pick me up – or I can call a taxi.'

'Please . . .' I felt her hand on my arm. 'It's only for one night.' Then, as we walked, she said, 'That's a nasty cut on your arm. We've cleaned it up and put a new dressing on it. How did you do it?'

I was thrown by her question. I still didn't remember how I'd been injured. 'I fell over . . . and caught it on something.'

'It's quite deep, isn't it? You need to keep an eye on it.'

I nodded, allowing her to steer me back to the bed, where

I sat awkwardly, hating how I felt I had no choice, when I heard my phone. Pulling it out of my pocket, I saw Erin's name on the screen.

'Hi, Erin.'

'Hannah, I'm at yours, with the police. Abe is fine, and so is Gibson. They're going to stay with me tonight. There's no sign of the man you saw earlier. Do you know how long you're staying in?'

'Only till tomorrow.' I glanced at the nurse, as Erin went on.

'Once Abe's gone to school, I'll come and pick you up, if you'd like me to?'

'OK.' I said it reluctantly, hating that it meant I was staying here.

'Look after yourself.' She sounded anxious. 'And don't worry about anything. I'll see you tomorrow.'

Ten minutes later, PC Marsh called me. 'Your friend seems to have everything in hand. I take it you're comfortable with that? It's certainly better for Abe that way.'

'Of course. You didn't see that man?'

'No, Ms Roscoe, there was no sign of him. I suggest you try and rest.'

'Yes.'

I ended the call, then I texted Curtis to tell him where I was, asking him not to call me as I was going to try to get some sleep. Then I lay there in silence, imagining Abe and Erin together, both of them talking to PC Marsh about me, not sure what they would have said. After the Facebook post and my students cancelling, the two strangers who appeared to know me, the strange noises outside my house at night, and now my accident, it was as though any control I had over my life was slipping from my grasp. I was being paranoid, I told myself. Abe was better off with Erin than with a stranger. But it was the way PC Marsh had spoken about her. *Your friend seems to have everything in hand.* It was me who'd told PC Marsh that Erin was my friend, and she was, but on the most superficial level. The truth was that we knew hardly anything about each other. I hadn't even told her about Matt until a few weeks ago, and then he'd left.

But at least the police knew what was going on. Most likely none of this was related, I knew that. The stranger was just a weirdo who got his kicks out of scaring women, and the Facebook post had been a childish prank. But it was the timing – everything happening at once. I couldn't shake the conviction that there was more to this.

Something was missing. Something that connected these seemingly unrelated events. Turning out the light, as I lay back in the darkness, the final moments before the accident replayed in my head. This time I remembered more clearly how terrified I'd been. I'd no idea why I was so frightened of that man, but it was fear that had propelled me onto the road without looking. I remembered the impact, the grating of metal on metal, hearing the thud of my head against the side window, then opening my eyes to see a face hanging over me.

I sat up with a gasp. It wasn't possible. I was sure it had been Nina's face, our eyes meeting for a moment, before I'd passed out again.

I'm getting closer, Hannah. I know about the Facebook posts, I've listened to what people are saying about you. Villages are full of nasty, vicious gossip, aren't they? It takes nothing to start small-minded people pointing the finger of blame. Unfair that someone should post a photo of you, wasn't it? But your drinking isn't a secret any more. It's about time people knew about it. When you teach the bright, impressionable teenagers entrusted to your care, don't you think their parents should know the truth?

Maybe they should know what else is in your past. What would they say if they knew how huge the lie was? Or about the other, bigger lies? Lies your whole life has been based upon. There's the other boy, too. The older brother. Jude. You tell yourself there's no reason for you to meet him, don't you? You've lost touch, after all. Anyway, he's not a child, he doesn't need you – and you believe that, instead of being honest with yourself. You're scared, aren't you, Hannah? Not just of what he might do, but of what he knows.

You want facts? About what happened the night you cut yourself? You didn't feel the sharp edge of glass cut through your skin, did you? Nor as it pressed deeper into your flesh, severing blood vessels, causing pain that was no different from the aching, gnawing feeling in your heart; both of them numbed by alcohol.

In between, while you're pacing around your house, neurotically checking windows, hearing imaginary noises, obsessed with yourself, have you stopped and thought about what the boy needs? You've lost your sister, but he's lost his mother. All that fuss you made about him going missing, when he hadn't . . . You didn't even notice the night he caught a late train to London, creeping along the street and letting himself into his old home. How does that make you feel? The thought of a teenage boy, battling with his grief, alone in the empty house where his mother was killed?

But you'll never know about that. As there always are, with the people in your life, you and the boy have secrets between you. He'll be OK, though – the boy. He has a plan, one you don't know about; he can feel change already in motion, change of which this short chapter is a brief but necessary part. It won't last long, it will soon be behind him. That's what he's thinking about, counting down each day at a time, looking forward.

You need to be careful, though, Hannah. He knows more than you think. Has proof that could give you nightmares, if he shared it with you, but the right moment hasn't come. Not yet.

Abe's read the letters. Bit of a game-changer, isn't it, Hannah? Out-secreted by someone who knows more than you thought? What if he tells someone else? Maybe he already has, like that woman who's been hanging around the village, asking about you. She's talked to the boy, waiting in your garden at night for the first stars to draw him outside. So easy when he's always alone, when you don't bother to go with him, but you wouldn't know she's been here, because so far he hasn't told you anything. He never does.

But why would he, when you're always on the defensive, always waiting for someone to catch you out? Always the victim? That's who you think you are – poor Hannah, with her estranged parents and broken marriage, and whose band fell apart; whom life has been hard to.

You're a victim only of yourself, Hannah. Of your life choices; of your own misjudged decisions. You're not poor Hannah. You need to know how it feels to have no one in the world, to have nothing. And you will.

16

Hannah

I knew my mind had been playing tricks on me and it couldn't possibly have been Nina's face I'd seen. My sister was dead. I'd identified her body. The only explanation was that, as I fell unconscious, my brain conjured up the one person – the only person – I'd most have wanted there.

I was too dazed, too confused to make sense of anything. The more I thought, the more I felt my life spiralling out of control. But everything that was happening to me had started since Nina's death; since Abe came to live with me. Maybe there was a link; maybe the police were missing something.

Counting the minutes away, desperate to escape the stark sterility of the hospital, I was relieved when Erin arrived. Climbing into her untidy car, I winced as my arm caught on the car door.

Erin noticed. 'Are you OK?'

'Bruised.' I didn't tell her the cut on my arm was nothing to do with the accident. 'I can't thank you enough for coming here.'

'Please, don't worry about it. I'm glad I could help. I left

Gibson at mine. I wasn't sure how long it would take for you to be discharged. Why don't you come and have some lunch, then I'll drop you both home after?'

I nodded. 'Thanks.'

The accident had affected me more than just physically. My nerves were on edge. Erin drove too fast for comfort and, as I sat in the passenger seat, my fists were clenched while unconsciously I stamped on an invisible brake.

'Abe was fine.' She glanced sideways at me. 'Do you remember anything about what happened yesterday?'

I nodded. 'Most of it. It was to do with this man I told you about, who's been hanging around. The first time I met him walking along a footpath on my way back from the village. Then yesterday I was on my way out, when I met him walking up the track towards my house. When he saw my car, he stood in the middle, blocking it.'

'You should have stopped and asked him who he was.'

'Really?' I stared at her, aghast. Is that what she would have done? 'You should have seen him, Erin. The first time, as we passed, he spoke my name. How creepy is that? I've never met him before. I wasn't going to stop. There's been other stuff, too. I just don't feel very safe at the moment.'

'OK.' She was quiet for a moment. 'You've been through such a lot, Hannah. I'm not surprised you feel so overwhelmed.'

Beside her, I felt myself stiffen. It sounded as though she didn't believe me.

Going on, she changed the subject. 'Abe's quiet, isn't he? It's not been easy for him, losing his mum and then moving here.'

'No.' But I was biting back the urge to shout at her, *Nor is it easy for me . . .*

'He talked a bit while we had a cup of tea. But that was about it.'

'What did you talk about?'

'Oh, not much really.' She sounded vague. 'About what it was like living in London, and how it was coming to live with you.'

I was quiet, imagining their conversation, uncomfortable knowing that they'd been talking about me. We drove the rest of the way in silence, while I took in the ancient beech trees on either side of the road, as we headed towards a part of the Forest I rarely passed through. Muted green shades gave way to earthy greys and browns, so that the landscape appeared almost monochromatic. Gazing out of the window, I took in the stretches of drab heather yet to burst into flower, where a few ponies wandered, before the road zigzagged ahead of us through more trees. Then, on the outskirts of a village, outside a terraced cottage, Erin pulled up at the side of the road.

'Here we are.' Only the roof of Erin's cottage showed from behind the tall beech hedge that flanked the road. Above, the branches of an apple tree were covered in buds that were just starting to flower.

'I hope this isn't too much trouble?' I felt awkward that I was putting her out.

'Of course it's not. It won't be anything fancy. I made soup earlier – if that's OK with you?'

'It sounds lovely.' Getting out of the car, I followed her through the white-painted gate and under the apple tree, towards the door set to one side of the house. As she opened it, two dogs rushed out.

'Gibson!' I was ludicrously pleased as my dog leapt around my feet, wagging his tail.

'He's missed you,' Erin called from inside. 'Though he and Abe seem to have hit it off. Come on in.'

With Gibson at my heels, I went inside, closing the door and finding myself in a small entrance hall. Erin appeared in a doorway. 'I've put the kettle on. What would you like? Tea or coffee?'

'Tea would be great.' I followed her into the kitchen, which was surprisingly bright and spacious, with faded wooden units and muted grey walls, which set off the crooked beams. 'Your house is gorgeous, Erin.'

'Thank you.' She looked pleased. 'You should sit down, Hannah. I'm sure the doctors told you to take it easy for a few days.'

I nodded, doing as she said and pulling out a chair at the table that was pushed to one side against the wall. 'They did.' I paused, frowning. 'What I don't know is what's happened to my car.'

'The police would be able to tell you.' Erin busied herself at the stove.

'PC Marsh didn't say anything last night.'

'Maybe she didn't know. Why don't you call the police station and ask?'

I nodded, getting out my phone, but the screen was blank. 'I'll do it at home. It needs charging.'

'You can do it from here, if you like. My mobile signal is rubbish, but you can use the landline. It's in my study – through here.' As Erin started walking towards another door, I got up and followed her into a sitting room, which was simply but comfortably furnished with a huge sofa in a soft shade of yellow and a patterned rug on the floorboards in front of the fireplace. Across the room, another door led into a much smaller room.

It was a cosy space, with a desk placed in front of the window, and Erin pulled out the chair. 'Help yourself.' She gestured towards the phone. 'I'll go and finish lunch.'

I walked over to the desk and sat down, gazing through the window at the front garden, which was screened from the road by the hedge, taking in the view of the apple tree and the white gate beyond, aware of how peaceful it felt here. And how safe, when my own home didn't feel safe. Remembering what I'd come to do, I picked up the phone. Then I put it down again. I didn't have the number – it was on my phone.

As I looked around, I saw Erin's laptop. The easiest solution was to google it. It wasn't something I'd usually do, but on the off-chance the computer wasn't password-protected, I turned it on. The screen instantly came to life with her Facebook page. But before I could open a new window, I noticed it wasn't Erin's page. Scrutinizing it more closely, I saw a name I recognized.

It was Cara Matlock's Facebook page. My blood froze as I remembered what she'd posted about me. But what did she have to do with Erin?

Suddenly I heard footsteps. Quickly I closed Erin's laptop, before she could see what I was looking at.

'Any luck?'

I shook my head. 'There was no reply,' I lied. 'I'll try them again when I'm home.'

'If you're certain?' I wasn't sure if I was imagining Erin's eyes lingering on me. Had she seen me using her laptop?

I got up. 'To be honest, I'm not feeling all that well.'

'Oh, Hannah.' Erin was all sympathy. 'You should probably be resting. Come and have a quick bite to eat, then I'll take you home.'

Back at home, as I watched Erin drive away, I let out a breath that I'd been holding in since leaving her study. Slumped into a chair, I rested my head in my hands. My stomach felt hollow. I hadn't been able to eat Erin's soup, blaming my lack of appetite on the accident, and hiding the truth gnawing at me: that I didn't trust her. Right now, I didn't trust anyone.

17

I must have dozed off, because I awakened feeling a familiar mistrust creep insidiously back over me, as I tried to piece together the events of recent days. The unexpected appearance of PC Marsh an hour later did little to help.

She stood on the doorstep, her eyes appraising me. 'I called in at the hospital earlier, but they said you'd been discharged. How are you feeling?'

'Not too bad.' Then I remembered my car. 'Do you know what's happened to my car?'

The police officer nodded. 'Actually, would you mind if I came in? I need to take a few details about the accident – if it's convenient?'

I hadn't even considered that the police would want a statement from me. Frowning, I stood back. 'Of course. Come in.'

She stepped inside. 'Thank you.'

Closing the door, I led her through to the kitchen. 'Have a seat.'

She nodded, pulling out a chair. 'Thank you. This shouldn't take long.'

I felt my stomach churn as I sat down opposite her, suddenly realizing that, with everything else that was going on, I'd given little thought to any consequences of my accident. There'd be an insurance claim, but surely that was all? I watched her get out a notebook.

'Can you begin by telling me what you remember before the crash?'

'I'll try.' I hesitated. 'I've told you about the man who's been hanging around here, haven't I? It was because of him.'

PC Marsh frowned. 'How, exactly?'

'He was walking up the track towards my house as I was driving down. I should point out that it isn't a public right of way. Then, when he saw me, he deliberately stood in the middle of the track and wouldn't move.'

'So what did you do?'

'He frightened me. I had to get away from him.'

She looked puzzled. 'What exactly was it about him that frightened you?'

I hesitated. How did I describe that it was the combination of his body language and the look in his eyes, which was almost triumphant, as though he knew something I didn't. 'I felt threatened,' I said. 'I'm sure he was trying to intimidate me.'

'Ms Roscoe, did he actually do anything?'

I stared at her. 'Yes. He blocked the track, then made his way towards me.'

'Why did you find that so worrying?'

'If you'd been there, you'd know exactly what I mean. It was his body language mostly. I just knew I had to get past him. I ended up driving on the verge against the hedge to get past. When I looked in the rear-view mirror, he was standing there, laughing at me.'

'Ms Roscoe.' PC Marsh put her pen down. 'Have you questioned whether your reaction was emotional rather than entirely logical?'

'What?' Her question startled me. 'What do you mean?'

She frowned. 'Well, to be honest, I find it strange that you didn't slow down and perhaps ask him what he wanted? Maybe there was a reason?'

It was what Erin had said. 'No.' I shook my head. 'No. You've got it wrong. There's no way I could have done that. This man . . . I've seen him twice. He's definitely trying to frighten me, and he's succeeding. Everything about him is designed to intimidate me – his body language, the way he stares, the fact that he knew my name. You must be able to understand that?'

She sighed. 'The problem is, he hasn't actually done anything, has he? If he really wanted to get to you, he'd have come to the house when you were at home – but he hasn't. I'm struggling to understand why you're so convinced of his intentions against you.'

I was on the point of saying that threatening behaviour didn't need to be physical, but I could tell she'd already made up her mind. I couldn't believe how unfair this was. I didn't know what else to say to her. I just stared at her, aghast.

'Would you be able to identify him?'

'Yes.' As I thought back, the man's face, his demeanour, the expression in his eyes – all were imprinted in my mind.

'Anyway, go on,' she said quietly. 'Tell me what happened after you passed him.'

'Is there any point?' I couldn't help myself. 'If you've already decided you don't believe me?'

'I'm not saying I don't believe you. I simply questioned your response.' PC Marsh paused. 'Please tell me what happened next.'

'I was terrified,' I said simply. 'I had to get away from him. I drove too fast, I know that. Instead of stopping at the main road, I pulled out, thinking I had enough time before the van reached me. All I remember after that is the impact. Then I must have passed out, because the next thing I remember is voices.' I nodded. 'Then—' I broke off, thinking about the face hanging over me.

'Go on.' She was watching me.

I shrugged. 'I saw a face I recognized. She reminded me of my sister.' I looked up at her. 'I know it wasn't her. I banged my head. I wasn't clear about anything. I still don't feel clear.' It was true.

PC Marsh nodded. 'I can imagine. A sample of your blood was taken. It is within the law in a case like this, when someone is unconscious,' she added, seeing my face.

I was incredulous. 'Why?'

'We needed to rule out whether alcohol was a factor.'

'But it was the middle of the afternoon. I'd hardly have been drinking.' I couldn't believe what she was suggesting.

'Then it will come back clear, and there'll be no problem,' she said, matter-of-factly. 'We'll let you know as soon as we have the results.'

'Do you know where my car is?'

'It was towed away. I'll check and let you know where. It was quite badly damaged. The van you hit . . . The driver was uninjured, but you did quite a lot of damage to his vehicle, too. His insurance company will be in touch. I assume you are insured?'

I nodded, dumbstruck.

She looked at me. 'He's within his rights to press charges against you. For dangerous driving.'

'What happens then?' My jaw dropped open.

'There'll be a court case. You might want to think about finding a lawyer.'

Summer

It doesn't take much, does it, Mother? To embellish the lie, layer upon layer, with pretty words and other lies, until a whole story's built around it; before the grain of sand becomes a pearl. Embedded in the past, its origin forgotten, the lie is buried; it is no longer.

What lie?

And things change, don't they, Mother? You're always telling us that. And sometimes we all remember things wrongly. My cat didn't really drown, did he? He must have run off, you told me, the day after I buried his lifeless body.

But you're forgetting. The most shocking memories – the most disturbing ones, seared irrevocably into your mind – they are the ones that never leave you.

Like your own and Hannah's little secret, Mother. I've watched you fabricate the story around it, weaving it into the past, so no one will know. But there are too many loose ends, Mother. Tattered edges. A pulled thread that will eventually come away, after other, smaller threads have worked loose, setting the scene.

The time isn't right. Not yet.

But soon it will be.

18

Hannah

After PC Marsh left, I felt another layer of insanity swirl like mist around me, as I sat in shock, digesting what she'd said. I'd always been such a careful driver. The thought of going to court horrified me. I was still sitting there, going through it all in my head, when Abe came in.

'Sorry,' I said. I meant about last night, for not being here. It was all I could think of to say. 'I'm really not feeling well. Would you mind taking Gibson for a walk?'

'OK.' He didn't ask how I was, just wandered through the kitchen and went upstairs, reappearing a few minutes later. 'I'll take him out now.'

'Thank you.'

Going into the snug, I curled up on one of the armchairs and closed my eyes. I must have slept, waking a little while later when someone knocked quietly, then let themselves in. Just as I was starting to wonder who was here, I heard Curtis's voice in the kitchen.

'Hannah?'

I was too tired to move. 'I'm in here.'

He came through to the snug. 'I wasn't sure you'd be home. You OK?'

'Not really.' I was tearful all of sudden.

He came over and put his arms around me. 'It could have been worse.'

Pulling away, I wiped my eyes. 'Not much. I don't have a car, and I may be facing a charge of dangerous driving.' Sitting down, I was shaking my head. 'It was because of this man who freaked me out. Everyone seems to think I overreacted.' My eyes searched Curtis's face. 'If I'm honest, I feel like I'm going mad.'

'Of course you're not.' He sat down next to me. 'It's probably the stress of losing your sister catching up with you.'

'There's a load of other stuff.' I was silent for a moment, hoping he wouldn't bring up the last time he was here. 'Not the stuff I've told you about. There's been this Facebook post about me drinking. I've had students cancelling. I'm finding Abe so difficult . . .' I was trying my hardest to hold it together, but my voice wavered. 'It's getting to me, that's all.'

'Right now, you need to recover from the accident,' Curtis said more firmly. 'Then you can worry about everything else later on.'

He didn't stay long. The reassurance that his presence generated quickly wore off after he'd gone. As the evening went on, I felt progressively worse. I put it down to a delayed reaction to the crash, which was causing my head to throb and my body to ache all over. But it was nothing compared to the stream of thoughts that galloped disjointedly, relentlessly through my head, not just about the accident, but about Nina. Then suddenly I found myself thinking of Summer, as everything I'd blotted out for years came flooding back.

In my mind I replayed a series of images, each fading into the next. The carefree, tangle-haired little girl who ran barefoot, getting older, more curious, with questions Nina had no answers for, becoming the angry teenager with flashing eyes, who wanted a world she felt she had no access to. What had been fine, when the children were young, hadn't worked as they got older. Nina had made a mistake.

Instead of calming me, the glass of wine I poured made me nauseous. I desperately needed to sleep, but as I got up to go upstairs, the room started to spin. Trying to steady myself, I reached out to grab the table, then sat again, heavily, just as Abe came into the room.

'*Thinking about Summer, Abe.*' I hadn't planned to say it, but my tongue seemed disengaged from my mind. I felt giddy all of a sudden, the room seeming to tip sideways, then start slowly rotating.

'Why?' The word sounded like an echo. As I looked at him, I tried to focus, but sitting across the table from me, instead of one Abe, there were two.

'*It was good . . .*' As the words came out, I couldn't remember what I was talking about.

Abe looked furious. 'You have no idea what it was like.' Then I thought I heard him say, 'I saw what happened.'

I caught his words as they died away. My eyelids were suddenly heavy, so that it was all I could do to stop them from closing. '*Help . . . me?*' I tried to say, knowing my words were slurred.

I blinked, trying to focus as he said something I couldn't hear. When I didn't reply, he repeated it, louder, but all I could make out was a single word: 'drunk . . .'

'*Not drunk.*' I tried to say, followed by '*bed*'. But too heavy for my lips to frame, each word remained silent.

As I sat there, I saw his face moving. I frowned. Why couldn't I hear him? Then he came over and, taking my arm none too gently, helped me stand, then slowly make my way upstairs to my bedroom.

I woke early the next morning with a blinding headache, noticing that the curtains hadn't been closed and that I was still in the same clothes I'd been wearing yesterday. Tentatively I tried to move, but I was in too much agony.

As I lay back on my bed, I remembered Abe helping me up the stairs. I'd felt so drunk, but I'd only had a glass or two of wine. It must have interacted with the painkillers the hospital had given me. I tried to remember what Abe had said to me last night, seeing in my mind his face, his mouth moving. Then I had a flashback, a single word in my head, as if whispered to me. *Summer.*

It was followed by another, Abe's words, his eyes blank as he spoke. *I saw what happened.*

My heart was racing. Is that what he said? Or, barely conscious at that point, had I imagined it? I closed my eyes. What had he seen? Or had he been telling me he'd seen what happened to Summer? Oh God, what if he had?

I sat bolt upright for a moment, then slowly lay back again, thinking of Nina's cottage, besieged by an unstoppable flow of memories, watching that night unfold all over again. Nina's and Summer's raised voices coming from her bedroom, escalating as I went in there; Summer's physical attack on her mother. Then silence.

It had been worse than their usual rows. Instead of letting

Summer say what she had to, Nina had been on the defensive and the most terrible argument had kicked off. I remembered going in there, as Nina yelled at Summer to leave her alone; Summer launching herself at Nina, tearing at her clothes in her desperation to be heard – my own attempts to intervene ineffectual. Hearing the commotion, one of Nina's friends had knocked on the door, but Nina had screamed at him, too. I couldn't remember exactly when it happened, but Summer had physically attacked her mother, scratching at her face and arms, drawing blood. She hadn't been strong, but Nina was bigger than her daughter. She'd shoved her away. Then Summer had come at her again, screaming in a way I'd never heard before. I could remember Nina's eyes – blank, defeated – as, with all her strength, she shoved Summer across the room.

I didn't hear the crack of Summer's head. All I noticed was how she'd stopped screaming. I'd gone rushing over to her, crouching on the floor beside her. Nina's words, spoken harshly, uncharacteristically: *Leave her there.* Getting up, hesitantly, noticing Summer wasn't moving; how her eyes were wide open, staring, unseeing.

Across the room, I watched Nina stagger as she took another swig from her glass, while I crouched down beside Summer again, trying to rouse her, my words becoming more urgent, until I was shaking her, more and more violently, then I heard the crash as Nina dropped her glass, falling to her knees beside me.

After the initial silence, I remember my sister's scream. For so many years I'd blocked the memory, never once considering that Abe could have been there, invisible, the way he often was. I had no memory of seeing him. The voice of reason kicked in. He'd only been four, I told myself. Too young, surely, to have coherent memories of that time.

A sinking feeling filled me. I knew that wasn't true. I knew, from my own childhood, that he had been old enough. It was the traumatic images that stuck and were the most difficult to shake. I had enough of my own.

The next day I'd heard Nina misguidedly lying to Abe, telling him that Summer had gone away, imagining every maternal cell in her body urging her to protect her son from the hideous truth about his sister – the same truth that had later derailed Nina. Now, I couldn't help wondering if it was herself she'd been trying to convince. But if he'd been there, all along, Abe would have known.

As Summer lay on the floor of Nina's bedroom, no one had suggested calling an ambulance, or even the police. A friend of Nina's – a man called Sam – had carried Summer's body outside. Then, with Nina's typical lack of regard for convention, her body had been buried in the woods near the cottage. Maybe too near, I'd wondered at the time. Even now, I could remember the small clearing where her grave was, and how the following spring it was covered in soft green grass and primroses; the sense of peace that tried to permeate me as I stood there, as rays of early-morning sunlight filtered through the trees. But the reality of what had happened was too brutal. It was the last time I ever went back.

It had been one unfortunate accident that had changed everything, leaving Nina no longer able to bear living in the home she loved, accelerating her descent into addiction, while all I'd done was hide – from Nina, from the truth, I could see that now. Instead of supporting her, I'd let her down.

And now it was all catching up with me, turning my world

into a place I no longer recognized. But it was what I deserved. As self-pity welled up inside me, I collapsed into uncontrollable sobbing.

Wrung out, I tried to pull myself together, wanting to work out what I wished to say to Abe. I knew life hadn't been easy for him since he'd moved here. If I explained how I hadn't been feeling well since the accident, I hoped he'd understand, or at least be prepared to hear me out. Managing to drag myself out of bed, I felt only marginally better after a shower. I glanced at the time. It was ten o'clock.

I had a window of opportunity to finish reading the letters, but as I got up to fetch them, I heard Gibson start barking. Going over to the window, I looked out to see Erin waving up at me. As I went downstairs to let her in, I was wishing I was more pleased to see her, but all I could think of was Cara Matlock's Facebook page on her laptop.

'Hi!' Erin greeted me warmly, kissing me on both cheeks. *A Judas kiss* . . . The phrase landed in my brain from somewhere, as she handed me a bunch of flowers. 'I brought you these. How are you today?'

'Not great.' Deliberately stand-offish, I didn't thank her. 'The police don't believe me about this man who's stalking me, and I may be facing a charge of dangerous driving.'

'Jesus, Hannah!' Erin frowned. 'Look, if you're having a rough day, would you rather I went?'

'No. I want you to come in.' It came out more forcefully than I intended. 'Actually, I'm glad you're here. There's something I want to talk to you about.'

'Really? I'm intrigued.' Erin followed me into the kitchen.

'You seem tense. Is everything OK? Stupid question – I know it can't possibly be. You just seem really on edge.'

'No. Not really.' Meaning nothing was OK. I went to fill the kettle. 'Tea?'

'Great.' She changed the subject. 'I love your house, by the way. Before the other night, I hadn't been here. But you're isolated, aren't you? Doesn't it ever worry you?' She pulled out one of the chairs and sat down.

'I've always felt quite safe – until recently—' I broke off. I couldn't pretend I was happy with Erin. I had to say what was on my mind.

'What do you mean?' She was frowning at me.

'It's everything. It started after Nina died. These two people in the village who say they know me . . .' Then I cut to the chase. 'The other day, when I was in your study, I didn't have the number for the police. Your laptop was there, so I thought if it wasn't password-protected, I'd google the number. I'm sorry, I know I shouldn't have.'

'It would have been better if you'd asked,' she said shortly. 'But it's a bit late now. I don't suppose it matters.'

'Actually, I'm not sure. I think it does.' I watched her face closely, but it was blank. 'Facebook was open. But it wasn't your page. It was a page belonging to a girl called Cara Matlock.' As I spoke, I watched her shift slightly on her chair, then glance away from me. 'You know her name, don't you? I take it you know what she's been posting about me?'

She looked slightly embarrassed. 'Abe told me that someone had written this malicious post about you. It was the other night, when you were in hospital. I thought I'd take a look, that was all. It was fairly vicious, Hannah.'

'I know it was. It was all lies.' I stared at her. I hadn't even told Abe about it. Suddenly, I realized, Erin was lying to me too. 'But Abe couldn't have told you. He didn't know. I never had the chance to talk to him.'

'Well, he'd found out somehow.' Erin sighed in exasperation. 'I'd hardly lie to you. It's not like you don't have enough to worry about right now.'

'So what about the conversation you and Abe had with the police? Did you discuss my so-called drinking problem with them? Over a nice, cosy cup of tea around my kitchen table? While drunk Hannah was conveniently out of the way? Is that how it was?' I knew I sounded paranoid, but I couldn't stop myself.

'Now, just a moment . . .' Erin was frowning as she got up. 'I'm not listening to this. You're out of line, Hannah. You know, it would be good for you to talk to someone. I'm saying that as a friend. You don't have many friends, do you? Because you don't trust people and you're suspicious of everyone – including me.' She started walking towards the back door, then just before she got there she stopped, turning to face me. 'Get real, will you? If not for yourself, then for Abe. You do have a drink problem. It's no secret. Half the village knows. They've seen you in the pub over the years. The only person who hasn't admitted it is you.'

It was like listening to Curtis all over again. I couldn't take it. 'Get out!' My voice was deadly cold. 'I thought you were on my side.'

'I'm not on anyone's side, Hannah. I wanted to help you. I've no idea what's happened in your life that stops you trusting people.' Erin's voice was sad. 'I was trying to be your friend. But the trouble is, friendship's a two-way thing, and you keep everyone at arm's length.' She shook her head. 'I'm sorry for you. So much has happened to you and I know you don't find things easy, but you have Abe to think about now. He's a good kid. You could be good for each other. Have you thought about that?'

'You don't know the half of it.' I spat out the words, but it was true. She didn't know anything about me, or Nina, or our past.

Erin looked at me oddly. 'How would I? When you don't share anything with me?'

'Everyone has stuff they keep to themselves.' What had happened in my life was none of her business.

'I'm sure you're right.' Her voice was quiet. 'I wish you well, Hannah. I won't come here again. I'd have liked to, but I don't think I can help you.'

Opening the door, she went outside, then closed it quietly behind her. As she walked away, I heard her footsteps fade, then a few seconds later the sound of her car starting. I sat down heavily, going back over what she'd said. I should have listened to my instincts. I'd been right not to trust Erin. She was no different from anyone else. She'd lied, it was obvious. I hadn't had a chance to talk to Abe about Cara Matlock. Erin must have found out from someone else. Unless . . . It couldn't be possible. Was there something I'd missed? Could Erin have been behind the post?

Her flowers were still lying on the worktop where I'd left them. Shaking with fury, I picked them up, dumped them unceremoniously in the bin, then went outside, breathing in the cool air, trying to calm myself down. I thought about taking Gibson for a walk, but I was put off by the thought of coming across that man again. Whoever he was, he seemed to know where to find me. I couldn't take the risk. I wasn't sure how much more I could cope with.

Instead I walked around the garden, breathing deeply and trying to shake off my anger with Erin, but there was a restlessness that wouldn't leave me, even as my eyes scanned the spring flowers, taking no solace from the freshness of the colours and the delicate scent that hung in the air. There were weeds that needed pulling up, something I'd usually be on to straight away, but I didn't care about them right now. There were more pressing matters preoccupying me.

The letters . . . As the thought flashed into my head, I turned and strode inside. I had time, I knew I did, before Abe was back. I needed to get to the bottom of what he knew.

19

After fetching the letters from Abe's bedroom, I sat on my bed and carried on reading the next one, hoping for something more conclusive, rather than another of Summer's bitter rants, which was what seemed to be a common theme:

26th February 2007
Dear Mother
I'm writing it all down so you don't forget. A letter's forever, isn't it? A record of events you'll never remember. It's not just for you, though. It's so one day everyone will know how it was.

What I wish is that Abe could remember when the house was clean. We had that lovely old sofa – a rich jewel shade of turquoise, the colour of optimism and laughter, which we'd pile onto, watching TV while you were in the kitchen, cooking supper for us all. Sausage and mash or shepherd's pie to fill our hollow stomachs, followed by home-made cake or ice cream.

Had you fooled, didn't I?

Didn't I??

I truly wish Abe could remember it had been like that, but none of us can, because it never was. But I don't need to tell you what home is. The leaky roof over our heads, the front door that flies open unless you bolt it. Walls that need painting, which you never get round to. A house full of drunk and stoned people. The dirt and filth that drinking blinds you to. It stops you caring, too. Was that your legacy from your parents? The only way to survive living with them? Get off your face. It works, doesn't it?

Was Summer suggesting that she'd followed in her mother's footsteps? I folded it and put it away, then read another:

2nd April 2007

Oh, Mother, you were good at so many things. At hanging up coloured lanterns and smiling blankly at everyone; at throwing parties and gouging out huge chunks of the past, so that when the raw, gaping holes scabbed over and eventually healed, all that was left was a tiny scar.

Scars that didn't fade, that you passed on to us, Mother. The one across your heart called loneliness; the blank eyes that mask your inability to cope with the world. We all have those eyes, Mother. That same smile, which hides a thousand feelings, so that no matter what happens, it's always the same.

Remember that photo of the four of us? The split-second moment the camera caught, a snapshot of unreality.

'In the photograph I'm fine.'

But I wasn't. None of us were.

Because a picture paints a thousand lies . . .

Do you remember why you had children, Mother? Don't most mothers want to protect and nurture, give their children the world? A bigger, better world than the one you grew up in? Be a better parent? Don't you realize you've done the same as your parents did to you? You've decided what's right for us, taken away our choices. You don't think you have, but you've clipped our wings, Mother.

Like you, we have nowhere else to go.

I knew the photo she was talking about. I'd seen it in Nina's shoebox, a typical family snapshot in which they'd all looked so happy. Nina had tried so hard to do the right thing for her children. I was filled with sadness that Summer couldn't see that.

The next letter was more of the same rant against Nina. However, this time it made my blood run cold:

9th May 2007

Dear Mother

How much longer does this go on? The hideous charade of your life? The meaningless people, the parties that are simply an excuse for drinking until you don't wake up, until the day after the day after. Who looked after us then, Mother? Not you. Ask Hannah, you breathed at me the last time, as I recoiled at the stink on your breath, your unwashed skin. Saw the clothes you hadn't changed for two days.

One of your better ideas, Mother. To ask the other damaged, fucked-up grown-up that's still a child. The one who throws up in the garden, who uses you whenever it suits her, blundering in with her tight clothes and failed music career. Who has the same blank smile.

You have a blind spot, Mother. Her name is Hannah.

When is a lie not a lie? When everyone around you believes it's true? Or when it's been watertight, nailed-down, buried under a ton of shit for so long, everyone's forgotten what the truth is.

Not everyone, though.

You're not the only one with secrets. I have one, too. You didn't know I knew, did you? But don't worry. I haven't told anyone. Not yet.

Are you worried? You should be. I'm on to you. I know what you and Hannah have been hiding, the lie you've been living. But the truth never stays buried forever.

The time is coming, Mother.

I put it down, mortified. I had no idea Summer had seen me that way. But it wasn't just that. It was the thinly veiled threat that lay in her words. What had she known? I hoped to God it wasn't what I thought it was.

I read the letter again, a sense of foreboding building in me. It was obvious that Summer had been jealous of me. Jealous of the attention Nina gave me. But at the time, Summer had been better off than she'd realized, I thought angrily, conveniently forgetting Lenny. She'd had a home and a mother who loved her – it was more than Nina and I had ever had.

Nor had she had any idea what I was going through. I sat there, not knowing what to do. I was faced with a dilemma. I had to put the letters back, or Abe would know I'd found them, but if the police got hold of them at some point, there'd be more questions – questions I couldn't answer.

Remember the script, Hannah.

Frowning, I knew there were gaps in Summer's narrative. Were there more letters? Still hidden back in Nina's house somewhere? Or maybe Abe had them. After putting back the ones I'd taken from his room, I was thinking of Nina's shoebox. I'd yet to finish going through it, and it was the obvious hiding place. Hurrying back to my bedroom, I sat down and started emptying it onto the floor, taking in the old photos, keepsakes, a lock of hair from one of the children. Right at the bottom was an envelope.

It was a similar envelope to the others. My hands were shaking as I opened it. I knew Nina must have had her reasons for keeping it separate from the others. Then, as I unfolded it and started reading, I felt my jaw drop. There was no misinterpreting what Summer had written. But how could she have known?

It was as though the years were unravelling around me, until I was seventeen again, in hiding at Nina's cottage, having just run away from our parents. I'd gone to the one person in the world I thought I could trust, and I'd thought Nina and I had been alone, but Summer must have heard me talking to her.

Suddenly I got it. She must have shared what she'd discovered with someone. Someone who, after her death, felt they had to carry out Summer's threat to disclose Nina's secrets.

Perhaps that was the real reason Nina moved without telling me. She'd been concerned for me, cutting me off because she didn't want me exposed to the same threat that she was. It was the kind of thing I could imagine her doing for me. Whoever it was, it had taken time, but they'd found her in the end. And, having got to Nina, now they were coming after me.

It was why those two strangers were here. They were part of it. Abe coming here had led them to me. I could feel my heart racing. I hadn't imagined a conspiracy against me; it was real. Then fear struck me, paralysing me. If I was right, I was in danger. But if I told the police, I would have to explain how Summer had died. And it was more complicated than that. As with the births of Nina's children, Summer's death had never been recorded. Even if I explained that it had been an accident, what if they didn't believe me?

I needed to talk to Abe, find out exactly what he knew. Maybe, between us, we could work out what was happening. But then my dream came back to me and, with it, words that had haunted me. *I saw what happened*. What if Abe had been there that night and had seen what happened to Summer?

There was nothing I could do. I couldn't go to the police and face the questions I knew they'd ask, as they dug into the events leading to Summer's death, in the process establishing me as an accomplice. I had to be careful what I said to Abe, too. But apart from him, there was no one I could talk to.

Other than talking to Abe, I could see that I had no choice but to stay silent. I was caught in the web of stories Nina had concocted, unable to break free, forced to watch the past closing in around me. I was a sitting target. Trapped.

Nervously, I waited for Abe to get back from school, my stomach lurching as I heard his footsteps outside. Coming in and closing the door behind him, appearing not to notice me, he started to head towards the stairs.

'Abe?'

He froze, then turned to face me. 'What?' His face was expressionless.

'Could I talk to you?'

He shrugged. 'What about?'

'Everything that's been happening. I've been trying to make sense of it all. I've even been thinking it's all linked to Summer.' Abe was frowning at me, as I went on, 'I know we were talking about her the other night. I'm sorry . . . It was after the accident and I can't remember what you said exactly.

These painkillers I'm on make me drowsy.' I looked helplessly at him.

'I don't remember.' There was disdain on his face. I waited for him to accuse me of being drunk again, but he didn't.

'Not any of it?' I faltered.

'I've no idea what you're talking about. Yeah, you weren't with it. You were fucking out of it.'

'Abe . . .' I gasped at the harshness of his words, but his face was implacable. I remembered the Facebook post. 'Erin said it was you who told her about Cara Matlock. But I know you couldn't have, because I didn't tell you. That is, I meant to, but I forgot. How did you know, Abe? Answer me that!' I was beginning to sound hysterical, but I couldn't help it. It was that constant feeling of being wrong-footed by him at every move.

He shook his head slowly. 'You think that came from me? Why?'

'How else would you know about it?' My eyes didn't leave his face.

'Just maybe it was something to do with the rumours flying around my school.' His voice was dangerously quiet. 'Embarrassing rumours. I talked to Erin because she was your friend. But you wouldn't have thought of that, would you? I know you think there is, but there's no conspiracy against you. It's drink that's doing this to you, just like it did with Mum.'

I stared at him. I wasn't like Nina. Desperate for him to believe me, I tried again. 'But there is a conspiracy. It's to do with Summer. It's why those strangers are hanging around. You have to believe me, Abe.'

He shook his head in disgust. 'This is pointless.' He started walking out of the room.

'Abe,' I called after him. '*Please* . . . I've no one else. I need your help . . .'

He stopped briefly in the doorway and then, without even looking at me, carried on walking.

Pouring myself a drink, I didn't hear him come back in, just heard his voice behind me.

'You've been in my room.'

I turned round, sloshing the contents of my glass. 'I haven't, Abe – only to open the window earlier,' I lied.

'It's closed.'

I floundered. 'I . . . I shut it again. I didn't want your room to be too cold.'

'You're lying.' There was no doubt in his voice. 'You've been going through my things.'

It was the moment to mention the letters, but suddenly I felt vulnerable, intimidated by the strength of his reaction. It was easier to lie. 'The police were in there the other day – you know, when I reported you missing.'

He looked incensed. 'They went through my stuff? Fucking great!' He threw his hands up in the air. 'You're insane, d'you know that? Look at you. It's just gone four o'clock and you've nearly finished a bottle of wine already. What about your students? Or have you cancelled them, again?'

I was shaking my head. 'It's not like that. I've had a glass, that's all.'

His eyes swung round to the empty bottle. He didn't say anything. 'Just so you know, I don't even know a Cara Matlock.'

'Nor do I. What's happening, Abe? First your mum, then those people hanging around, the Facebook post, my accident

. . . The police don't believe anything I tell them.' I hated the tears welling in my eyes.

'Then stop drinking,' he said harshly. 'If you did, you might find things change.' He walked towards the back door. Then he stopped suddenly. 'Where's Gibson?'

Wiping my face, I looked up though my tears. 'I don't know.'

I started walking towards the back door, but Abe was there first. Flinging it open, he marched outside. 'Gibson? *Gibson?*'

I waited for a scurry of feet as my dog ran up the path, but there was silence. Abe came back in. 'When did you last see him?'

I tried to think. He'd barked when Erin arrived. Had he slipped out when I opened the door to let her in? 'This morning? Erin was here briefly.'

As I thought about the row we'd had, I felt sick all of a sudden. Would she have taken him? Out of spite? It was ridiculous, I told myself. 'I'll call her – just in case she remembers seeing him.'

'I'm going to look for him.' Abe disappeared back outside.

Fetching my phone, I found her number, but my call didn't even go to voicemail. Instead I heard a recorded message, as it sank in. Erin had blocked me.

20

Abe and I searched the surrounding fields for Gibson, walking further than I usually went and reaching the edge of the woods. Standing under the canopy of branches, I called, then listened, but heard nothing. Eventually the light started fading around us, the cooling air growing damp, and I turned back, but even as it grew dark, I stood in the garden, calling his name. There was no sign of him.

'Either he's trapped or someone's taken him.' Forced to give up, we stood outside the house. In the distance, I heard an owl hoot. I was worried. Gibson had never gone off like this before. I was sure something must have happened to him.

'You don't know that.' Abe shook his head. 'Maybe he went after a rabbit.'

'He's never run off like this. Not once.' I paused. 'I'm going inside to call the police. See if anyone's found a missing dog.' I turned and started walking back to the house, finding my phone and calling the number of the local police station.

But when I got through, no dogs had been found. I knew it

was too late to try ringing round local vets. I'd have to resume my efforts in the morning.

Gibson's absence forced an uneasy truce between us, Abe silently cooking beans on toast for us both, a gesture I was grateful for. Afterwards, he went outside again. I didn't ask, just assumed he'd be stargazing.

'Will you listen out for him?'

He nodded.

I was in bed by the time Abe came in, listening hopefully as he shut the back door, then clattered around in the kitchen for five minutes. Then I heard his footsteps on the stairs and my hopes sank. If he'd found Gibson, I was sure he would have told me.

I slept intermittently that night, finding myself awake uncharacteristically early the following morning. As the dim light filtered through the curtains, I remembered Gibson. I hurriedly pulled on some clothes and went downstairs, hoping that maybe he'd got shut in somewhere and that there'd be a hungry, grateful terrier waiting on my doorstep.

As I opened the back door, relief filled me as, across the garden, I saw his familiar shape lying underneath one of the trees.

'Gibson? Here, boy . . .' I waited for him to get up and come trotting over to me. When he didn't move, I called him again. Feeling my heart lurch, I pulled on my boots and ran over to where he was lying.

'Gibson?' But I knew before I reached him, from his unnaturally hunched shape, that he wasn't going to get up. I fell to my knees beside him. '*Oh, Gibson . . .*' Tears streamed down my cheeks. '*What happened to you?*'

His body was stiff, his coat cold. He'd clearly been dead for some time. As I knelt on the ground beside him, I became aware of Abe standing behind me – my cries must have woken him.

His voice was low as he bent down next to me. 'What happened to him?'

'I don't know. He was so healthy. I need to carry him nearer to the house.'

'I'll do it.' Abe stood up. Then, as he turned Gibson's body to pick him up, he paused. 'He's been shot.' His voice was tight.

'No.' I was hysterical. After everything else, now this. I couldn't take it. 'We have to tell the police. I'll call them.' I was sobbing uncontrollably. 'It was probably that man . . . Maybe now, everyone will believe me.'

I was in shock as Abe silently carried Gibson over to the house and laid him on the grass. Stumbling inside, I looked around for my phone, then suddenly remembered how early it was. Too early to call the police. Slumping into a chair, I leaned forward onto the table as grief consumed me.

'Why would someone shoot him?'

I hadn't heard Abe come in. I saw his face, mutinous, before he disappeared upstairs without waiting for an answer. A few minutes later he came back down and put the kettle on, letting me sit there while he made us cups of tea.

'I could take the day off – if you want.' His eyes flickered towards me briefly.

Taken aback, I shook my head. 'It's OK.' Then I added, 'It's probably best if you go to school.'

He shrugged indifferently, then got up, putting on his jacket, gathering his school things together. As he closed the back door behind him, I couldn't help wondering if I should have taken him up on his offer, watching from the window as he walked down the track to catch the school bus. Then, remembering I had to tell the police, I reached for my phone.

I got straight through. After giving my name, I was put through to PC Marsh.

'Ms Roscoe. How can I help you?'

'My dog's been shot.' My voice wavered. 'I've just found his body in my garden.'

'When was this?' Her voice was suddenly sharp.

'This morning. He went missing yesterday.'

'You're sure he was shot?'

'Abe looked at him.' My voice broke. 'That's what he said . . . Sorry, I'm really upset about it.'

'Of course.' She sounded slightly more sympathetic. 'You don't think he could have been worrying sheep?'

'There aren't any for miles. The land round here's too wet at this time of year. He's never wandered. I'm sure someone's done this to get at me.'

'What makes you say that?' Her voice was sharp again.

'I've been attacked by a stranger on Facebook; there's been a man and a woman hanging around – as you know,' I reminded her. 'And now Gibson – my dog . . . Someone's done this deliberately, to upset me.'

'I'm afraid we need to establish what he was shot with. Would you be able to take him to your vet?'

'I don't have a car.' It was true. Ever since the accident I'd been disorganized.

She paused. 'Are you at home this morning? If there's a police car in your area, I'll see if they can come and pick him up.'

*

While I waited for Gibson to be collected, I tried to distract myself by going outside, wandering around the garden, pulling up some weeds and picking a bunch of spring flowers, with each step thinking of my dog, missing his presence at my heels. My sorrow turning to anger at whoever had done this to him, I was surprised when, only a few minutes later, a police car drew up.

Expecting it to be a local police officer, I was taken aback when DI Collins got out. She was followed by the detective chief inspector who'd been here with her before. I assumed they'd come here about Nina. I walked across the garden towards them.

'Ms Roscoe? You remember Detective Chief Inspector Weller? Sorry to spring this on you, but we'd like to ask you a few questions. Would you mind if we came in?'

I swallowed. Did I have a choice? 'Of course.' I led the way towards the house, holding the back door open for them, following them in and slipping my boots off as I closed it behind me. If either of them noticed Gibson's body, neither of them said anything. 'Come through to the kitchen.' I walked across to the sink, where I left the flowers, before turning to face them.

'Would you mind if we sat down?' DI Collins asked.

'No. Of course. Please . . .' I gestured towards the chairs, flustered. There was a gravity about their demeanour that was making me uncomfortable. As they sat down, I pulled out a chair opposite them. 'What's this about?'

DCI Weller leaned forward. 'Ms Roscoe? Can you tell us where you were the day your sister died?'

'What?' His question took me completely by surprise. Why was he asking me? An uneasy feeling filled me. He almost made it sound like I was a suspect.

'You drove to London that day to pick up your nephew. Can you remember what time you set off?'

Of course I remembered driving to London. It was after the phone call from DI Collins. I'd been driving in the dark. *The M3, heavy rain, the onslaught of headlights.* 'Seven?' I said blankly, then more decisively, 'I'm not sure exactly. I know it was early evening. I left straight after DI Collins called me.'

My answer seemed to satisfy him. 'What about earlier that day?'

I blinked, as across the table DI Collins's face swam in and out of focus. I was exhausted, upset about Gibson and I'd hardly slept. 'Sorry?'

'The day your sister died, what were you doing earlier that day?'

I tried to think, and failed. But it was obvious. Before Abe moved here, my days were all the same. 'The same as any other day. I got up and took my dog for a long walk.' My voice wavered as I thought of the dog walks I'd never have again. 'Then I was at home.'

'Did you see anyone that day? A neighbour? The postman even?'

I stared at him, puzzled. Why did he want to know? 'No, I don't think so. I often don't see anyone. Does it matter?'

He glanced at DI Collins. 'The thing is, we have reason to believe you were in London earlier that same day. Your car registration was photographed by a speed camera.'

'No . . .' I shook my head. 'There must be a mistake. It couldn't have been my car. I was at home.'

'I can assure you there was no mistake. Is there a possibility someone else could have been driving your car?'

I sat there, trying to cast my mind back to what I'd been

doing before I received the call about Nina, as Matt came into my head. Matt sharing my life. Matt leaving. Tears pricked my eyes, too many to blink away as they overflowed, running down my cheeks. 'If you must know—' my voice wavered again and I broke off, trying to control my emotions, 'I did drive to London.' I hesitated, knowing I had to tell her. 'I was going to see my ex-partner.'

'And he can vouch for this?' Her pen was poised. I swallowed, dreading what I knew she was going to ask. 'Could you give me his name, please? And a contact number?'

'Matthew Elliott.' I paused, trying to work out how much to say, needing her to understand how it was between us. 'I went there. But in the end, we didn't actually meet.'

Her pen hovered above her notebook. 'But he knew you were coming?'

I shook my head. 'Not exactly.' I knew how it sounded, but I could explain. 'We hadn't spoken for a while. Rather than call him, I thought I'd just catch him at lunchtime.'

'So where had you planned to just catch him?'

'He works in Shepherd's Bush. I got – was going to get – there for lunchtime.'

'You drove all the way?' DCI Weller was watching me intently.

I shook my head again. 'I parked at the services at Heston. I got a bus, then the Tube.'

'And then you went to meet Mr Elliott?'

I remembered standing across the road from where Matt worked, looking up at the window where I knew his office was, waiting for his familiar figure to walk out through the glass doors, being filled with a sense of anticipation.

'He wasn't there. He was probably at a meeting.' I faltered

and then, feeling their eyes on me, added, 'It really isn't how it looks.'

They exchanged glances. 'How does it look, exactly?'

'I wouldn't want you to think I was stalking him.' I wasn't entirely serious, but their faces remained deadly earnest. 'We were living together. He left unexpectedly and there are things we haven't had a chance to talk about, that's all.'

DI Collins looked at me. 'Could you give me Mr Elliott's phone number?'

'You don't have to talk to him, do you?' I felt anxious all of a sudden, my eyes darting between them, not wanting Matt to know I'd been there that day, waiting for him. 'There's no point, is there? He didn't see me. He won't be able to tell you anything.'

'Maybe not. But I still need it for our records.'

Reluctantly I recited the number. 'He may not answer. He doesn't always. You know how it is. He's busy.' I tried to sound nonchalant, hating the thought of them contacting him. I'd no idea what he'd think, if the police called and asked questions about me.

'What did you do next?'

'I got the Tube and the bus back to where I'd parked my car. Then I drove home.' I'd waited outside Matt's office for about an hour. After that, I could remember feeling disappointed, numb, light-headed; how my legs had felt weak as I walked back towards the Tube station.

'You're sure that's all you did?' DI Collins frowned. 'You didn't by any chance decide to call in on your sister – at the same house you alleged you'd never been to, before she died?'

'What?' I looked at them, aghast. 'You think I went to Nina's that day?'

'Did you?'

'I've just told you, I went home.' But I could tell from the way they were looking at me they didn't believe me. Alarm bells started going off. I looked at them uneasily. 'I hadn't seen her for ten years. I didn't know where she lived.' I paused, then added, 'I'm not lying.'

'No one's suggesting you are. I've no doubt you did go home. I'm merely asking if, between going to see Mr Elliott and getting the Tube back to where you parked your car, maybe you'd called in to see your sister. It would be a normal enough thing to do, especially if you were upset.'

I stared at her, frowning. How did she know I'd been upset? 'But I didn't.'

'Maybe you've just forgotten.'

I shook my head. 'No,' I said firmly. 'What makes you think that?'

This time, it was DCI Weller who spoke. 'Ms Roscoe, we have someone who looks rather like you on CCTV, walking away from the Tube station near your sister's, early that afternoon.'

I felt my blood chill.

'I'm asking you again. On the afternoon your sister died, did you call in to see her?'

'I already told you. No.' But my hands were shaking. As I looked at them, I was afraid of saying the wrong thing. But even worse, suddenly I knew. No matter what I said, they'd made up their minds.

Relief flooded over me when we were interrupted by a knock on the back door.

'Excuse me.' I got up to answer it, opening the door to find a uniformed PC I didn't recognize standing there.

'PC Marsh asked me to call in. Something about a dog?'

'Yes.' I gulped. 'Thank you. He's down there.' I pointed to where Abe had left Gibson's body. Suddenly tears were pouring down my cheeks again. 'I'm sorry.' I wiped my cheeks with one of my hands. 'Are you OK to take him?'

'Sure.' His manner was kindly. 'I'm taking him to the vet in Lymington – near the station. I think they're going to X-ray. Would you like him back?'

'Please.' I nodded through my tears. 'Sorry . . . I'm in the middle of something. Can I leave you to it?'

As I went back inside, DCI Weller and DI Collins were talking quietly. As I walked across the kitchen to get some tissues, they stopped.

'Is everything OK, Ms Roscoe?' DI Collins had clearly noticed I was upset.

'My dog went missing yesterday. I found his body this morning. He'd been shot.'

'I'm sorry.' She frowned. 'Do you have any idea who might have done it?'

I was shaking my head. 'None. The local police are looking into it. That was one of them picking up his body to take to the vet. I don't have a car at the moment. I was involved in an accident.' It came out without thinking. I hadn't planned to tell them, but I didn't suppose it mattered. It wasn't exactly a secret. Both of them were frowning as they looked at me. I sighed shakily. 'A man's been hanging around. He's been trying to intimidate me. He was the reason I had the accident. I've told the local police about him.' I stopped. Had I said too much?

'Who's been dealing with it?' DI Collins had her pen poised again.

'Sergeant Levigne and PC Marsh.'

'Has this man caused you any harm?' DCI Weller spoke carefully.

I looked at them bleakly. 'No. It's more psychological. He plays mind games. He's intimidating. He frightens me. I'd never seen him before, and yet somehow he knew my name.' I paused for a moment, then added, 'But I don't suppose it's anything to do with Nina.'

'Probably not.' But DI Collins looked thoughtful.

I'd already told her about the other stranger. 'There's the woman I told you about, too. I wondered if she might be a journalist. She hasn't been here, but she's been asking about me in the village.'

DI Collins nodded. 'I remember you mentioning her.'

After she'd noted it down, DCI Weller cleared his throat. 'I think we've got what we need – for now. We'll leave you to it. You've obviously got a lot going on.' They stood up. 'Thank you for your time.'

I stared at them. Was that it? 'What? I mean . . .'

'This is standard procedure, Ms Roscoe.' DI Collins saw my discomfiture. 'Your sister's been murdered. We have to talk to anyone connected, however unlikely their involvement. That's all it is.' She started walking towards the door, then stopped briefly, turning towards me. 'By the way, I'm sorry about your dog.'

'Yes,' I muttered. 'Thank you.'

After they'd gone, I closed the door behind them. Going to the fridge, I got out a bottle of wine and found a glass. I stared at it for a moment. I had to break this pattern somehow. It took all my willpower to put it back.

My legs were shaky as I walked through to the snug and sat

in one of the armchairs, feeling for the throw that was draped over the back, folding it around me, remembering DCI Weller's words. *I think we've got what we need – for now.* The implication, which had remained unspoken, that they'd be back, with more questions. Was I considered a suspect? I shivered at the thought. I couldn't be. It wasn't possible.

I needed to think more clearly, but I couldn't. Everything was too complicated, too disjointed. Too painful. Wherever I looked, there were no answers. And all the time I had to think of Nina. I couldn't let her down. *I had to keep to the script.*

But the pressure was too much, pushing me over the edge. I no longer cared about the script. Something had to give. I couldn't go on like this, constantly tense, on edge, waiting for something else to happen. Why had someone shot my dog? Suddenly I felt dizzy again. Then, as I sat there, I felt my body go slack, before it lightened, then I seemed to be floating above it. It was all I was aware of as my mind emptied, then went blank.

Summer

Such a twisted web you weave, Mother, of lies and secrets, woven double-thickness, unbreakable, with Hannah's lies and secrets.

It was always the same. So much to be said, words that would fall on deaf ears and a closed mind, just as they did the night Lenny raped me. The night you didn't believe me. It was when I knew I had to get away from you.

Did you keep my letters? Read the dates, remember what had happened? Feel the anger in your daughter's words, the pain scored into the paper, in her desperation, the only way she could think of to reach you, before pouring yourself another drink and letting them fade away into oblivion.

Have you missed me at all, Mother?

Have you and Hannah had enough time to think about what happened? Have you wallowed in enough guilt? Did you think at all about justice? Wait, how could I forget? Nina and Hannah have their own rules. Rules to live by and rules to die by, all neatly tied up, making perfect sense in your warped, twisted little worlds.

You were unreachable, Mother. There in body, but gone, deep inside your head, where the world couldn't hurt you. Forgetting your children; forgetting everything. It was all too much for you. You existed. You didn't live.

But you didn't deserve to. Not after what you did. You and Hannah, blood thicker than blood, protecting each other, when your own daughter had been brutally raped. Partners in crime.

Murderers.

So what now, Mother?

The punishment should fit the crime.

Who is guiltiest? Of murder, of neglect, of abandonment? The mother or the sister? Does it really matter? How can you tell which is which?

21

Hannah

After that, my recollection of events was blurred. It was as though I was watching things unfold from a distance. Time drifted in such a way that I didn't register day or night, just Abe's comings and goings, eating little, spending most of the time sleeping.

I gave no thought to my remaining students, although I remembered Abe telling me that when a few of them turned up for their lessons, he let them know I was ill. He must have called Curtis, too. He'd come here, concern in his eyes as they stared into mine. His voice seemed to come from miles away.

'*Hannah . . . I'm going to help you up. You need to eat something.*'

I'd let him take my arm and help me through to the kitchen, where he put a mug of tea in front of me, then a plate of toast, which I ate, unable to understand his concern. But I was emotionless, anaesthetized, unaware of anything being wrong, so that when DI Collins and DCI Weller returned, I felt no shock.

As they followed me inside, I was still spaced out, barely

registering as they watched me closely and asked if they could sit down.

'Of course.' I wandered over to the kitchen table and joined them.

'We wanted to ask you more about the day your sister died.' The DCI seemed to be gathering his thoughts. 'We've been going through the CCTV footage, from two areas in particular. The first is near your sister's house. I think you already know that we picked up an androgynous figure in jeans and a bulky hoody, who arrived and left at times that corresponded with your sister's death.'

'Yes.' They'd already told me this. I felt myself swaying in my chair.

'Ms Roscoe, are you feeling all right?' DI Collins looked at me sharply.

'I'm fine.' I sat up straighter, trying to clear my head.

'Are you sure?' She was frowning. 'You look a little shaky.'

I nodded. 'I'm all right. Really.'

It seemed to satisfy her. She went on. 'The second is the area around where Mr Elliott works.'

'Matt?' At the mention of his name, the haze in my mind cleared. Instantly I was alert. I didn't understand why they were looking there. 'But Matt didn't even know Nina. Why?'

DCI Weller paused. 'We managed to identify a similarly dressed figure in the locality of his office. They seemed to arrive by Tube and hang around for an hour, after which they got in a taxi.'

I was uncomfortable all of a sudden. Matt had nothing to do with any of this. 'Can you tell me what this has to do with Nina?'

He cleared his throat. 'We traced the driver of the taxi, who unfortunately wasn't much help, other than to tell us he took a girl in a hoody to a street in south London.'

'Which street?' I cried. 'You're going to tell me it was Nina's, aren't you?' I knew I shouldn't be speaking to him like this, but I was outraged.

'Ms Roscoe, where were you the afternoon your sister died?'

Hadn't they already asked me that? I stared in horror, my eyes widening with shock as they shifted between him and DI Collins. 'I don't understand.' I shook my head. 'You can't think I—' I broke off, flabbergasted.

'Would you mind answering the question, Ms Roscoe?'

Another layer of unreality settled around me. In that moment, I knew for sure they saw me as a suspect. I began to panic. 'No. This is wrong . . .'

'Ms Roscoe, answer the question, please.'

'Where was I? I was here – all day – until I got the phone call telling me about Nina.'

'You've already told us you went to meet Mr Elliott that lunchtime. At about twelve thirty, when you waited for an hour or so for him to come out of his office, before you got in a taxi and left?'

I stared at them, starting to panic. Had I said that? Or were they lying? 'When?'

DI Collins spoke. 'You told us, last time we were here. Don't you remember?'

I stared blankly at her. I had no recollection of what we'd talked about.

She went on. 'Also, Mr Elliott saw you from his office. He didn't want another confrontation with you, so he worked through lunch that day and didn't go out until after you'd gone. He happened to see which taxi firm it was. Also, I believe you made one or two calls to his secretary.'

I could feel the heat rising in my cheeks. I remembered how that stuck-up bitch had been so rude. She shouldn't be working there. 'I wanted to talk to him, that was all. When he didn't come out, I was worried about him.'

'So why lie to us, Ms Roscoe?'

'Sorry?'

'You've clearly lied about your whereabouts on the day your sister died. What did you do next?'

'I asked the taxi to drop me near a Tube station. Then I went back to my car. I swear it's the truth.'

It was like trying to remember a dream, pieces of which were coming back out of sequence, while the rest hovered in my consciousness out of reach. I stared at them both, wanting them to stop, to give me a chance to gather my thoughts, but DCI Weller was straight in with another question. 'Why did you bother with the taxi? Why not just get the Tube in the first place?'

'I wanted to get away from everyone,' I muttered. 'Quickly. I was upset. I wasn't thinking straight.'

'And it was a coincidence that the taxi happened to drop you near your sister's house?'

I stared at him. 'Yes, it was. I didn't have her address. You gave it to me . . .' That much I did remember. I turned to DI Collins. 'You phoned me that evening. I told you I didn't know where Nina lived.'

DI Collins glanced at the DCI. 'You're quite certain about that, Ms Roscoe?'

'I've already told you. When she moved, she didn't tell me where she'd gone.'

'What were you wearing that day?' I could feel her eyes scrutinizing me.

'I don't know. Jeans?' There must have been tens of thousands of people wearing jeans in London that day.

'And?'

'A jumper, I think. A red jumper. It was tied around my waist until I got off the Tube.'

'Did it have a hood?'

I closed my eyes briefly. 'Yes. My jumper has a hood.' My voice was dull.

'Ms Roscoe, we have in our possession a letter to your sister. It's dated the fifteenth of October, last year.'

'What?' I was incredulous. 'I haven't written to Nina since . . . I don't know when.'

She passed me a photocopy. 'Would you say this is your handwriting?'

'Yes. It looks like it.' I scanned the piece of paper, then noticed the date. I looked up at her. 'But it can't be.'

'Are you saying someone's forged this letter to your sister, to make it look like you sent it?'

'Yes.' I was confused. 'They must have. It's the only explanation.'

'What about this?' She passed me a photo of a woman in jeans, wearing a hoody. Her face was mostly shielded by the hood, with enough of her hair visible around her face to make out its colour. Looking more closely, I managed to make out the shape of her chin. 'Is there any chance that's you?'

I stared at it, then shook my head. I could see why she was saying that. The hair was a similar colour, even the shape of the figure, in as much as it was possible to see it, under the shapeless clothing. I shook my head. 'It isn't me. I don't even have clothes like that.'

'You've just told us you were wearing jeans and a red top with a hood.'

These words they were making me say . . . It wasn't how it was. They were wrong. I was shaking my head again, wishing I could remember more about that day. 'I never wear the hood up. It's just not something I'd ever do. It isn't me.'

'When we spoke to Mr Elliott, he told us he almost didn't recognize you, before he went to lunch. Not until he looked more carefully. There was a reason for that.'

As she looked at me, I knew that whatever she was about to say wasn't going to help me.

'Your hood was up.' She paused, then put her notebook down. 'You've consistently lied to us, even when presented with evidence to the contrary. I'm suggesting you went to your sister's house that afternoon. Perhaps you had a few drinks, then you argued. Then you lost control. Unable to listen to her any longer, while she was sitting on her bed, you hit her on the head from behind and then, as she fell, she hit her head a second time on the chest, before collapsing on the floor.'

I gasped. I couldn't believe what I was hearing. She was so wrong. I had to stop this, somehow, but before I could speak, she went on.

'Hannah Roscoe, I'm arresting you on suspicion of the murder of Nina Tyrell. You do not have to say anything. But, it may harm your defence if you do not mention when questioned something which you later rely on in court. Anything you do say may be given in evidence. You have the right to consult with a lawyer and have that lawyer present during any questioning. If you cannot afford a lawyer, one will be appointed for you, if you so desire.'

'You can't do this.' My voice was shrill as I stood up. 'You haven't any proof.'

'We have a statement from Mr Elliott and the CCTV footage, which – along with what the taxi driver told us, and your own inconsistencies – is enough to hold you.' DI Collins spoke quietly. 'Unless there's anything you can tell us that proves otherwise?'

You're so like your sister, Hannah. Both of you existing in a dream world of distorted facts and crazy conspiracy theories; where you see yourselves as powerless, surrounded by circumstances beyond your control. But we both know you're not.

Being a victim is a let-out, Hannah. Makes it too gloriously easy to pile up reasons why not to do something. To say I can't, or it isn't possible, when if you want something enough, you should make it happen.

But you and your sister are the same. Any excuse to escape reality, because confronting the truth is too painful. Drugs and alcohol are a safe place to hide, until they become more than that, taking over every aspect of your life, ruining everything, because although you won't admit it, you're an addict.

You'll close your ears, refuse to face the truth, but then you hide from everything that's difficult. Like the past, all there, folded away in the drawer in your sitting room – your old photos of the band you were in, the interviews ripped out of magazines. Your glory days of fame, the dazzling future that was so full of promise. With so much going for you, what could have gone so wrong? But that's there, too. The press cuttings, the speculation about why the Cry Babies only had one hit.

It took a while, but in the archives of your life, the vague online references, the grainy photos, in other people's indiscretions, in the

232

most subtle details, I found it. The real reason the Cry Babies fell apart. And it's not good, is it, Hannah, because it's you; it shows a person you're not proud of, reminds you of the most selfish decision you've ever made – not that you can ignore that any longer, not with the boy in your house. No wonder the chinks in your armour are showing. It's impossible to keep up the pretence.

Be careful. Once or twice, you've almost given yourself away, creeping around his room, going through his stuff, convincing yourself you're tidying up – that you're really not invading his privacy; that if he didn't want you to find things, he'd have hidden them out of sight, wouldn't he? I'm talking about the letters, Hannah, but you know that. Do you wonder if he reads the guilt written on your face; if he knows you've sneaked them out of his room to read them?

He knows everything. And the letters tell a story, don't they? A story of lives you had a part in; a story you know so well, of a time you wish hadn't happened. But it's a story that, much as you want it to be, isn't quite over. Not yet. While you're fumbling along trying to make sense of these strange things happening around you, you don't imagine there's a purpose to it all; that the final chapter is being written.

But somewhere inside, you have a sense of time slipping through your fingers, of the past creeping closer. It's in your shifty glance, your restlessness; your sense of ill-ease; the dim light in your kitchen at night, the air of oppression that pervades your house. It's no coincidence that so many strange things are happening around you. They're called justice, Hannah. Karma. You've been deluding yourself for years. It was inevitable that at some point the past would catch up with you. Ten years of nothing and now, every day, it seems there's something.

The boy's seen it too, in the way you speak, the way your mind works, twisting everything, trying to make it fit, until you start to question your sanity. It's a feeling that leaves you on edge – one that, when it gets too much, you numb in the comfort of alcohol; where, in the haziness of your mind, it's easy because anything makes sense; where words churn around, their meaning changing, until you turn them into something you can live with.

While all the time the boy watches you. You tell yourself that it's taking time, that things are getting easier between you, but you don't see him go up to his room, throwing open his window, now that he's alone letting the chilled night air flush away your slurred words and the memory of your breath; clinging to the sense of peace that steals over him. You didn't see his face when he found out the police had been; but you'd been taken away by then. Have you thought about how he felt, poor Abe, whose mother was killed and whose aunt has been arrested? About how, apart from his absent brother, he has no one?

But he has a strength that would scare you, if you knew about it. Somehow he holds on to a kind of faith, because the truth is slowly coming out, the way it has to. He knows he has to let things unfold the way they're meant to. What matters most is that his mother's killer is found. And he knows, if he bides his time and tells the police what he knows, it's only a matter of time before it happens.

22

Hannah

Arrested on suspicion . . . I played the words through in my mind, over and over. The police believed I killed Nina. I didn't understand. Why would they think that? It made no sense. I could never have hurt my sister.

Feeling like a criminal, I was escorted by DI Collins and DCI Weller out to their car, then driven to Lyndhurst, where my mobile phone was removed from me and I was taken into custody. When I was asked if I wanted to make a phone call, I thought of Curtis. But I couldn't run the risk of him not answering, which happened so often. The only other person was Erin. Not recognizing the number, mercifully she answered.

'Erin? Please don't hang up . . .'

There was a brief silence. 'What is it, Hannah?' Her voice was neutral.

'I'm with the police, Erin. They've arrested me. It's a mistake . . . But could you meet Abe after school? Explain? I'm sorry to ask you. Hopefully it will be cleared up soon. And I'm sorry, about the other—'

But she interrupted. 'I'll meet him.' She spoke abruptly. 'As long as you understand, I'm doing it for Abe.'

Her words stung. I knew what she was saying. She was prepared to put herself out for Abe, but I could rot in hell. She hung up before I could thank her.

After taking photographs and my fingerprints, a DNA sample was taken. Then I was led to a small room, the door locked behind me, and I was left to wait. As I sat there, listening to the unfamiliar sounds that echoed though the building, the realization of where I was started to sink in. I had no way of contacting anyone. I was alone. It was too much and I felt my mind start to close down again, until it became blank, so that I stared at the wall in front of me, thinking of nothing.

I had no way of knowing how much time had passed, when my door was unlocked and a police officer came in. 'Ms Roscoe? Would you come with me, please?'

Getting up, I blinked, trying to remember where I was. As it came back to me, a nauseous, light-headed feeling washed over me. Then, as he escorted me along the corridor to a small interview room, thoughts were tearing through my head again. This was a terrible mistake. I had to tell someone, make sure they realized that.

The room was dingy, with a dirty table stained with coffee. As I went in, a man was already in there, waiting for me. When I was first brought in, I'd been asked if I had a lawyer. As I didn't, legal representation had been arranged for me. I had a sinking feeling as Julian Hill, the duty solicitor, introduced himself to me. Even as he outlined what the police had found, and explained that I could refuse to answer any questions unless he was there, nothing about him instilled confidence.

'I shouldn't be here,' I told him urgently. 'This is a mistake. The police have missed something . . .'

'Ms Roscoe, if that's the case, all you need to do is answer their questions honestly and it will be resolved.'

I knew from the way he spoke, his defeated manner, that he wasn't going to be much help to me. He should have been asking me why I thought the police were wrong. I needed someone stronger, more dynamic, who understood, who was more obviously on my side.

'You should probably sit on one of those.' He indicated one of the four mismatched chairs, arranged in pairs on either side of the table.

I sat down. Nervously I tried to gather my thoughts. It wasn't long before DI Collins and DCI Weller joined us.

'Is this necessary?' Standing up, I blurted it out, not sure of the form.

'Ms Roscoe, would you sit down, please? We'd like to get started.'

Out of the corner of my eye I saw Julian Hill nod, as DCI Weller sat down opposite me while DI Collins went over to the tape recorder and turned it on.

'This interview is being tape-recorded and may be given in evidence, if your case is brought to trial. We are in an interview room at Lyndhurst police station. The date is the fourteenth of April and the time by my watch is three p.m. I am Detective Inspector Collins. The other police officer present is Detective Chief Inspector Weller. Please state your full name and date of birth.' She paused, looking at me.

'Hannah Emily Roscoe.' My voice sounded small. 'The eleventh of July 1985.'

The DI went on. 'Also present is Julian Hill, duty solicitor.

Before the start of this interview, I must remind you that you are entitled to free and independent legal advice, either in person or by telephone, at any stage. At the conclusion of the interview I will give you a notice explaining what will happen to the tapes, and how you or your solicitor can get access to them. Caution: you do not have to say anything. But, it may harm your defence if you do not mention, when questioned, something you later rely on in court. Anything you do say may be given in evidence.

'Ms Roscoe, we've spoken to Matthew Elliott. He's confirmed that he was unaware you were planning to meet him, the day your sister was killed.'

I stared at DI Collins, not sure what she wanted me to say.

'He did also say that you'd been calling him constantly since he left you. It's why he blocked your number.'

I frowned at her, then shook my head. She'd got this wrong. I put her straight. 'Matt hasn't blocked me. He's been busy, that's all. He must have told you that.'

'Is this relevant, Detective Inspector?' My solicitor's interruption bought me time for what she'd said to sink in. Not even Matt was on my side.

'I believe it is.' She paused, picking up a piece of paper. 'This is a list of calls you've made to Mr Elliott's number, at all times of the day and night. There are over three hundred of them. He said that you were calling him at work, too. We've spoken to the receptionists and they've confirmed that.'

'I didn't realize it was that many.' Embarrassed, I raised my head to look at her. 'Isn't it understandable, in the circumstances? After he left me, my sister died. I needed someone to talk to. I thought he cared . . .' My voice faded to a whisper.

'Most of these calls were before you knew about Ms Tyrell's

death. He also mentioned that he hadn't known you had a sister. Not until the day he came to your house to pick up his things, when you told him your nephew was staying. Was there a reason for that?'

It was of no importance that I hadn't told Matt about Nina. Couldn't she see that? But as DI Collins watched me, suddenly I saw how, by adding in or leaving out the smallest fact, she could make my behaviour sound the way she wanted it to.

When I didn't answer, she went on. 'He did also mention that he was concerned about your drinking.'

Again, I couldn't help wondering if DI Collins had asked a loaded question, or if Matt had volunteered the information. There was a world of difference, and I was fairly sure I knew what the answer was. Matt would never intentionally say something untrue about me. 'Yeah.' I said it with sarcasm.

'You still haven't told us why you didn't tell him about your sister.'

'There was no reason to.' I folded my arms. Why wouldn't she let it go? 'Nina and I hadn't seen each other for so long, we were no longer in each other's lives. She moved about ten years ago, but she didn't tell me where she'd gone. I suppose I should have tried harder to find her . . .' I let the sentence trail off, ashamed. Embarrassed again. 'So often I'd wanted to find Nina, but so much time had passed. And she'd made it clear she didn't want to be found.'

'We've spoken to Jude.' She paused. 'He wouldn't tell us much. He said he was hardly ever at her house.' Then she frowned. 'What with Ms Tyrell moving and not telling you, along with her eldest son's absence from her home, what exactly was going on in your sister's life, Ms Roscoe?'

I rubbed my arm. My skin was prickling, as though I'd

brushed against stinging nettles. Did I get stung? Yesterday? *What happened yesterday?* Why couldn't I remember? A sense of panic started rising in me. It was as though yesterday had been erased. What day was it today? Hadn't DI Collins just said? What was happening to me?

Suddenly I had to get away from them all, out of this stuffy, featureless room that had no air, and go somewhere I could breathe. 'I need the bathroom.' It was a lie. What I needed was a closed door between me and DI Collins, where no one could see me, so I could think.

As she stood up, I could tell she didn't believe me. 'I'll take you,' she said shortly, pausing the tape. 'We'll carry on when we come back.'

I followed her, putting one foot in front of the other, my thoughts becoming more confused as my sense of panic intensified. Then I felt as though hands were twisting my insides, the pain agonizing, excruciating. By the time I reached the toilet, leaning against the door as it closed behind me, I couldn't even remember where I was.

'Ms Roscoe? *Ms Roscoe* . . . Open the door, please.'

Still dizzy, my fingers fumbled with the bolt on the door, as I opened it to find DI Collins standing there. She frowned. 'Are you all right?'

I nodded. 'I think so.' I felt strange, detached, light-headed. Light.

'We need to continue the interview.' She sounded impatient.

I nodded again, washing my hands and following her out.

Back in the interview room, I sat down, staring at the table, waiting for DI Collins to resume her questioning.

'I'm curious,' she started, 'as to why you and your sister lost touch for so long. We have a witness who says that you used to spend a lot of time with her when you were younger. You lived there for a while, didn't you?'

I stared at her. Who was the witness? 'When I left home,' I said at last, 'I stayed with Nina. I didn't have anywhere else to go.'

'Where did she live?'

I was shaking my head. 'I . . . does it matter?'

'Please answer the question, Ms Roscoe.' It was the first time DCI Weller had spoken.

'She had a cottage in the countryside. In Hampshire. I couldn't say where exactly – it wasn't in a village.' I frowned. 'I remember driving through South Harting. It was probably a couple or so miles from there.'

'And she lived there for how long, roughly?'

I tried to work it out. 'About twelve years? Maybe thirteen?'

'And you went to live with her when you left home?'

I nodded. 'Yes.'

'How old were you, Ms Roscoe?'

'Seventeen.'

'And what was your life like while you were there?'

I thought back. 'Free and easy. Happy.' After leaving my parents, I'd felt free for the first time.

'And were you in the band at that point?'

I frowned at her. How did she know about the band? 'Yes.'

'The Cry Babies. I looked them up. You were quite successful, weren't you?'

'Almost,' I said quietly. 'We had a hit single. We were offered a record deal, but after that, things went wrong.'

'I would imagine that was quite devastating.' I knew she wasn't being sympathetic. 'What did you do after that?'

'I was married at that point.'

'Yes – we have here that you were married to a Nathan Roscoe. Is that correct?'

'Yes.' I nodded.

'And divorced two years later. He left you the house?'

I frowned. 'Yes. He did.' Why did that matter?

'Tell me about your sister. Did she like Mr Roscoe?'

I was about to protest, tell her how Nina liked everyone. Then I thought better of it. 'Not really.'

'How long were you and Mr Roscoe together?'

'About three years – since the band started playing around the country.'

'You didn't have children in that time?'

I shook my head. 'No. It wouldn't have worked with our lifestyle.'

'No. I can imagine.' DI Collins paused. 'But you'd known him longer than that?'

I frowned. 'I suppose. I don't know exactly how long. Four, five years maybe.'

'When your marriage ended, I imagine you would have needed your sister's support – emotionally, I mean. But that was when you lost touch, wasn't it?'

'About that time.' I nodded.

'And since then, you hadn't spoken. Is that correct?'

'Yes.' I glanced at the solicitor sitting next to me, as a wave of nausea came over me. 'I'm sorry, I'm not feeling well. Could I have a glass of water?'

'Let's take five minutes.' Getting up, DI Collins went over and paused the tape, then fetched me a glass of water. While

I drank it, she and DCI Weller turned their backs, talking in low voices.

I turned to Julian Hill. 'How much longer?'

'Hard to tell.'

'Can I go home?'

'Not yet.' He paused. 'If you're really not feeling up to it, I could ask them to stop and they can carry on tomorrow.'

'Tomorrow?' I was horrified. I couldn't spend a night here. I knew I'd been arrested, but I assumed that, after answering their questions, they'd realize their mistake, everything would become clear and I'd be free to go.

DI Collins turned to face me. 'Are you ready to continue?'

I stared at her. I genuinely wasn't feeling well, but if I wanted to get this over with, I didn't have a choice.

23

An interrogator is like a killer, stalking its prey, waiting for a moment of weakness, before pouncing.

DI Collins restarted the tape. 'Going back to before your sister moved to London, when she had this idyllic country life you described to us just now, why did she move?'

'I don't know.' One of my shoulders twitched. Why were they asking this? 'She didn't say, and I never had the chance to ask her.'

I used to think DI Collins was sympathetic, but I knew now, she wasn't. 'I don't understand. Two sisters, who to all intents and purposes were close . . .'

I nodded. 'Yes.' The word had less impact if I mumbled it.

'She took you in, shared her home with you. Then, out of the blue, she moved away without telling you why. She didn't tell you where, and you didn't go looking for her. I have to ask: why?'

I knew what she was doing. I wanted to stop her, but instead I was forced to listen to the sound of metal on metal, as the handle turned, slowly opening the can of worms.

Then she added, 'Or am I missing something?'

I flinched. 'I don't think so.'

'Tell me more about your relationship with your sister.'

'Nina and I . . .' I stopped. *How much should I tell her?*

'Nina and you what, exactly?'

'We were close. But we didn't agree on everything.' I stared at my hands, clasped on the table in front of me.

'Such as?'

'I didn't agree with her way of parenting. Her children needed to go to school. To make friends and pass exams and . . .' I floundered.

'So before she moved, her children weren't at school?'

'No.'

'Go on.'

'She wanted to home-educate them, but she was too busy. She didn't really have enough time. There were all these other things she had to do. It wasn't fair on them. I tried to tell her, but she wouldn't hear it . . .'

I couldn't tell where the voice in my head came from, full of scathing contempt. *Pathetic, Hannah. Lies, lies and more lies. You didn't even think about the children going to school. You were too wrapped up in yourself.*

It took all the restraint I could muster to stop myself putting my hands over my ears. 'It was too late for Jude by then.' I had to stop myself mentioning Summer. 'But there was Abe. I suppose Nina got fed up with me talking about it. It was easier for her to cut all ties with me. Of course she was drinking by then, which didn't help . . . Nina wasn't good at facing things.' I'd no idea where this was coming from. *Why am I lying to the police? Perverting the course of justice? That is a crime, Hannah. But you know all about that, don't you?*

'Mr Elliott told us something quite interesting. He found out – not from you – that at some point you'd been pregnant. When was this?'

Matt knew about that? I was flabbergasted, but even before she'd finished speaking I was shaking my head. 'It isn't true.' Then I swallowed. *Lie carefully, Hannah.* 'I mean, I was pregnant. But I lost the baby.'

'You had a miscarriage?'

Wasn't my solicitor supposed to intervene at moments like this? Beside me, he shifted slightly in his chair, but made no attempt to speak. I nodded numbly. A head movement could be misinterpreted. At some point I'd be able to look back and tell her I never actually said 'yes'.

'How old were you when you miscarried?'

I stared at her. Why did she have to ask? 'Young. Too young. God, I was in the band at the time. I must have been no older than seventeen. The miscarriage was probably best for everyone. I was a child . . .'

'Even so, it must have been traumatic. How far along were you?'

My lips were dry. 'I can't remember exactly, but not far. Four months? Roughly?' As I looked at DI Collins questioningly, a heaviness came over her face.

'Ms Roscoe, we have a photo of you. I'm not an expert, but it looks as though you're in the latter stages of pregnancy.'

'I couldn't have been.' I denied it hotly. 'I've just told you when I lost it. You can't tell from a photo.' I was offering her a way out.

But she didn't take it, just leafed through the papers on the table in front of her, then silently passed me a photograph.

I stared at it, feeling the years, one by one, peel away, until

I was back in Nina's cottage, with a group of people whose names I couldn't remember. We were at one of Nina's parties. I could date it by the glittery silver tiara on Summer's head, which I used to wear on stage, along with my skin-tight leather jeans and a tightly laced corset, all black of course. It had been deliberate, an ironic gesture. *Innocence corrupted*, I'd thought at the time, liking how it sounded. The innocence of my childhood had been the iron bars of a cage. I'd thought of corruption as representing freedom.

Of course DI Collins would have had no idea who Summer was. As I stared at the photo, I picked out Nina. That smile . . . There were others standing around her, then right in the middle was me. But I'd changed since then. Fifteen years had passed. It was easy to imagine it was someone else.

DI Collins read my mind. 'It may be a long time ago, but it's definitely you.' She paused, long enough for me to register that she had no doubts.

I started to feel dizzy, then my hands began to shake. I dropped the photo on the table. Then my whole body seemed to go slack, as the light around me dissolved into holes and faded to black.

When I came round, I felt detached, as though I was coming out of a dream. I couldn't make out my surroundings. Where was I? Then, as it slowly came back to me, as the faces hanging over me came into definition, I felt the churning feeling inside me start again, as I remembered.

'I think my client has been through enough for one day.' It was my solicitor's voice, coming from somewhere above me.

'Yes, I think that's fairly obvious, Mr Hill.' DI Collins

sounded irritated, then she spoke more quietly. 'Ms Roscoe? Can you sit up?'

Slowly I pulled myself up, feeling more and more nauseous. 'I need the bathroom.'

She nodded, taking my arm and helping me stand up, getting only a few feet along the corridor before I was violently sick.

24

As I lay on the narrow bed in my cell that night, I thought of my house, empty and dark, then of Abe, in Erin's warm, cosy home. After this was over, I wondered how many students I'd have left. Then, as I imagined what people would be saying about me, the blankness came back, so that I was aware only of sounds coming from other cells, the echo of footsteps as people walked past my door; the coarseness of the blanket under which I was curled into the foetal position, trying to keep warm. But nothing more.

I wasn't aware of my tears, soaking into my pillow, my hair, just felt myself drifting, wanting to be back in Nina's fairy tale, in our own little world where we were safe.

The next morning I was aware of someone shaking me, then of a distant voice. Thinking of Nina again, I pulled the blanket higher over me, as my head filled with memories of the early days in her cottage, when life had seemed so free and easy. *Nina's world was where I belonged. It always had been.*

'Ms Roscoe?' The voice intruded into my thoughts. 'Ms Roscoe?'

'Yes?' Still thinking of Nina, I murmured the word through a smile.

'You need to wake up.' The voice was too loud. 'There's some breakfast over there.' Opening my eyes, I blinked in the daylight. I wasn't at Nina's. The room was too small, bare. Looking across at the tray with a mug of tea and a couple of slices of toast, the full horror of yesterday caught up with me.

'How are you feeling today, Ms Roscoe?'

'Not very good.' I hadn't been able to eat the breakfast that was brought to me. I felt weak, light-headed, detached from reality.

'Are you happy to continue, or would you like us to organize a doctor to see you?'

I shook my head. 'I'm OK.' A doctor would only delay things further. The sooner this was over, the better.

'Let us know if you want to stop.' The DI glanced at me. 'I'd like to begin with a comment made by one of Ms Tyrell's neighbours. You told us earlier that you and your sister disagreed on the matter of her children's schooling. Well, it sounds as though she had a change of heart. It was something Ms Tyrell said recently, about how she wished she'd sent them to school. She was talking about her children. When the neighbour reminded her that Abe was attending the local school, apparently Ms Tyrell said, *Not Abe, the others . . .*'

I felt my insides tighten. *You slipped up, Nina.* It was here. The moment that was never supposed to happen; that Nina and I did everything we could to prevent from ever existing. The blood in my veins turned to ice.

'Ms Roscoe, do you know who your sister was talking about? One of them was obviously Jude. I wondered if the other could have been you, but of course you'd left school by the time you went to live with your sister.'

I frowned at her, trying to work out what to say.

'So there was clearly someone else your sister was concerned about. Do you know who that was?'

I tried to look puzzled. 'It must have been before I moved there. Maybe another child lived with them for a while. Nina was always taking in waifs and strays. It could have been a friend of Jude's.' I seized on the idea. 'In fact, I'm sure that's what it was. Come to think of it, I remember her mentioning him . . .'

DI Collins didn't look convinced. 'But whether the friend went to school or not would hardly have been your sister's responsibility.' She scanned the piece of paper in front of her, then looked at me. 'Is it possible she had another child? Obviously I'm guessing, but perhaps they left and went to live with their father?'

I swallowed. 'It's possible.' *It isn't a lie, Hannah, not exactly . . . It's perfectly possible. Even though you know it didn't happen.*

DI Collins leaned forward. 'Don't you think you would have known?'

In the silence that followed, I didn't answer.

She went on. 'You and your sister were close, weren't you? She didn't do what most people did. Instead, she fought against convention to give her children the childhood she believed was best for them. It can't have been easy. It rather suggests a mother who cared deeply for her children.'

I nodded silently. 'She did care. A great deal—' I broke off. *Hannah, be careful what you say.*

'But?' DI Collins prompted.

My sigh was shallow, fluttered in my throat. 'She . . . she had a lot going on. People coming and going. She grew a lot of their food – it took up her time. And there were parties . . . I don't think she gave the children what she'd set out to. That's probably why she made that comment to her neighbour.'

'When we first spoke, you denied that your sister had a drink problem. But something clearly wasn't right. Looking back at her life then, which do you think was the case?'

I couldn't understand why DI Collins seemed so disproportionately interested in Nina's drinking. 'I don't know.' I shook my head. 'I mean, she did drink and take pills occasionally. But it wasn't a problem.'

'Did it ever get in the way of her caring for her children? For example, was there always enough food there? Were their clothes washed? Did she care for them?'

'Of course,' I said hotly, rising to Nina's defence. 'Of course she cared.'

'That's not really what I'm asking, Ms Roscoe.' DI Collins paused. 'I'm trying to establish if their needs were being met. Try to think back for a moment.'

I cast my mind back, for the first time seeing how it really was. Jude and Summer with their tangled hair and grubby clothes; how many times there wasn't enough food, and my arrival would be greeted by Nina's exclamations of how chaotic she was, how wonderful it was that the children could run free, and could I nip to the shop and get a few things? How she'd pay me back. At the time, I'd thought nothing of it. She never did pay me back, but it didn't worry me. Given the amount of time they spent outside, I'd simply accepted Summer's and Jude's voracious appetites as completely normal. At no point had it entered my head that they'd been starving.

'I think . . . Nina maybe had money problems,' I said at last. 'At the time I didn't notice. But I know life was difficult for her. It always had been. Our parents . . .'

'About your parents,' DI Collins's eyes bored into me, 'what's the story with them? It's only a small thing, but that night you collected Abe and took him to live with you, you told me you'd let them know about your sister's death. Did you?'

I shook my head. 'No.' It stuck in my throat.

'Did you ever have any intention of telling them?'

I shook my head again.

'So you lied?'

I sat there, slumped. Should I explain to her that a part of me knew what was expected of me and was prepared to carry it out, but before I could, suddenly it was too much. I couldn't. Did that make it a lie?

'I didn't intend to.' This time I looked at her. It was true.

'Why were you and your sister estranged from your parents?'

Just thinking of my parents was like a stranglehold, choking the air from my lungs. Fighting to control the violent cough erupting from me, I looked at her. 'Whatever they might tell you, they were cruel. They used to beat Nina and lock her in her room without food. Then, after she left, they did the same to me.'

She looked surprised. 'I've spoken to them. I told them about your sister. They sounded upset.'

I stared at her, shocked that she'd spoken to them, but

knowing how quickly they'd have forced the expected reaction to news of the death of one of their daughters. 'Of course they did,' I said bitterly. 'But guaranteed, they faked it. After everything that happened, they didn't want to know. I don't suppose they asked about any of her children?'

From DI Collins's silence, I took it that they didn't.

'Why did you even try to find them?' My words held a ring of desperation. What had happened to me and Nina was best forgotten. Why couldn't the police leave our parents out of it?

'Your nephew found their address. A few years back, when your sister's problems were getting worse, he contacted them. I suppose he was hoping they might help.'

I shook my head. 'He didn't mention it to me.' But it was believable, that if Abe didn't know his grandparents, that if he was desperate enough, he'd have tried anything. I could imagine what they'd have said to him, about his mother and his aunt, about how both of them had got what they deserved. They wouldn't have helped him. Then I frowned. 'But when I came to get Abe, he'd already told you he didn't know his grandparents.'

'It wasn't Abe who told us. It was Jude. Apparently, they didn't want to know about your sister's problems.' The DI's eyes scrutinized me.

'They wouldn't,' I said tightly, clamming up. 'They didn't care.'

Slumped in my chair, I folded my arms tightly in front of me. I didn't want to talk about my parents. When the police didn't believe me, there was no point.

'I've been along to the AA group your sister had joined. It seems she'd turned a corner, as far as drinking was concerned.

She'd been sober for weeks. Some of them said she was a real inspiration.'

I looked up at her.

'Does that surprise you?' DI Collins's eyes were on me.

I frowned. 'Was she still taking drugs? And I thought she'd been drinking the day she died?'

'She had.' DI Collins frowned. 'Not heavily, but given what her AA group had to say, it was her first lapse since she'd been going there. Perhaps something difficult happened that day, which she couldn't cope with. Or maybe someone she didn't want to see turned up. I think the empty bottle was supposed to distract us from what really happened.'

It didn't make sense. No one, least of all a murderer, would be stupid enough to imagine the police wouldn't carry out tests. 'But it's obvious, isn't it? That tests would be carried out?'

DI Collins looked at me thoughtfully. 'You'd think so – unless the murderer was either too naive or too disorganized to think it through.'

There was a short break then, during which DI Collins stopped the tape and went outside with DCI Weller.

I turned to the duty solicitor. 'I want to go home. How much longer can they keep me here?'

'It depends.' He paused. 'If they don't have any more evidence, then not much longer. We'll find out soon—'

He broke off as DI Collins and the DCI came back, restarting the tape before sitting down.

'The problem is . . .' DI Collins hesitated, then she sighed. 'Ms Roscoe, I don't know what to believe. What you say one day, what you say a different day, what Abe's told us, what Mr Elliott's told us – they're all different things. Somewhere in it all there's the truth. But right now, I'm not sure what that is or how we get to it.'

I was on edge. As I sat there, it was as though the walls were closing in. What had Abe told them? *What else had Matt said?* DI Collins leafed through the papers in front of her, then seemed to find what she was looking for. 'Let's talk about Cara Matlock.'

I should have learned by now to expect the unexpected. A sinking feeling filled me as I thought about the content of her Facebook post, then I glimpsed a chance to prove the conspiracy against me – my escape route. 'I've never met Cara Matlock.' Then I paused, frowning. 'How do you know about her?'

'Your nephew mentioned that you'd been the subject of some vindictive Facebook posts. What were the posts about?'

I shrugged. 'It started with a bitchy remark – probably someone meaning to be funny. It was to do with my past.' I frowned, not sure why Abe would have told the police about the posts.

'You're saying you don't know Cara Matlock?'

'No. In fact, until I was told about that Facebook post, I'd never even heard of her.'

'That's not strictly true, is it, Ms Roscoe?'

I gasped. I wasn't lying. 'It absolutely is. I swear.'

DI Collins looked at me wearily, as though she didn't believe me. 'She isn't one of your students?'

'No.' For once, I looked directly at her. 'Erin,' I said softly. She'd denied it, but after seeing Cara Matlock's Facebook page on her laptop, I was still convinced there was a connection. But why?

'Who's Erin?'

'A friend.' Only she wasn't, not really. With everything that had happened, the way she'd spoken to me, she'd proved as much. It was clear now: Erin had lied to me. 'She picked me up from the hospital and took me back to her house. She had Cara Matlock's Facebook page on her laptop.' I stared at DI Collins. 'She told me it was because Abe had been talking about it. But they'd obviously cooked something up between them. You see, it wasn't me who told Abe about it. You need to talk to her. Don't you see? She obviously knows something.'

DI Collins looked confused. 'Can you give us your friend's full name and address?'

'Of course.' I recited them, feeling hope rising in me. If I was proved right about this, maybe they'd believe everything else I told them.

She looked at me questioningly.

'That's all, really.' But it was eating away at me. 'Actually, what she wrote ended up costing me a number of students.'

'Really?' DI Collins reached into the bag on the floor beside her chair, then got out an iPad. 'Would you be able to identify Cara Matlock?'

I nodded, shame flushing my cheeks as I thought about the false accusations posted for anyone to read. After a couple of minutes she turned the screen to face me. 'Can you tell us which is Cara Matlock?'

On the screen were a number of profile photos. I recognized her instantly. 'This one.'

'You're certain?'

I nodded, watching as she touched the screen and the Facebook page opened, flinching as I recalled Cara's words, waiting as DI Collins scrolled down the posts. 'How long ago did it happen?'

'Just over a week?'

Eventually she looked up. 'There's nothing here.'

For a moment I was relieved not to have to go through the humiliation of her reading the post. Then I looked at her in disbelief. 'There must be.'

'The last post was a month ago. She's not very active. Are you absolutely sure it's her?'

'Let me see.' I pulled the screen towards me, staring at the girl's face, her eyes seeming to taunt me. It was definitely her, but DI Collins was right: the last post was a month ago. I looked at her. 'She's deleted it.'

Through the silence I heard a whisper. *No one believes you, Hannah. The police, your solicitor, they've all worked it out. They all know. You made it up.*

'Talk to Erin,' I said desperately. 'And Abe.' Then I frowned, remembering something. 'The mother of one of my students called me to tell me. She sent me a screenshot – by email. It will be on my laptop.'

'You can log in from here.' She gestured towards the iPad.

I shook my head. 'I think I deleted it. But I would have saved the screenshot.'

'I see.' She paused again. 'We'll be talking to Ms Bailey.'

'Can't you see there's a pattern?' I said desperately. 'The strangers, my crash, the Facebook post leading to my students cancelling, my dog being shot . . . It's like there's a conspiracy against me.'

Nobody said anything. DI Collins leaned forward, resting her elbows on the table. 'I can see why you might say that, but the evidence isn't exactly cut-and-dried. And the question is, Ms Roscoe, why? Can you think of any reason why someone might want to cause you so much trouble?'

I stared at her. There was a reason, one that had to remain unspoken; a promise to Nina that must remain unbroken.

I followed it with the lie, as convincing as I could make it. 'No.'

Everything's changing, isn't it, Hannah? The police have inter-
viewed me, did you know that? At Erin's house. How does that make
you feel . . . ? The friend you suspect betrayed you, befriending the
boy you don't trust, both of us talking to the police?

The policewoman sits there, writing with a cheap pen in her
notebook with the black cover, as she listens to what Erin says.
Erin's honest about her concerns about your drinking; Erin, your
friend, who might as well be stabbing you in the back, for all the
favours she's doing you. Then it's my turn. I've half expected it, ever
since you were arrested. I'm ready for their questions, to hand over
the letters to them, even though I can guess what they'd make of
them.

It wasn't right to hide things, so this was it: the moment that
could make all the difference. The truth needed to come out. You
committed a crime, you had to pay. It's how it worked.

It was me who told the police about how I found the letters; how
my mother had hidden them; how you had read them. No surprise
that they ask about Summer. I hold my breath. What to say . . . ?
But Jude and I have discussed this. There have been too many lies for

too long. *They have to stop somewhere. And I still have one last letter.
I stare at the police, watching the expressions on their faces, as I tell
them.*

*If only you'd been honest, Hannah, years ago, you and your sister.
All of this could have been avoided.*

25

Hannah

Back in my room, I knew I'd done the right thing. When the police had asked me if there was anyone who might want to cause me trouble, I'd had to lie. But it wasn't as if I could name anyone. It was speculation at this stage that it was someone who'd seen what happened to Summer and wanted justice, but it made sense. I couldn't think of any other explanation.

No matter what, it wasn't right for anyone to judge what had happened in Nina's life. They didn't know how hard it had been for her. So she'd made a decision to live unconventionally, but she was still a good person. She may not have lived according to the rules most people abided by, but she'd never intentionally done anything wrong. But there was too much I was holding back. One by one, I felt the doors around me closing, until I was left with only one.

After the break, I was led back to the interview room.

'Ms Roscoe.' DI Collins paused. 'Going back to the Facebook post, your nephew found out about it when he heard rumours going round his class.'

'Are you sure?' I glanced away from her. It was what he'd said to me, but I was sure he'd been lying.

DI Collins leaned forward. Her eyes were merciless. 'We've spoken to your friend, Erin Bailey. She confirmed his story. She told us what she's already told you. The night you called her from the hospital and she went to check on Abe, he told her about the Facebook post. Then when she remembered, sometime later the next day, she looked up Cara Matlock. She says she hardly uses her laptop. In fact she said she was sure her laptop had been switched off. She said you must have switched it on . . .' She looked at me questioningly.

'I did.' I cast my mind back. 'My phone was dead. I'd gone to her study to use her phone to call the police about my car. But I hadn't got the phone number with me, so I turned on her laptop to google it. I suppose I should have asked her.'

'I see.'

Did DI Collins believe me? Did I believe Erin?

'Ms Bailey did express her concern about you,' DI Collins went on. 'She said that you're finding it difficult looking after your nephew. I had a word with her as we walked outside.'

I nodded. 'I am. He's quite aggressive sometimes – and he won't talk to me, about anything.'

'Apparently he told Ms Bailey he was worried about you. She was going to talk to you about it, but she said she was concerned about having the conversation – she knew you'd be angry with her.'

'Angry? Why would I be angry?' Inside, I was seething. How dare Erin tell the police that. Calm, successful, confident Erin, who was so believable, who was everything I wasn't. I spoke as neutrally as I could. 'And I've no idea why Abe should be worried about me.'

'Ms Roscoe, it seems apparent to everyone we've spoken to that you have a problem with alcohol. A problem you yourself seem oblivious to. But surely, if you're honest with yourself, you must be aware of it?'

As she spoke, I shook my head. 'That's ridiculous. You must see that? How would any of them know? Abe spends the evenings outside, and I hardly ever see Erin.'

'I thought Ms Bailey was a friend?'

I was silent for a moment. 'Not really. We used to walk our dogs together now and then. That was about it.'

DI Collins made no attempt to hide her exasperation. 'Ms Roscoe, a few hours ago you described Ms Bailey as your friend, and now you're telling me she isn't. Which of these is correct?'

I stared at her helplessly, dammed if I lied, dammed if I didn't. I struggled for a word. 'I should have said "acquaintance" rather than "friend".'

She went on. 'It wasn't just your nephew and Ms Bailey who expressed concern about you. There's also your ex-partner and a number of people in the village.'

'What?' I felt my face grow hot. 'Who's been talking about me?'

'Ms Roscoe, it doesn't matter who. Suffice to say, enough people have seen you walking your dog, apparently the worse for wear. Then there's your accident.'

'It's all hearsay. You have no proof of any of this.'

'Not until your blood results come back.'

'Talk to Curtis. He'll tell you how wrong you are.' I lapsed into silence.

'Curtis?'

'He's a friend. He's known me a long time – longer than Matt and Erin. He'll tell you the truth.'

She looked at me. 'Maybe we should. Can you tell us how to contact him?'

'His number's on my phone.' Which the police had taken. 'His name is Curtis Dalton.'

She wrote it down. Then, turning to DCI Weller, she mumbled something I couldn't hear, before continuing, 'We're still going through the CCTV footage in the area where your sister lived, from the day she died. But also . . . we checked the services where you allegedly parked your car. For some reason it wasn't caught on the way into the car park, but it was on the way out. At three thirty that afternoon. If, as you say, you were waiting outside Mr Elliott's office at lunchtime, some two hours must have elapsed between you leaving Mr Elliott's office and driving out of the car park. Where were you during that time?'

'I don't know.' I looked from her to DCI Weller. 'I can't remember.'

'It was the day your sister died. I can't believe you don't remember every minute of what happened.'

I shook my head, numb. 'When I went to meet Matt, I was early,' I say at last. 'I stopped for something to eat. That's where the time went.' I'd found a pub just around the corner from where Matt worked, where I ordered a sandwich and a gin and tonic. As I'd sat looking out of the window, across the street I'd caught a glimpse of his profile as he walked back towards the office. Getting up, I'd rushed outside, stopping in my tracks when I saw he wasn't alone.

I could remember the acid rush in my throat, so that I'd turned to find somewhere to vomit. When I looked up again, he'd gone. A waitress had coming running after me at that point, but I'd never intended not to pay. I'd gone back to the pub, where I'd ordered another drink and then, after settling my bill, I left.

I waited across the road from his office, hoping Matt would come back out for lunch, devastated when he didn't. In the end, I'd been forced to give up and start for home.

As I walked away, I thought of the woman I'd seen Matt with. She looked young and pretty, smartly dressed. Jealousy had raged through me, then the most desperate sense of loneliness had filled me and, with it, a longing for human comfort. In a world that had set itself against me, there was only one person I could turn to.

I knew what DI Collins would ask if I told her that. *Could I have started making my way towards Nina's house? In the digital age isn't it possible to find anyone, if you look hard enough? What if I'd found her address?* Then she would twist my words again and make them mean what she wanted them to mean. Her blood was up. She was on the scent of a murderer.

'There's a problem, Ms Roscoe.' DI Collins spoke quietly. 'Because, every time we speak, your story changes. Nothing you say matches anything anyone else says, plus it's obvious you're hiding something. I'm going to suggest that you're assessed by a psychologist, because it's almost impossible to treat anything you say as reliable.'

A psychologist's assessment? What was going on? I was trying to answer her questions, but it was difficult when I was having trouble remembering.

She hesitated. 'One other thing . . . In the time you've been here, it's been noted that you've shown no concern about your nephew's well-being. After losing his mother, have you thought about where he is and who's looking after him? Or how traumatic this is for him?'

Had I thought of Abe? He was central to this, but her words pierced the last of my defences. As they were peeled away, suddenly I felt myself, my past – everything I'd tried to keep hidden – exposed.

'He's with Erin,' I muttered.

'Yes. After you asked her to look after him that first day, Ms Bailey has very kindly agreed for Abe to stay there as long as necessary.'

'What do you mean? I'm going home.' I had to. If they didn't let me go, today, I would have to tell her everything. But now, more than ever, I couldn't. 'You've nearly finished, haven't you?'

'Not exactly.' The DCI's voice filled the room.

'But I've told you what I know.' My eyes flitted from DI Collins's face to the DCI's. 'This is ridiculous. I want to leave.' I started to get up.

'Ms Roscoe, you're not going anywhere.'

26

Faced with another night in the small room where I'd been held since my arrest, as I sat on my bed, my head was buzzing with too many questions. How had Matt had found out I'd been pregnant? Who told him? And why? The police were supposed to be investigating Nina's murder, yet somehow the focus had turned on me. I couldn't understand why.

After the last interview I'd wanted to speak to my solicitor, alone. After the police officers left us, I'd asked him, 'Why are they so convinced that I'm connected with this, when I'm not?'

His eyes had been cold and mildly disinterested as he'd looked at me. He was going through the motions, no more than that. 'Is there anyone from the past who might have an axe to grind? Like from your days in the band?'

But I'd already thought about that. 'There's no one. The only thing I can think of is that, for a while, I've been sure there's some kind of conspiracy against me. So many things have happened – you heard about the Facebook post, but before that there were these strangers hanging around. Then my dog was shot . . .'

He'd raised his eyebrows. 'But this isn't new. You've already told the police all of this.' He'd paused, then added, 'It doesn't help that they suspect you have a drink problem. I'll be honest with you, when you start talking about conspiracies, you run the risk of sounding paranoid. I'm afraid . . .'

'What?' I'd stared at him. 'You're supposed to be helping me. I'm not an alcoholic and I'm not paranoid. I'm telling you this is what's been going on.'

'Ms Roscoe . . .' He'd held up one of his hands. 'Please, take my advice and do as I suggest. At the moment they believe they have evidence and, until they've finished questioning you, there's not much I can do. Any solicitor would tell you the same.' Then he'd added, 'As I've already said, if you really have nothing to hide, your best course of action is to answer their questions truthfully.'

I'd nodded, then looked away, realizing how pointless it was, expecting him or anyone else to understand what I was going through. No one had any idea how impossible this was. Nor could I tell them.

The next morning, I was taken back to the interview room again. I'd lost track of how many times I'd been in here. I didn't have to wait long. DI Collins and DCI Weller were right behind me.

'Your nephew told us there are letters,' DI Collins said, after we'd sat down and she'd started the tape.

Oh no, Abe, no . . . Why? Can she see my heart hammering inside my ribcage? My face was a mask. 'I'm sorry?'

'We were talking to him last night. When you went back to

your sister's house, he found some letters that were written to his mother. He brought them back with him to your house. We're sending someone round there to pick them up. Did you know about them?'

'Not really.' I paused, filled with dread. 'I did notice something in his room that could have been letters. But I didn't want to go through his things.'

She frowned. 'You haven't mentioned them before. Why not?'

All I could do was tell another lie. So many lies – one more would make no difference. 'Like I said, I didn't even know they were letters. I wasn't in the habit of going through Abe's belongings. They're nothing to do with me.'

'No.' She paused. 'Of course not. It was just that he did say he thought you may have read them.'

My fists were clenched as I tried to stop the rise of heat through me. I shook my head. 'Why would he think that?'

'Abe told us the letters were from his older sister, Summer. Clearly you must have known about her. Why haven't you mentioned her before?'

At the mention of Summer's name, I froze. I couldn't understand why Abe would have brought her up. I paused, trying to buy time to think, then muttered the only thing I could think of. 'She wasn't around.' I paused. 'There was an accident.'

'Your niece was in an accident. Can you tell us what happened?'

That moment again, welling up inside me. A memory I could mould, or even stop, right now, but once it was out, I could never take it back. I nodded miserably – at my betrayal of Nina, of Abe's privacy, of myself. 'I'm not sure exactly what happened. Nina was devastated. It was a long time ago. Abe was too young to remember her. I can't understand why he would have kept her letters.'

DI Collins glanced at DCI Weller. 'So when I asked you about the comment that your sister made to her neighbour, about *the others*, is it reasonable to assume she meant Jude and Summer?'

I was silent for a moment. Then I said quietly, 'I suppose so.'

'In other words, you lied.'

'Not really,' I started. 'You asked if it was possible Nina had another child who might have gone to live with their father. I said it was—'

DI Collins interrupted. 'Ms Roscoe. It must have entered your mind that your sister was talking about her daughter. So why didn't you say so?'

Rigid as I was, somehow I contained the panic rising in me, so that my shrug was barely perceptible. 'It was years ago. It didn't seem relevant to what happened to Nina.'

She frowned. 'Maybe not, but it seems that you've gone to great lengths to hide the existence of your niece. Presumably there's a reason for that.'

I stared at her. 'It wasn't intentional. It's just . . . it was distressing. Like I said, there was a tragic accident. Summer died. Dragging it up now doesn't change anything. All it does is bring back memories of the most horrible, upsetting time—' I broke off, the words sticking in my throat.

'How long ago did your niece die?' DI Collins paused for a moment.

'It was the thirtieth of June, 2007,' I said quietly. Whatever else I couldn't recall, it was a date that was carved into my memory.

'How old was she?'

'Almost fifteen.'

'Can you tell us exactly what happened?'

They were firing questions at me. I stared at my hands, clasped in front of me. As I spoke, my voice shook. 'She and Nina had a fight. Summer was the most angry I'd ever seen her. They had a horrible row, during which she attacked Nina. Nina pushed Summer away and she fell. She hit her head . . .' Hot tears pricked my eyes. 'It was terrible. We sat with her for hours.' My voice broke as I was transported back to Nina's cottage, the two of us beside ourselves as we knelt either side of Summer's body. 'Nina was out of her mind – with grief, and guilt. She felt it was her fault . . .' I shook my head.

'It sounds as though it was,' DI Collins said matter-of-factly.

'It was an accident.' I stared at her. 'She didn't mean to.'

But DI Collins ignored me. 'What happened next?'

'A friend of Nina's was staying that night. He carried Summer's body away and buried her in a clearing in the woods. It was really beautiful there . . .' Tears were streaming down my face as I recalled going there with Nina the following morning. If Summer's life had leached Nina's vitality from her, then her death had drained what little had remained, leaving Nina a shell.

She looked disbelievingly at me. 'So no one was notified? The police weren't called? There was no death certificate?'

I shook my head, numb.

'And you and your sister were OK with that?' This time, it was DCI Weller who spoke. He sounded incredulous.

'What were we supposed to do?' I sobbed. 'We couldn't bring her back. All Nina wanted was for Summer's body to be laid to rest somewhere beautiful. Nothing else mattered. It was a horrible accident. There was no one who'd care about what happened – except us.'

'In other words, she was invisible.' DI Collins spoke calmly.

'I suppose she was. It's what the rows were about. Summer wanted more. Nina had tried to give her children the kind of life she thought was best for them. She couldn't bear that Summer hated it.'

'There were no neighbours, or anyone who'd have missed her?'

Tearfully I shook my head. 'Summer and Jude knew other people, but they weren't nearby. Nina's neighbours were at least two miles away, so they wouldn't have seen them often. Then she moved . . .'

'And no one missed them,' DI Collins said quietly.

DCI Weller spoke. 'The friend who was there the night Summer died, what was his name?'

'Sam.' I paused. 'That's all I know about him.'

'I suppose you've no idea where Sam lived?'

I shook my head. It was the truth.

'And then your sister carried on living the life that was so important to her.'

But I was shaking my head. 'She couldn't. She fell apart. It was not long after that she moved. After losing Summer, the dream was over.'

DI Collins frowned at me. 'This cottage in the middle of nowhere, is that what it really was? Her dream? Because it sounds like a strange environment to bring a family up in, if you cared about them getting an education, making friends, having a future?'

'You don't understand.' I hesitated, not wanting to explain further about my own and Nina's childhood. 'She honestly did what she thought was best. And in so many ways it really was wonderful . . .' It was how I'd always seen it, as the opposite of our own childhoods. 'She didn't want them to suffer the way we did.' After what we'd been through at the hands of our parents, I could only admire her for what she did.

'You've said very little about your parents, Ms Roscoe.'

I nodded. 'I know. Oh God . . .' I couldn't help the shudder that ran through me. Suddenly I needed her to understand, even slightly, how it was for us. 'They were cruel,' I said simply, watching her face. 'Our parents expected us to be *the good children*, and when we weren't, we were punished. If we did something they didn't approve of, they thought nothing of locking us in our bedrooms without food or water – for something like a school grade that wasn't high enough, or having a friend they didn't like. We're talking days – Nina was once left for four days. If we didn't do what my father wanted, he used to threaten us. He'd beat us when he was drunk. He used to beat our mother, too, if she didn't go along with him, but she was weak. Too weak to leave him.'

DI Collins turned to the DCI and murmured something. Then she frowned. 'You didn't tell anyone?'

'When you're a child, who do you tell?' There had been no one Nina and I could have turned to. 'It's always the problem, isn't it? Maybe today someone would listen, but not fifteen years ago.' I shook my head. 'People who didn't know him liked my father. And he was always so believable. My mother was just too frightened to speak up against him.'

DI Collins changed the subject. Was she doing it on purpose? Trying to catch me out? 'Abe told us the letters are behind his wardrobe, at your home.'

My heart quickened. Then I remembered the tape recording my every word. I tried to remember what I had said about them before. 'I wouldn't know. To be honest, I'm still not sure what this has to do with anything.'

'Without reading the letters, it isn't possible to comment. Wouldn't you agree?' If DI Collins had guessed that I'd read them, she wasn't saying. 'I take it you know where they are, as you've already said you thought you'd seen them.'

I swallowed. I was giving myself away – I had to be more careful. 'Yes.'

'Where was your niece buried?' DI Collins's tone was sharp.

I frowned. Her questions were jumping about again. 'In a clearing near Nina's cottage.'

She looked incredulous. 'I can't believe neither of you thought to report her death.'

I spoke under my breath the truth I'd told myself for years, a whisper that was barely audible. 'It was an accident.'

'Ms Roscoe, your niece died as a direct result of your sister's actions. Had the police been informed, she would have been arrested and, on the strength of what you've told us, quite possibly charged with manslaughter – if not your niece's murder.'

I sat there, shaking my head, staring at the table.

'If we drove you to where your sister used to live, would you be able to point out where your niece was buried?'

I was still shaking my head. 'Maybe. I don't know.'

'I'm making a note that at some point this is something we

need to do. Ms Roscoe, is there anything else you should tell us about?'

At last, a question I could answer truthfully. 'No.'

I was growing more uncomfortable as each minute passed, hating the way DI Collins was tainting the past. Even now, years on, the time I'd spent with Nina was the most real my life had ever been. Yet progressively throughout the interview I'd started to feel like an onlooker, as though I was someone else sitting there, listening to DI Collins pulling Nina's life apart.

But soon she'd be reading the letters, assembling more pieces of the puzzle in the wrong places. I dreaded to think what lay ahead.

'I haven't had a chance to read the letters yet.' The interview had resumed after a break for a lunch that I couldn't eat. 'We've arranged for you to see a psychologist in the morning.'

As I stood up, Julian Hill was muttering at me to sit down. 'What do you mean? I can't stay another day. I have to go home.'

'Ms Roscoe, I'm afraid you're not going anywhere just yet.'

'I want a better solicitor.' My voice shrill, I stood there, trembling. 'I have rights, don't I?'

'Ms Roscoe, please sit down. This isn't helping.'

I turned on Julian Hill, suddenly frustrated beyond belief and grabbing him by his lapels. 'You're supposed to help me.' I knew I shouldn't be doing this, but I couldn't help it. The unfairness of it all was catching up with me.

DI Collins stood up. 'Ms Roscoe, please sit down.'

But I ignored her. 'You're supposed to help,' I shouted, lowering my face closer to his. 'You've done fuck-all.' Letting go of him, I turned to face DI Collins, utterly exhausted. 'I demand a different solicitor.'

The room was silent as she hesitated, then nodded towards Julian Hill. He looked ashen. 'I'll see what I can do.'

27

Even without the delay I'd caused, I faced another night in the cell, but when I was escorted to the interview room the next morning, to my relief I was met by a different solicitor. I was praying he couldn't be worse.

'Phil Bannister.' He regarded me suspiciously. 'You're lucky Mr Hill isn't pressing charges.' He sounded disapproving, but at least Bannister had a voice.

I looked at him disbelievingly. 'What do you mean?'

'Apparently you assaulted him yesterday.' Bannister stared coldly at me.

'I didn't *assault* him.' I looked at him in disbelief. What was he talking about? 'Who told you that?'

'Legal definition of assault, Ms Roscoe: an attempt to cause harm . . . You got him by the lapels, I'm told.'

'It was hardly an assault.' This was insane. I'd been pushed to my limit and Julian Hill had sat back and let it happen. It was hardly surprising I'd lost it with him. 'I had no intention of harming him. He was supposed to be helping me and he was useless. It was a . . . difficult moment.'

There was hostility in his eyes, as Bannister stared at me. 'Let's hope there are no such difficult moments with this morning's proceedings. I'm less, shall we say, forgiving than Mr Hill.'

I'd been naive to hope that a new solicitor would make a difference. As he sat down next to me, organizing the papers in front of him, I realized I was no less alone than yesterday. Horribly aware of my stomach churning, I waited in silence.

As DI Collins and DCI Weller came in and sat down, I instantly recognized the envelopes DI Collins had in front of her. Then, as I stared more closely at them, I went cold as I saw Nina's diary underneath them. She started the tape.

'The psychologist hasn't been able to make it. The appointment will be rescheduled for a later date.'

My heart sank. Did that mean I'd have to come back?

'Carrying on from yesterday, about the letters, Ms Roscoe.' DI Collins went straight to the point. 'It's very clear that your niece – Summer – was angry with her mother. Were you aware just how angry?'

I nodded. 'I heard them argue several times. It was usually about Summer wanting to go to school.'

DI Collins frowned. 'I'd say it ran a little deeper than just wanting to go to school. There are references to Ms Tyrell's drinking and her lack of attention to her children. These were mostly written around 2007, in the months leading up to your niece's death.' She paused. 'She's quite damning about you, too, wouldn't you agree?'

'I always thought we got on well,' I said defensively. It was true. 'It was probably written after a particular party that got out of hand.'

'Just the one party?' DI Collins sounded sceptical. 'Was that the party where one of your sister's friends drowned Summer's cat? And your sister was oblivious to it? Were you there when it happened?'

I gasped. Here, in this room, in front of the police, I was aware of how unforgivably cruel it sounded. 'By the time Nina knew, it was too late to do anything about it. It wasn't her fault.'

'Not directly. But if she had been sober, don't you think she might have listened to her daughter and intervened?' DI Collins stared at me. 'Or perhaps you might have, if you'd been sober?' When I didn't reply, she added, 'I assume, from your silence, that both you and your sister were out of control?'

Beside me Bannister sighed, then he surprised me. 'Detective Inspector, I take it you have evidence of this?' He sounded disinterested, bored.

'I think what we're establishing here is a history of drug and alcohol abuse, which aside from affecting the behaviour of both Ms Roscoe and Ms Tyrell, certainly affected Summer and her brothers. According to Jude, his mother's drinking was the reason he spent as little time as possible with her. He remembers it being worse when you were there.' DI Collins looked at me expectantly.

Had it been? I frowned. 'I'm not sure that's right. He was only nine – and he was hardly there.'

I saw her look of frustration with my answer, before she went on. 'In one of the letters, Summer talks about "blood being thicker than blood" – she goes on to say, "One day, you'll have to tell him what you've been keeping from him. Can you do that? Be brutally, heartbreakingly, self-sabotagingly honest?"' She looked at me. 'She was referring to Abe, wasn't she? Do you have any idea what she's talking about?'

Glancing around the room, I was too hot. 'Can you open the window?'

Getting up, DI Collins looked exasperated as she walked across the room and cracked open the window. The smallest ripple of air reached me. She sat down again, glancing at DCI Weller.

He cleared his throat. 'The letter, Ms Roscoe. What was your sister hiding from Abe?'

'I don't know.' I looked desperately at Bannister, not sure if I imagined his smirk. 'I wasn't always there. I didn't know everything that went on in Nina's life.'

'That line about blood being thicker than blood.' DCI Weller's eyes didn't leave my face. 'I didn't get it to start with, but she's talking about you, isn't she? It's Summer's way of saying that her mother put her loyalty to you above that to her children.'

'No, that's not it.' I was shaking my head. He was wrong. 'Her children always came first. It was what she always said. They were the most important thing in the world to her.' I was aware of my voice rising.

There was a pause before DI Collins spoke. 'There's another letter. It makes me think we're missing something. Maybe you know what that is.'

I listened with dread as she started reading:

You're weak, Mother. You run away from problems, leaving them piled up behind you, instead of facing them. You don't realize there are things you can't run from.

What about being honest? Telling the truth, Mother? Getting real?

Too hard for you?

But not everything's easy. I remember you saying how everyone was different; it was up to us how we looked at things. Then you'd give me that smile and tell me, a lie isn't always a lie . . .

You and Hannah rewrote the rules, didn't you? It meant you could do what you like. Lies weren't lies, if there was a good reason for them. The two of you always had such good reasons.

And now, it has to end here: the lie that isn't a lie, because I can't keep your secret. But you and Hannah were never thinking of Abe. You were only thinking of yourselves.

My mouth was dry. 'I've no idea what she means.'

'Ms Roscoe, we've been in touch with your ex-husband. He's coming in to answer some questions later today.'

'Nathan?' I was stunned. How could he possibly help with this? Since the divorce I'd completely lost touch with him.

We were interrupted by a knock on the door. 'Excuse me.' DI Collins got up to answer it, speaking in a low voice to the uniformed PC just outside, before coming to sit back down. She looked at me. 'Apparently your nephew has found another letter.'

'He isn't reliable – you do know that, don't you?' Agitated, I looked at each one of them in turn. 'He has—' I started to add, but Bannister interrupted.

'Ms Roscoe, whatever this is about, can I suggest we discuss it in a moment?'

'No. I need to say it now . . .'

He was shaking his head. 'Ms Roscoe, I strongly advise you wait.'

DCI Weller got up and walked towards the door. 'If I were you, I'd take your solicitor's advice.'

As they walked out, the door closed behind them, leaving me alone with Bannister.

'You're making this unnecessarily difficult.' He regarded me coldly.

'I don't think I am. It's important that they know what people are really like.'

He shook his head. 'I think you'll find they're more than capable of judging that for themselves.' Then he sighed wearily. 'Ms Roscoe, if you've really nothing to hide, for God's sake why don't you tell them the truth?'

After DCI Weller was called away on another matter, I was led back to my room. Alone, I was trying to work out where to go from here.

Keep to the script, Hannah . . .

Tell them the truth . . .

I was torn. The script wasn't working any more. Nothing was going as it should. I hadn't lied exactly – not about anything important. I'd just left out things that weren't relevant. But my only hope now was to tell them everything.

At least an hour must have passed, possibly longer, before the interview was resumed. I knew what I had to say.

'I want to tell you about that afternoon – the afternoon of Nina's death.' I was calm as I addressed DI Collins and DCI Weller. I hadn't eaten the sandwich I'd been brought at lunchtime. Instead I'd rehearsed what I was going to say, trusting that this time they'd see I was telling the truth.

'The day I went to meet Matt, I was early. I went into a bar. I had a sandwich and a drink, planning to stay there until the time he usually went for lunch. But I saw him walk past with a woman—' I broke off. The memory was too vivid, too painful. I banished it. I couldn't mess up. Not now. 'They went into his office together. I tried to call him, but he didn't answer, so I waited. Then, when he didn't come out at lunchtime, I called reception.'

'Go on.' DI Collins was watching me intently.

'I was still waiting, about an hour later, when I had a call from Nina. It was the first time I'd heard from her in years – that's the honest truth. She sounded distraught. And drunk.' I tried to remember her voice. She'd been crying, slurring her words. 'She begged me to go and see her – something had happened, but she was too upset to talk about it over the phone. Then she gave me her address. I got in a taxi and went over there.

'I'd had a couple of drinks while I was waiting for Matt, and just before the taxi got to Nina's house, I asked the driver to pull over.' I paused. Had it been near a Tube station? I couldn't actually remember. 'I'm not sure exactly where we were. I asked him which way Nina's street was, and he pointed me in the right direction.' I swallowed. 'When I got out, it was cold. I'd had my hood down in the taxi, but once I was walking, I suppose I pulled it up again. The photo you showed me, taken by CCTV, that was me.'

Looking at them, I faltered. It was impossible to tell from their faces if they believed me or not.

'Go on.' DCI Weller broke the silence.

'I got to Nina's house. I rang the doorbell, but there was no reply. Then I noticed the door was ajar.'

'Did you think that was odd?'

'Not really. When she lived at the cottage, Nina never locked her door.' I shook my head. 'But that was in the middle of the countryside. I suppose, for London, it was odd, but I didn't think so at the time. I pushed the door open and went inside. I called her, but she didn't answer. Having heard how drunk she sounded on the phone, I was thinking it was possible she'd passed out. I checked each room downstairs, but there was no sign of her, so I went upstairs. She was in her bedroom.' I felt far away all of a sudden, remembering the shock I'd felt when I realized my sister wasn't breathing, as it slowly sank in that she was dead.

'She was already dead?' DCI Weller's voice was sharp.

I nodded. 'Yes.'

'Do you know what time this was?'

Staring at them blankly, I shrugged. They already knew the answer. 'Whatever time your CCTV says it was.'

'Did you touch anything?'

'I picked up the bottle. I drank what was left in it,' I said distantly, without shame. 'I think I was in shock. I put it back where I found it. Then I left.'

'Didn't it occur to you to call the police?'

'It did . . . There's a reason I didn't.' I frowned, trying to remember. Had I been frightened of the exact scenario I now found myself in, suspected of killing her?

'But you can't remember.' DI Collins's eyebrows were raised. 'How convenient, Ms Roscoe.'

I was taken back to my cell, where I sat on my bed. Now that they had the truth, I was waiting for the police to let me go. An hour passed, then another. I didn't understand why I was still here.

Eventually I heard someone walking down the corridor. I jumped up. 'Excuse me, can you tell me when I can go?'

It was a uniformed officer I'd seen once or twice before. My heart leapt. At last I was getting out of here.

'Can you come with me, please.' He opened my door, but instead of taking me outside, he led me back to the interview room. Bannister was in there, waiting for me.

'What's going on?' I wasn't expecting to be brought back in here again. 'I thought I was going home?'

He looked evasive. 'They'll be here in a minute.'

Filled with unease, I sat down. They'd asked enough questions – unless Nathan had thrown them something new against me, but I couldn't imagine what. Almost immediately DI Collins and DCI Weller came in. DI Collins turned the tape on.

'We've spoken to your ex-husband, Nathan Roscoe. He confirmed that you were pregnant. It was before the two of you were married, soon after you went to live with your sister. Apparently you were worried that a baby would ruin your music career. Is that correct?'

'Yes, but . . .' There was no way I could have gone on tour with a newborn baby. 'I miscarried, so it was never an issue,' I reminded her.

She frowned. 'That isn't how Mr Roscoe remembers it. He says you had the baby, and that three weeks later you were performing again. So my question is: why have you lied about it? What happened to your baby, Ms Roscoe?'

I stared at her incredulously. 'Nathan was permanently stoned in those days. You can't believe anything he remembers from that time.'

DI Collins looked unimpressed as she nodded. 'He seemed perfectly clear about it when he spoke to us. We've managed to track down a couple of other members of your band, to see what they can add about what was going on at that time. We spoke to one yesterday, and there's another being interviewed later today.'

'Oh my God!' I stared at her, aghast. More buried memories were coming to the surface, as I felt the blood drain from my face.

'What is it, Ms Roscoe?'

'The band,' I gasped. 'I know what went wrong. It was my fault. Everyone blamed me. Maybe that's what this is about.'

DI Collins frowned. 'I hardly think they'd wait all this time if they had a grudge against you. As I said, we'll be talking to them.' She paused. 'There's also the matter of this other letter. It's dated the twentieth of June 2007. I'll read it to you:

Dear Summer

I'm begging you, for Abe's sake – for all our sakes – not to tell anyone. You were never supposed to find out. Imagine what it will do to him to know I've been lying all these years – and if he finds out who his mother really is.

It was my decision. I tried to do what was right. Not just for me, but for all of us, Hannah included. You have every right to be angry. I know I've failed you – you in particular, more than Jude. All I ever did was try to give you what I never had.

You may think there is, Summer, but there is no right answer. No solution that will remove the lies that Abe's life's been built on. Life isn't always as simple as right or wrong, black or white.

I sat there in shock. This letter hadn't been with the others in Abe's room. Where had it come from?

'I find it odd that your sister thought that keeping the lie going was better than honesty? Many children find out they

287

are adopted. They cope with it. But I don't think this was ever about Abe. Your sister was protecting you, wasn't she, Ms Roscoe?' DI Collins's words hung in the air between us. 'Why was that?' She paused.

Staring at the table, I shook my head.

'Then shortly after that, Summer died, didn't she? The problem disappeared. It would have stayed that way, except that Abe found the letters.'

I heard a sharp intake of breath, then realized it was my own. All the time Abe had been living with me, he must have known. I stared at her. 'If Abe knew, why didn't he say anything?'

Her expression was unreadable as she looked at me. 'If you put yourself in the shoes of a fifteen-year-old boy who suddenly finds himself living with his birth mother – a woman who hasn't been in contact for ten years – wouldn't you expect her to have made the first move?'

I stared at her blankly. 'But I didn't know he'd found out.'

'You're missing the point.' DI Collins sounded exasperated. Shaking her head, she gave me another of her looks. 'We've gone over everything you've told us,' she said slowly. 'You've told us about this so-called conspiracy against you. We've spoken to Cara Matlock. She told us that a woman approached her and offered her some money if she wrote that Facebook post about you. She realizes she made a mistake. She has nothing against you.'

'But who asked her to do that?'

'It turns out it was a Ms Olivia Elliott – Mr Elliott's ex-wife. She's the woman who's been hanging around your village, trying to stir up trouble. She's been cautioned. It was also her who sent Mr Elliott the photo of you when you were pregnant.

She had it in for you, make no mistake. But I don't suppose even she imagined the consequences her actions would have.'

I felt my jaw drop. 'So are they . . .' I couldn't bring myself to say *back together*.

'I have no idea,' the DI said drily. 'And it's of no consequence—'

'But that man,' I interrupted. 'The one who caused the accident . . .'

'He's a friend of Ms Elliott's, who agreed to help her. And you can hardly blame him for the accident. That was entirely your own doing. We're not sure yet if they played a part in the death of your dog.' She paused. 'I can understand how you might have found them intimidating. They certainly set out to cause you trouble. But your paranoia was almost definitely aggravated by alcoholism. These last few days have been difficult for you, haven't they? Not sleeping, the feelings of anxiety, your nausea, sweating, tremors . . . they're all withdrawal symptoms, you know.'

I stared at my hands, trying to stop them shaking, then looked up at her. 'I know I've been drinking too much, but I've been cutting down. I really do want to stop.'

She ignored me. 'We've spoken to Mr Dalton. It was interesting. He admitted that he, too, found it hard to relate to your nephew, but he was more concerned about you. He said something about pictures being moved, and a gash on your arm you didn't remember happening. He also had concerns about your drinking, but said you were adamant you didn't have a problem.'

I couldn't speak. I couldn't believe Curtis had said all this.

'Did you make it up – about the paintings? To add weight to your conspiracy theory?'

I just stared at her. This was insane. I couldn't speak.

'Your old band member shed some light on things, too.'

Startled, I looked up at her again. 'Apparently the reason you fled to Nina's was because your father kicked you out. I believe he found out you were pregnant. They went on to say you drank your way through your pregnancy, and by the time you'd given birth, you had a serious drink problem. That's the real reason why the band broke up, isn't it?'

As she stared at me, the fight went out of me. All these years I'd tried to hide it. Nina had, too. Right after the Cry Babies released their hit single, I'd had a fling and got pregnant. 'I had morning sickness.'

DI Collins raised an eyebrow. 'Really? Are you sure you don't mean you were constantly either drunk or hungover?' When I didn't say anything, she went on. 'Who's Abe's father?'

I gasped. 'No. No!' My eyes flashed wildly between them. 'No . . .' I couldn't go there. Not ever. They couldn't make me. It was the worst of the worst. Triggered memories I was so ashamed of.

'When we first met, you told me Jude was Abe's half-brother. I assumed they had different fathers, but I was wrong, wasn't I?'

Under her gaze, I shrank lower in my chair, conscious of all of them watching me.

'Abe and Jude didn't share the same mother, did they, Ms Roscoe? They have the same father. You slept with your sister's boyfriend.'

I opened my mouth to speak, to tell her it wasn't how it looked, that Nina and Ed had problems.

But she didn't give me a chance. 'You owed her far more than simply looking after Abe. As well as taking on your child, she'd forgiven your betrayal and given you a roof over your head.'

I slumped even lower in my chair. *Wasn't that what sisters do for each other?*

DI Collins continued. 'You've told us, at considerable length, about your sister's problems: her unreliability, how she wasn't there for her children. Her drinking . . . But these aren't just your sister's problems are they, Ms Roscoe? They're clearly your problems, too. It's you who's unreliable, who has a drink problem. You've told us yourself that your sister always did her best for her children – albeit in a limited way. She would never have abandoned her child, would she?'

I felt myself go numb as I turned towards her.

'You admit to being at your sister's house the afternoon she was murdered. Your fingerprints are on the bottle that was found in her room. One of her neighbours says they heard women's voices shouting.'

I gasped. 'But that proves I didn't kill her. Nina was dead by the time I got there.'

She ignored me. 'What happened, Ms Roscoe? Another violent argument like the one in which, all those years ago, you killed Summer?'

I looked at her, horrified. 'It wasn't me. It was Nina.'

You didn't do it, Hannah . . . Keep to the script.

'Oh, but you did,' she said quietly. 'There was a witness. When Summer attacked your sister, they saw you pull Summer away and shove her across the room.'

'No! It was Nina who pushed her.' This wasn't right. 'It wasn't me. And no one was there, I know they weren't . . .' I let my words trail off, suddenly remembering they weren't true; that Abe could have been there.

291

'That's not what our witness says. It's no wonder you weren't in touch with Ms Tyrell. You and your sister concocted the lie – your sister protecting you again, for reasons I don't understand – and you let her.

'Then recently, sober for the first time in a decade, maybe the burden of lying got too much for her. Maybe, like Summer, she wanted Abe to understand, to know the truth. But you were never able to accept responsibility for your mistakes, were you, Ms Roscoe? That was how you saw Abe – your biggest mistake. When you accidentally fell pregnant, rather than let it ruin your music career, your sister selflessly stepped in and offered to bring Abe up as her own. It was *you* who cut *her* out of your life until – out of the blue – she contacted you. But you couldn't take the risk, could you, especially when you were still hoping to be reunited with Mr Elliott? If he found out you hadn't told him about Abe, you believed it would ruin everything.' She paused. 'Strange how, in spite of your best efforts to arrange everything the way you wanted it, your music career failed, Mr Elliott left and Abe's ended up living with you. There's a certain irony in that, wouldn't you say?'

She was doing it again, twisting everything, until it was wrong – so wrong I didn't know where to start. I shook my head. 'It wasn't like that.'

'There's the small matter of the murder weapon. Your property is being searched as we speak. So far we've found a small statue with what looks like dried blood encrusted on it. Is that what you used, Ms Roscoe?' Both pairs of eyes were boring into me. 'It's the perfect size – big enough to deliver a fatal blow, but small enough to hide under loose-fitting jeans and a hoody, so that you could take it home with you and hide it.'

'No . . .' My heart was racing out of control. They couldn't believe I killed Nina. 'It wasn't me who killed her.' I paused, catching my breath. 'You've missed something.' Suddenly I realized what it was. 'My shed was broken into. About two months ago. Whatever you've found, someone must have been planning this! I've been set up . . .' It was all falling into place. 'You have to believe me! Please . . . Can't we go over this one more time?' But as I stared at them, slowly it dawned on me. It was too late.

'So you can change your story yet again?' The DI paused. 'You've had more than enough time to tell us what happened. We have more than enough evidence against you, including the tapes, which will in due course be examined by a forensic psychologist. Hannah Roscoe, I am charging you with the murder of Nina Tyrell. You do not have to say anything. But, it may harm your defence if you do not mention when questioned something which you later rely on in court. Anything you do say may be given in evidence. You will be remanded in custody until a court date is set.'

As she spoke, I felt the blood drain from my face. Shaking, I sat there, until a few minutes later a uniformed officer came in and led me away.

From the first night in your house, I've watched you, Hannah. Even if you hadn't given yourself away, there was always a paper trail to the truth about Summer. You thought you'd stumbled across those letters, didn't you, by accident, when all along you were intended to, in sequence, at the right time. It was carefully planned, Hannah. None of it left to chance.

There's one last letter I was tempted to leave for you to find. A letter dated a year after Summer's death – imagine reading that, Hannah. Imagine how you would have felt. I was tempted, part of me wanting to watch as you took in the impossible, as fear screamed through your brain, then denial, confusion, guilt, piling in on you, tipping you over the edge. But in the end I didn't need to. You were your own undoing. The letter has stayed hidden, at least for now.

I've always known you're my mother. That you abandoned me with your addict sister; that you hadn't wanted anything to do with me. Neither of you had – not really. You are the reason I was drawn to the night sky: so vast, it reminds you how small people are, confirms the transience of the human condition. People don't really matter. I don't matter – not to you or your sister. Nor do you. None of us are important. It might feel like an eternity, but in the grand scheme of things, life is short.

And some lives are shorter than others.

You didn't know when I bunked off school and met up with Jude for the first time in ages. He told me how the police had asked him to take them to where Nina's cottage used to be. They wanted to find Summer's grave. But when they got there, the woods had been bulldozed and a vast housing estate built. Jude grinned. As far as the police were concerned, Summer's grave was lost forever, somewhere underneath it.

Jude was a step ahead of them, of course. He hadn't really taken the police to where the cottage used to be. Instead, he'd done his research into housing estates built in recent years on woodland sites. There had been a couple – Jude had picked the biggest. The police were hardly going to dig up a whole housing estate to look for one grave. They were never going to know he'd lied.

Jude's found a job and he's been renting a room in a mate's flat, with room for me if I want it. It's an option, but it isn't what I've had in mind. There's another option, one I can't quite picture yet, out there in front of me, shrouded in mist.

From behind the locked door of your cell, I wonder if you even think about what's happened to me? If you'll find out that Erin asked me to stay on with her. I almost believed she wanted me there. Almost . . . I let myself imagine how that felt, being wanted by someone, but only for a minute. You've ruined that for me, Hannah. No one's wanted me before. Why would anyone want me now?

Instead, I talked to Jude. He gets it. 'You know, after everything that has happened, it would be good to make a clean break . . .'

Erin looked disappointed when I told her, but she nodded. She understood, maybe she was relieved, even. But I didn't want to get to know her. It's easier not to have people in your life. You let people in, they ask questions: about your plans, where you're going. This way, I don't have to explain myself to anyone.

Before I left, DI Collins stopped by to talk to me, about being called as a witness when your case goes to court. But I don't have to stand up in front of everyone, she told me. I can be questioned via a video link from another room. Think of it like this, Hannah. Mother. Chances are you'll never see me again.

I didn't say much to her, just gave her Jude's address, telling her I was moving. I thought of your house briefly. If you're sentenced, as you almost certainly will be, what will happen to it? Will it stand there empty for years? Have you thought about what happens to it when you die? I even thought about staying there for as long as you were being held by the police, maybe with Jude, the two of us breaking in. You have no idea how easy it is to break into your house, Hannah. No one would have known we were there. It was Jude who persuaded me against it. And he was right. It will be better to move away from all the people around here. When the press get hold of it, they'll all know what's happened, gossiping behind their closed doors and windows, in the village shop, in the pub. Far better to disappear.

After I packed my stuff, it was Erin who drove me to the station. As I got on the train, for the first time in my fifteen years I knew what it was like to feel a sense of control. At last I could make my own decisions, plan my future. Watching the fields and houses flash past, it seemed like no time before I was at the station where Jude was waiting.

Jude's immensely proud of his little Vauxhall Corsa, zigzagging it through the streets, until he pulled up and parked outside his house. He helped me carry my stuff inside – then straight out again, through a door at the back of the house, where there was another car.

You couldn't be too careful, Jude explained. So, just in case, he'd borrowed the car from a mate who owed him – he didn't say what for. After loading it up, he threw me a beanie hat, telling me to pull it down over my face. Then we were driving.

The journey, which had passed so quickly on the train, took much longer going the other way. Jude took no chances, taking the back roads, talking constantly about not wanting to be picked up by the cameras on the motorway; about how it was cool, wasn't it, that he was old enough to be my guardian? But then he started to talk more seriously.

If I wanted, I could have a new name, he told me. Jude had paperwork – a birth certificate; it was one of the advantages of being inside, he joked. You made useful contacts. I could disappear forever, or become Aidan – not too different, just in case I slipped up. Abe sounded a bit like Ade . . . Aidan Rodgers.

I don't have to decide, not yet. And it wasn't much further, Jude assured me. I shivered, feeling a sense of déjà vu as we drove through countryside I didn't recognize but that somehow looked familiar, while Jude kept talking. It would be worth it. He might have lied to the police – we both had. We'd had to. But there were to be no more lies, we'd agreed on that. Going forward, we had to be straight with each other.

As the roads got quieter, a sense of calm came over me. Jude was edgy, excited, telling me how I'd done the right thing, leaving the letters for you to see, then handing them to the police when I did. It might have been years ago, but you'd done something terrible when you abandoned me. You should have known what my life would be like and you'd turned your back on me. And now you deserved to pay. Thanks to me, there's little doubt that you're guilty.

But I knew all of that. And you are guilty – as hell. Of leaving me in the hands of your alcoholic, drug-addict sister, not giving any thought to what lay ahead for me; of only thinking about yourself. I had no qualms about feeding you the letters the way I had, then doing the same to the police. That last letter had been a stroke of genius, but you've no idea how good I am at forging handwriting;

about the years of faking your sister's signature when she was off her face. No one will ever be able to tell.

In the same way I forged the suicide note, sitting beside your sister's body, needing the police to see that her killer was erratic and naive. It was after I'd hidden it – intentionally not too well – that I called the police. Then later, when I met you, I knew how perfect it was. You fitted the profile flawlessly.

It was me who swapped your paintings around and generally fucked with your head, but you've had it coming to you for years. Not that it took much. You were unhinged before I got there.

It was so easy, so instinctive, to play to your fears, your neuroses; to manipulate you. You didn't know that, from the beginning, a process had been set in motion, at the end of which there'd be justice. You deserved no sympathy. I had no hesitation about cutting your arm that night. You were so drunk, you didn't feel me press the glass into your skin, cutting deeper until the blood started to flow. The next day you hadn't remembered anything.

I'd even planned to kill Gibson, but presumably someone else got there first – probably that woman who'd been hanging around. I saw her once or twice – she was almost as mad as you. I'd planned to strangle the dog. I'd thought many times about how I'd do it. I'd have been doing the dog a favour. There's no place for Gibson where you're going.

Those nights I stood outside I was doing so much more than watching the stars; in my head, I was running through every detail of what lay ahead; each step discussed with Jude; dispassionately, painstakingly waiting to be set in motion. I felt no guilt about what I was doing. It was simply a means to a better end, ridding the world of two broken human beings, whom everyone was better off without.

I'd known for some time I had to start looking out for myself.

Remember that awful night, when you attacked Summer? I was four years old, Hannah. The most vivid memory of my childhood, after which things had gone from bad to worse. All your sister's money had been spent on drink. There was never enough food, but you wouldn't want to know about that. Or how I was saved when we moved to London and I went to school, where at least I got one square meal. Otherwise, I would have starved.

Right now, for the first time, I have a chance to put it all behind me. Maybe I'll take a new name. Coming here is a fresh start. And if it doesn't work out, I'll deal with it in whatever way I have to.

This was it . . . Jude turned up a narrow track, flanked on either side by the dark trunks of tall pines, their branches tangled overhead. The little car bumped along it for what must have been at least a mile, before the trees started to thin out and then eventually, up ahead, they cleared.

A brick-and-timber cottage came into view. In front, two large pots were planted with brightly coloured tulips. Slowing right down, Jude stopped to one side of it. As I sat there, looking around, my head was filled with memories. Not all were good.

Then Jude switched off the engine. For a moment, neither of us moved.

'Don't worry, dude.' He nudged my elbow. 'It won't be like that. You'll see.'

After what I'd survived, the cottage in the woods didn't worry me. This couldn't be worse than what had already happened. As I got out of the car and stood there, breathing in the pine-scented air, I had a sudden sense of coming home. Then, as I looked up, I saw a ghost.

Summer

Your Three Musketeers, Mother . . .

If only you'd known.

But the only way was your way. Lies layered on more lies. You taught us well.

I can remember when it wasn't like that. For a while, when it was just you, me and Jude, there were days when your magic was like a shimmering cloud, woven around us, enthralling us, protecting us. Then Hannah moved in, casting her blackness, pulling you into her dysfunctional world, demanding you all to herself.

Poor Hannah, whom the music industry ate up and spat out. So talented . . . talented at dragging everyone she met into her madness. But you were bonded by the abuse you'd suffered. Hannah was you, and you were Hannah, born to parents who didn't love you, who starved you and hurt you, until they broke you.

And then you buried it, Mother, your blank, blind eyes hiding your pain, only seeing what you wanted to see, just as you buried the truth in your lies. And Hannah did the same.

You'll never know that your fucked-up little sister's attempt to kill me turned out to be my lifeline. While the two of you crouched over my body, you were too drunk to notice my whisper-breath, the flutter of my eyelashes. After almost killing me, you almost buried me alive, except that Sam saw. Sam carried me away from you. It was Sam who dug my grave and buried rocks in it. Sam, not you, who gave me freedom.

I couldn't come back. I couldn't do anything, just wait until I was older. But I was lucky, Mother. I had Sam to take care of me. Sam, who persuaded me to stay with him, who made sure I was safe and warm, who taught me about art and English; who protected me. But I couldn't rest, Mother – not ever. How could I? Not with my brothers still in your so-called care. Jude was older, tougher, but Abe was vulnerable. You didn't care, did you? I wanted to find you and try to get custody of him. Sam tried to talk me out of it. Sam who was under your spell, even after all this time; who said you'd suffered enough. But when I came after you, you'd disappeared.

You know how I found Jude? When he was sentenced and it was in the press. Angry Jude, whom no one had time for. I went to see him, Mother. I knew you wouldn't. But it wasn't just about me and Jude, was it, Mother? There was the secret, invisible child in the background. Abe – Hannah's child. And all the time you thought we didn't know.

Then all we had to do was wait. For Jude to get out; for things to start falling into place. Everything in life is about timing. Death too, when that moment comes – that something can go on no longer. Has to end, here. Now.

So it was for you, Mother. Brutal but essential, the termination of your slow decay, of the misery you left in your wake. But you were already dying, all three of us knew that. Those last minutes you saw me in your house, I read your life story in your eyes – regret, anger, guilt, pain, weakness; they were all there. But it was too late by then. The Three Musketeers had their own, painstakingly constructed, perfectly orchestrated plan. The plan was in motion, the perfect weapon chosen. The time had come.

You first, Mother. The older sister does everything first. Paves the way.

The first to lie. The first to betray.

The first to die.

One sister followed by another sister . . .

Hannah was next. Hannah who was born to be a victim. Selfish, irresponsible, weak Hannah, guilty of condemning Abe to fifteen years of misery, of not caring about her only child. She could have redeemed herself when he went to live with her, but she chose not to. What kind of person could do that?

But after her failed music career, after hiding away for years, she finally had a starring role that served a dual purpose. By becoming Hannah, the killer of her pathetic sister, she earned a punishment that fitted both her crimes.

Watching from a distance, I knew Hannah's every movement. Took my time when she went out, picking the lock on the door of the shed, where I found the murder weapon. She never knew I'd been to her house, just as she'll never know it was me who called her that day, Mother. Your last day. I pretended to be you – you were too drunk to notice. You didn't take much persuading, did you? You needed a drink for the shock, I could hear you telling yourself.

And, as always, Hannah couldn't help you. She never could, could she? Not even when you really needed her. By the time she arrived, you were dead. I watched her arrive from across the street, then leave minutes later. She didn't even stop to think of Abe, about to come home from school and find his mother's body. But as we all know, Hannah only thinks about herself.

I shouldn't have gone to her house that day, but Hannah drew me to her like a moth to a flame. By chance, or maybe it was destiny,

I was there when she crashed her car; leaned over her barely conscious body the way she had over mine, all those years ago, the night she thought she'd killed me. I made sure she saw me, Mother. Gave her another ghost to haunt her nightmares; to make her question her sanity.

My one regret was what Abe had to go through to get to this point. Abe, who was innocent, who had to stay with your fucked-up sister. But one of us had to be there. It was the only way the plan would ever work.

But it's behind us. Now, in this cottage you escaped to all those years ago, is where it ends, Mother. Your own and Hannah's crimes of neglect, your web of lies. The perpetrators have been sentenced. The penalty delivered by the victims. Justice perfectly carried out, in as much as it ever can be, without winding back the past and rewriting it.

And, as all endings are, this is a beginning. The start of the rest of our lives. That's what this was about, Mother. The suffering is over, for Abe and for all of us. The baby no one wanted now has freedom.

I've just watched him and Jude arrive in the car that Jude's borrowed. Abe's face is blank, the way it's always been. He's carrying a huge black rucksack, walking slowly as he looks around at the cottage, then at the trees, stopping for a moment. I'll have to ask him what he remembers about living here. Jude looks cocky. Pleased with himself – perhaps he should be. While for me, seeing them here, at last there is peace. Hope, too, for all three of us.

Abe doesn't know that there's a fridge full of food and warm covers on the beds. Sam's fixed the windows – we can close them now. I want to tell Abe all of this. He needs to learn what it means, to have a home, to feel safe, to be loved.

I'm going out to meet them now. I'm not Summer any more, by

the way. I haven't been for years. I'm Jess. Our future begins in your old cottage, Mother. But I don't know how long we'll stay. There's the shadow of history repeating itself. Sam owns it, says it's mine for as long as I want it. Is that how it started for you?

But the similarities end there, Mother. Our lives are going to be real. Coming here isn't about running away. There will be school, work, people. But we'll never be free of you. Not entirely. You've left us with our own secret. The ultimate lie, the one that put an end to your lies; that made it possible for us to be here.

But no more lies, Mother – or lies that aren't really lies.

No regrets, no remorse, no guilt.

Those days are behind us.

We've changed the script.

ACKNOWLEDGEMENTS

As always, I'm hugely grateful to my brilliant, insightful editor, Trisha Jackson, who is a joy to work with and to all the team at Pan Macmillan. My books have a wonderful home with you. I'm also lucky to have the support of the best agent a writer could ask for. Thank you, Juliet Mushens, for everything you do.

I'd also like to thank my sisters and my friends, for support and spreading the word and being with me along the way!

Huge thanks and much love to my children, Georgie and Tom. I had a crisis of confidence during the writing of this book and being the brilliant people they are, we sat down together and brainstormed a solution I wouldn't have found without them.

And finally, the Cry Babies played in 1980! They wrote some great songs and it's too good a name not to be immortalized in print. Thank you Martin! x

the
BONES
of YOU

The Sunday Times bestseller

A community in shock

When Rosie Anderson disappears, the idyllic village
where she lived will never be the same again.

A family torn apart

Rosie was beautiful, kind and gentle. She came from
a loving family and had her whole life ahead of her.
Who could possibly want to harm her? And why?

A keeper of secrets

Kate is a friend of the family. She's convinced the police
are missing something, and she's certain someone
in the village knows more than they're letting on. As the
investigation deepens, so does Kate's obsession with
solving the mystery of what happened to Rosie.

the
BEAUTY
of the
END

I was fourteen when I fell in love with a goddess . . .

A love he'd never forget

Ex-lawyer Noah has never forgotten his first love. When, years later, he hears that she's suspected of murder, he knows with certainty that she's innocent. With April on life-support and the evidence pointing towards her guilt, he's compelled to help her. But he's also unprepared as he's forced to confront what happened between them all those years ago.

A secret she would never reveal

April Moon had loved Noah. She never wanted to hurt him. But there was something – and someone – dark in her life which made happiness together impossible.

A family she could never forgive

Ella is a troubled teenager with her own secrets to tell. But no one will listen. What Ella knows holds the key to finding the killer. But as Noah, April and Ella's stories converge, shocking revelations· come to the surface. The truth is obvious.
Or so everyone believes . . .

the DEATH *of* HER

You thought you knew her.
You were wrong.

A woman is discovered on a Cornish farm, battered and left for dead in a maize field. As she's airlifted to hospital, her life hanging in the balance, no one's sure who she is. Three days later she comes round, but her memory is damaged. She knows her name – Evie – but no more, until she remembers another name. Angel – her three-year-old daughter.

As the police circulate Evie's photo, someone recognizes her. Charlotte knew her years ago, at school, when another child went missing. Leah Danning, who vanished whilst in Evie's care.

When the police search Evie's home, there's no sign of Angel. More disturbingly, there's no evidence that she ever lived there, forcing the police to question whether Evie's having some kind of breakdown.

But even from the darkest place she's ever known, Evie believes her daughter is alive. The police remain unconvinced – unaware that on the fringes of Evie's life, there's someone else. Someone hiding, watching her every move, with their own agenda and their own twisted version of reality.